NIAGARA TUNNELS
SECRETS REVEALED

Margarete Ledwez

ELM GROVE PUBLISHING

San Antonio, Texas, USA

ISBN 978-1-943492-47-3 (hard back)
ISBN 978-1-943492-48-0 (soft cover)

Front and back cover photographs © 2019 by Shawn Ledwez.

Book and cover design by **designpanache**.

ELM GROVE PUBLISHING
San Antonio, Texas, USA
www.elmgrovepublishing.com

Praise for "Niagara Tunnels Secrets Revealed"

"Margarete has done it again! In this fast-moving and entertaining book, the characters jump off the pages and come to life as new horrors are discovered and secrets are revealed. A fascinating and wholesome read for all ages."

— Sue Augustine
  Best-selling author of "When Your Past is Hurting Your Present"

"Everyone will enjoy this true reading experience as we are skillfully transported from home base to around the world and immersed in the brave, ingenious and emotional life stories of a growing cast of characters. It begs a third book."

—Tammy Chilcott

"This second novel builds on the suspense and adventures of the family as they uncover more of the past that is hidden in the tunnels. An enjoyable and unexpected read."

— Dave Elford

"In this, the sequel to 'Past Secret, Present Danger,' the main characters once again explore the mysterious and dangerous tunnels of Niagara. The non-stop action in Niagara, Pennsylvania, Berlin and Venice make this book a real page turner."

—Heidi Klose
  Author of "Darkness Falls on Niagara"

This is dedicated to all my grandchildren. For those of you who have this wonderful addition to your families, you realize how much they have enlarged your capacity for love and life. Your limitless love can be expressed in ways you never thought possible.

I would like to acknowledge that Josh has continued to grow into an outstanding young man and I anticipate reading one of his published books in the future.

I am featuring another group of grandchildren in this book. They will recognize themselves by more than just their names, Dustin and Mitchell. Brianna, named Bee in the book, included. They have all excelled in their lives, overcoming, adjusting and striving to finish their education. They have secured great jobs and found their one love to share their lives with. Giving me great joy and so many smiles, from engagements to sharing weddings, and watching their lives unfold, as they walk life's journey.

I will acknowledge the third set of grandchildren in my next book, which will complete this trilogy. They will be last, but not least, as they are my first as well as last of this precious gift, "grandchildren." I look forward to honouring them.

Contents

Previously in *Past Secret Present Danger*

Exploring secret passages in the long forgotten tunnels beneath Niagara Falls, Josh and his friends Mac and Mark have made a series of startling discoveries about his family's history.

Caught between the horrific events of the past and the ever-increasing sense of present danger, the youngsters have uncovered an evil plan that was put into action long before he was born. Finding the past catching up rapidly with him, Josh realizes he needs to act quickly or risk mortal danger.

In *Niagara Tunnels Secrets Revealed,* our intrepid heroes are drawn deeper into the mystery of the tunnels. A series of clues leads them to travel to Europe in search of answers. They've come too far to turn back now, but the Niagara tunnels do not give up their secrets easily, and danger is never far away...

Foreword

My love for travel, and for meeting people, has allowed me to introduce the Niagara Falls tunnels to others all over the world. Though most people are familiar with Niagara Falls, few have heard of the tunnels beneath. The tunnels have a way of reaching out far into the imagination of strangers with their dark tentacles.

My story is an adventure in fantasy, but my characters are based on real people with real, everyday concerns, and I hope readers, wherever they may be, can identify with them as they enter this dark world. Each of us faces difficulties in our daily lives, but by embracing these challenges, we can face the truth of who we really are and how we got to where we are in life. In the story, Josh and his friends are continuously drawn back to the Niagara Tunnels, where the mystery began, to face new challenges. With each new discovery, and in spite of their peril, they keep going back to search for more. They find proof of a massive conspiracy and follow their conscience in doing what is expected and what is right.

I have been fortunate in being able to travel, and I have set parts of the story in places where I have spent time, including Germany, its quaint villages and beautiful countryside forming a backdrop for its own wartime secrets. Venice, one of my favourite places, gives life to one segment in the book as the backdrop for a close look at some of it's inhabitants and their everyday battles.

Some things never change, and the depiction of a fleeing refugee family, and the hardships they encounter, is sadly still an everyday experience for far too many people.

The tunnels bring people from all walks of life together in ways I could never have imagined.

– ML

Characters

Alice—*rock climber*

Andy Shantz—*intruder*

Angelica, or Angela—*Mark's mom*

Barry—*police officer*

Bee—*Josh's sister*

Bella Shantz—*Andy's sister*

Carmela—*Carmelita's daughter*

Carmelita Fry—*Mrs. Fry*

Chelbee—*Amish Baby*

Clara—*Lovlyn's baby*

Daniel—*Pa's uncle*

Dustin Schwartz—*Great Grandson of Mitchell Schwartz 1*

Eckhart Kempt—*prisoner*

Eli— *Kelvin's youngest brother*

Friedrich—*Pa's uncle*

Fritz—*Stephan's son*

Fry—*prisoner*

Grammpy—*Josh's grandfather*

Grammy—*Josh's grandmother*

Hannah—*Carmela's granddaughter*

Helmut—*soldier*

Herbert—*Pa's father*

Herman Wolfgang—*guard soldier*

Jake—*Amish driver*

Jervaih—*squatter*

Joseph Schultz—*prisoner*

Josh—*main character, 17 years old*

Kelly—*short for Kelvin, Bee's friend*

Lovlyn—*squatter*

Mac— *Josh's friend*

Marion Lutz—*Amish mother*

Mark— Josh's friend

Mary—*Schwartz mother*

Mel—*gondolier*

Mitchell Schwartz I—*prisoner*

Mitchell Schwartz II—*son of Mitchell Schwartz 1*

Mitchell Schwartz III—*grandson of Mitchell Schwartz 1*

Mitchell Schwartz IV—*great-grandson of Mitchell Schwartz 1*

Mr. Bernhardt Eisenhouwer—*Jewish father*

Mr. Fritz Friezen—*grandfather of Stephan Friezen*

Mrs. Semph—*neighbor*

Natasha—*Jewish child*

Nerissa—*Josh's mother*

Omz—*Josh's grandmother on his dad's side*

Pa—*Josh's grandfather*

Pilser—*Carmela's last name*

Rachel—*Bee's Amish friend*

Ritmeir Brothers—*prisoners*

Romona—*Jewish wife*

Rudy Kempt—*prisoner*

Shawn—*Josh's father*

Stephan—*descendant of Friezen*

Sweetheart— cougar cub

The Suit—*man found in expensive suit*

Vanessa—*Mac's mom*

Vinnie— *Angelica's relative*

CHAPTER 1

Tunnel Secrets Alter the Future

Another school year had gone by, and we were all kept very busy with everyday life and our list of things to do in the secret tunnels. It took some time before the townspeople settled in and stopped looking over their shoulders for the evasive cougar. The cougar was blamed for Vinnie's death and that of the man found in the expensive shredded suit. We knew the cougar was harmless to us, but no one else was aware of this fact. Their deaths, caused by falling over the edge of the cliff, were also, now, things of the past. Although the police had released Vinnie's friend's name, he was still called, "The Suit." After the paper wrote an article about the two in coercion to murder—not only once, but twice—the fear grew even more in our close-knit town and neighboring Niagara area. The suspicion of the homicide of Omz, my grandmother, made the news once more. It had never made sense until now, when the circumstances were adding up to her murder. We needed the proof of foul play to put our minds at rest.

Mark, still my best friend, became known as, "The one that got away." He was fortunate to escape from Vinnie's terror and beating, even to his near death. Many friends came by to give their deepest regrets regarding Omz's death. The new information in the papers sparked new interest. It rekindled the feelings of those days from the past. Her accident driving over the gorge didn't make sense to anyone. Being confronted with the past came with healing gestures and comments, all filled with love and compassion, easing the pain of those memories.

Mom, Dad, Bee and I went on with our lives, and we became accustomed to the abnormalities of hiding and guarding every word when outside of our home. Mac, one of my closest friends, became great buddies with Bee. Pa, my grandfather, was stopped and asked about his time away, constantly being prodded for more details. He covered up the fact that he had been hiding in the tunnels below our grand mansion. Lies were hard for him to remember, so he gave as little information as possible. Pa, Dad, and I spent hours in our secret tunnels, organizing the information we found. We were looking for hidden evidence of the men who created them. I couldn't believe it had only been a year since Mac and I had discovered the secret entrances to the tunnels and the rooms below. They were now a familiar place, and we knew the passageways like the backs of our hands.

We found and continued to follow primitive maps of the passage ways. Pa shared the names of the ancestors he had already researched, as well as established the countries their descendants now resided in. We took day trips down below to areas I had never seen, to retrieve the papers that Pa had recognized as valuable and hidden well in the darkness. He did this in those long days spent in isolation underground, hiding from the danger that turned out to be Vinnie. These documents needed to be protected for the future, so I assisted in the transfer of information to a USB. We were very careful to do our backups. All the papers that we knew of were now in one place, organized and ready to study when time allowed in the hidden underground living room. We had discovered the underground living area last year, and it was still one of my favorite places below. The animal furs on the cold stone walls gave us a cozy feeling. The old, worn chairs from days gone by still drew us into them as we studied the papers. It was the most natural place to do this. Dad and I moved an old bookcase downstairs. It did nicely to house the collection we had acquired.

CHAPTER 2

To Our Surprise

One excursion was to the tunnel that connected the horrid water tunnel from under the graveyard to our hideout. I felt anxious again, remembering that I had almost died. That time, I was nearly taken by the tremendous water current over the edge of the gorge. We entered it from the underground living room this time, from behind the old hutch and hanging furs. With our flashlights off, but in our hands, ready at all times, we used a couple of lanterns to give us much needed visibility. By now, we had added a couple of battery-operated lanterns to make our work easier. A year ago, in the darkness, I stumbled on something in that black, cold tunnel, after I was almost pushed over the edge of the gorge. It felt hard, and I had to know what it was. I could still recall the hard kick by my boot. It seemed stuck well, or was it a rock?

Pa found an old tin can along the way. It seemed to be solidly stuck in the ground, but I strongly protested, that it had not tripped me. I would have recognized the feel and sound of a can.

We kept on looking. There seemed to be an abrupt dip in the tunnel floor. It could hide something until you were right on top of it.

I tripped and stumbled, catching myself. Déjà vu. This felt like the first time I tripped. We all looked down at what caused the clumsy step. It was dark, dirty, and had a rectangular shape. Was it an old brick?

Dad tried to pick it up with both hands and grunted, "This is stuck!"

I kicked it hard with my steel-toed exploration boots. It didn't loosen, or even budge!

"Dad, let me see if my pocket knife can clear some of the dirt away," I said, digging through the bag hanging by my side.

While scraping away some of the earth from around this mysterious piece, my knife accidently hit the hard surface. The light of the lanterns immediately illuminated a bright yellow glow.

Pa rubbed his chin with a, "Will you look at that?"

Dad got on his knees and bent low to have a close look, then announced, "I think it's gold!"

I worked even harder to free what was to become our newest treasure. Dad picked it up and declared that it was heavy. We scratched, scraped, and rubbed it, even using spit to expose its brilliance even more. Yep, we all decided, it definitely was a brick of gold!

Pa spoke with a furrowed brow. "I didn't see this the last time I came through the tunnel. I was so upset about Omz and wanted to protect the rest of my family. I must have been in a daze as I walked through here to get to the tunnel under the graveyard. All I wanted to do was close up the access to the living room and the tunnels from the cemetery. I knew it would keep everyone and everything safe. The access to the secret tunnel needed to be kept from intruders."

"Pa, do you mean you actually walked to under the graveyard from here? What about the water? It is so dangerous!" I added, in a not-so-polite manner.

The dreadful experience still threw me into an emotional spin.

Pa looked perturbed and replied that he wanted the grave and the memory of his beloved wife to remain undisturbed. I told him I realized that and understood. I wasn't trying to be rude towards him or Omz's memory.

As he put his hands on my shoulders, he said, "I know, Josh, you loved her too and you would never be disgraceful to her memory."

I gave Pa a huge hug. He returned it, and I enjoyed the strong feel of his arms around me once more, even at the age of seventeen. Dad's voice brought us back to the task at hand. My thoughts hid under the amazement I felt right then. Family had trumped gold once more—I realized we had forgotten all about the bar we had just found.

"We should go back and get a shovel to dig some more," said Dad.

"But Dad, can't we look around some more before we go back, please?" I pleaded.

We held our lanterns so we could get a better look at the ground. It appeared to have been dug lower for some reason. Of course, it was well compacted after all these years. My experience taught me to look everywhere. Hard walls and a ceiling of rock created the rugged tunnel. Suddenly, my eyes caught sight of a dark shadow in the rock. It was a crevice, and Pa saw it too as his flashlight passed over that spot. The light penetrated the crevice and lit something inside.

"Well, will you look at that?" Pa once again used his favorite saying.

There was a rustic handle of some kind inside at the back of the opening.

"It looks like there could be something attached to it," Dad added.

Pa tried to reach it but could not. The crevice opening was very narrow, but I was anxious and needed to give it a try. My body was long and lanky. On my knees, I squeezed my shoulders in sideways. This allowed the upper part of my body to enter the now dark opening.

"I think I've got it!" I exclaimed, pulling hard. My side position made it an awkward maneuver.

With accomplishment, I shouted, "Here it is!"

"Let's see," Dad and Pa spoke in unison while looking over my shoulders, as it was released from the large slit in the rock.

It was a handmade pick, forged like those of years gone by. The handle was crafted out of a single rustic piece of wood.

"Do you think this was used when they dug the tunnels, and do you think this dug the hole the gold was in?" I questioned.

I placed my lantern on the floor of the opening inside the crevice. Dad carefully scanned the walls and the ceiling with his flashlight.

CHAPTER 3

Confirmation

At the highest point of the rift in the rock, Dad noticed a minuscule piece of material. It seemed to be carefully worked into the crack and was barely visible.

"Look up there!" Dad shouted. "It's a good thing we checked this place over before leaving!"

After a quick peek, I searched my bag for some tweezers. My tweezers could get a hold of the corner and pull it out if I was very careful and didn't rip the old cloth.

"That is a great idea, but be gentle," Dad prompted.

I got a hold of a very minute corner and pulled very gently. It came out just about an inch. The piece that was exposed made it easy to pull again. Quite a bit more was released. Getting a hold of the material with my fingers, I was mindful that I was touching a hidden bit of history. Gingerly, a little at a time, I released the entire cloth from its years of isolation. I opened it carefully, while Dad and Pa leaned in close to get a better view. I was actually nervous and felt my stomach flip a couple of times. I should have been used to these unexpected moments by now.

It looked like the sleeve of an old shirt. The cuff was still attached and in good condition, though it was stained and dirty. You could tell it was a hand sewn cuff with very intricate stitching. Instead of a cuff link, it was held together with a piece of string tied in knots. The lanterns flickered and we felt a slight breeze.

"What was that?" I asked.

We went back to the task at hand: finding out what the sleeve was all about, or if there was a clue to tell us why it was hidden there. It looked like it had been torn from the shirt at the shoulder. The rustic drawings and some writing held our attention. I couldn't make it out, but Pa recognized the German. He would have to read it in better light. We gathered the new-found pick, gold, and latest clue, as well as our lanterns. Our hands were full.

Back in our cozy room, we closed the door and put the furs back as well as the cabinet, always erring on the side of caution. After soaking the gold bar in a pan of water, its former brilliance was exposed. At that moment I couldn't think of anything that would consume me more and attract my attention. This was gold!

Pa was reading the German writing on the cloth. He seemed so intense, and his face looked strained.

He read to himself, *Mein Name ist Friedrich Wittfoot.* (My name is Friedrich Wittfoot.)

Ich bin in Gefangenschaft. (I am in captivity.)

Mein Bruder ist Herbert Wittfoot. (My brother is Herbert Wittfoot.)

Mein Bruder Daniel ist in Deutschland im Gefängnis gestorben. (My brother, Daniel, died in prison in Germany.)

Ich habe mein Geld heimlich versteckt. (I secretly hid my money.)

Bitte gib das Geld zu meinem Bruder Herbert, und seinem Sohn. (Please give the money to my brother, Herbert, and his son.)

Ich war für fünf Jahre hier. (I have been here for five years.)

Mein Gott hat mir so weit geholfen und ich werde Ihn bald sehen. (My God has helped me this far, and I will see him soon.)

After sitting frozen for a time, Pa's eyes overflowed with quiet tears. Dad and I both took note and prodded to know what was going on. What was on that piece of cloth?

Dad took the cloth out of Pa's hands but couldn't read enough of it to make sense of it.

"Pa, tell us what the note said," Dad almost commanded.

After trying a couple of times, Pa pulled himself together and started to talk. He told us who wrote it and that it was his missing uncle.

I wondered how this could be and asked, "He was one of the prisoners working in the tunnels?"

It was his farewell note to the remainder of his family, Pa's Dad and Pa. He told us about Pa's uncle Daniel dying in prison in Germany just as rumors in their hometown in Germany had forecast. He went over to the gold, stroking it with love, knowing very well his uncle had touched it and they had taken his life here in the tunnels. Friedrich said Pa should have the money he hid. How could this be? We all needed time to digest this one.

Dad directed, "We should hide the gold and the cloth in this room and call it a day. Pa, you need to rest a while and recuperate, as well as gather your thoughts."

Dad was looking at the map that had been drawn under the hand-written letter and wondered what the lines represented. He would find out another day.

It seemed like a long way back to the study. Pa was lagging behind, and we made sure we slowed down to stay with him. I hoped the news wasn't too much for him.

When we reached the secret entry, I took note of the clipboard, pencil, and flashlight. After our experience today, our rules sure made sense. The family had created a firm household rule. This was so no one would disappear down below. We would keep track of our comings and goings by signing the clipboard inside the secret door from the study. There hung a flashlight, pencil, and the paper. We signed our name, time, and return time. I signed us back and noticed how late it had gotten. We were never to go further than the storage room or living room by ourselves. It was a not physically written in stone, but it made that kind of impact on us. We were to enter our hideaway with another person if at all possible. I liked that loophole, "if at all possible." Today, it made total sense to obey every detail. You never knew when someone might need that extra support.

Mom left the study just as it was, enjoying the typewriter, clock, and Pa's old Bible on the shelf once again. Pa didn't use the ancient typewriter any more as he had mastered the computer. It was kept for nostalgic reasons. The old Bible was taken down daily, of course, and never got a chance to gather dust. Pa sat in his chair after dinner and read his precious book consistently. He was always willing to stop and talk about the insight he had gained reading. I would pop in on him often, as I knew full well I could count on him being there. Our conversations never disappointed me, and Pa continuously gave me more insight into God's character. I was going to research God for myself and get to know Him in these ways too. I used modern technology by downloading an app onto my computer and phone to read online or listen to an audible version. I wondered if Pa would be in his usual chair this evening, after the shock of his uncle living and then dying below in the secret tunnels.

Mom had rearranged the house, just a little, just enough to suit our belongings. It was full of life again. Pa enjoyed watching his family interact and fill the old place with so much warmth and love. We often heard him say that he wished that Omz could have seen her home now. He never stopped insinuating that he felt Omz was still alive. We chalked it up to wishful thinking or old age.

It was almost suppertime, and we would tell Mom and Bee all about our ancestors then. For now, we were too deep in thought to discuss anything.

We had chosen our bedrooms, as there were five in total. I took the one facing the gorge, and Pa's room was next to mine, also having the same view. Bee had picked the one on the left coming up the stairs, which overlooked the gully and gazebo. Directly across the grand staircase was the only spare room left. Mom and Dad's room was at the top of the stairs, overlooking the coach house and driveway.

Pa and I also shared a bathroom with a door from both bedrooms, giving us ensuite privileges. We still had one secret between the two of us. A wall opened in both of our closets, joining our rooms. We visited now and again but were careful not to be found out. We would sit at the window and look at the hydro plant up the river and talk about all the mysteries we still haven't uncovered.

Bee and Mom decorated her room. She chose black, white, and

a trendy turquoise color. From what they reported, it reflected her room at Grammy's place. She seemed to enjoy herself there, even without Dad and me. I thought she would be bored, but apparently this Kelly fellow kept her pretty occupied. Every time I saw her, she was texting or video chatting him. I would have to check this guy out some time. After all, he seemed to have the total attention of my sister.

The house was spacious, and we didn't have to run into each other if we so desired. Of course, that was not the case, and we met around the large home crafted oak table every chance we got. Pa had witnessed the gigantic tree being hit by lightning when he was a child. It had stood close to the house, so his dad had it cut down and made a table out of part of the massive trunk. It was worn, but completed the kitchen with warmth, style, and functionality.

The aroma of coffee, pancakes, or bacon and eggs often beckoned our arrival. Mom would make a special breakfast, but, if not, Pa or Dad would do the honors. As well as breakfast, we would make an effort to have supper together. Today we would all be there. Sometimes Bee's job would make it impossible for her to feast with us. There was usually someone else to take her place. Mark and Mac joined us when they were over, but Bee got plenty of leftovers.

CHAPTER 4

Vinnie

This evening, just before dinner, Barry delivered the report on the investigation regarding Vinnie. According to the documents, he emigrated from Germany in 2004. He spoke English and had no problem fitting into the Niagara on the Lake way of life. He tried to secure a job with the hydro plant. He started a business in the area during the early years, delivering water to homes with cisterns. He was known for his oversized and overly modified truck. He pushed other vehicles out of the way when he felt like he wanted to. The police were called on several occasions regarding the matter. Vinnie was careful to never leave a dent or even a mark on the vehicle, so he was never charged.

The people that were interviewed regarding Vinnie were quick to add that he asked a lot of questions about the German folks in the area. It was said that he seemed to be searching for information regarding someone, but he would never say who.

He had a list of names of German immigrants who had purchased properties since 1943. No one could figure out what the list was for, except that he could be looking for a relative. This was how he found his distant cousin, Angelica, Mark's mom. She was of German origin and thought all of her relatives had passed away. Her grandfather was arrested during the war, as he had disobeyed orders to turn in his Jewish friend who was hiding. He was subsequently sent to prison. No one ever knew what happened to him. We had his name on our list of tunnel workers, or, rather, prisoners. Angelica came to Canada, having no known remaining family. She arrived as an immigrant with her French husband. They worked on the farms to make a living, until Mark's Dad became ill with cancer and passed away. Mark and his mom lived a humble lifestyle. They had rented the little farmhouse where they now lived for many years. Their landlord treated them with overwhelming kindness.

When Vinnie's body was finally recovered, they found a very old, worn piece of paper on him. You could make out that it was sent from Queenston. Nothing else was legible in the letter. It was so old and had deteriorated, as it appeared to have been carried in Vinnie's wallet for years. This information made us believe that Mark was a direct descendent of one of the murdered tunnel workers. He would be one of the first to receive his share when it was ready to be divided. The fate of life had a way of correcting all wrongs, or maybe God had ordained this, just like Pa repeated over and over. Mark's great granddad was imprisoned, sent here to work against his will, and died here, and Mark was to inherit the fruits of his labor. Maybe he and my relative were friends. Chills ran through my body, leaving me cold. Did they work side by side and talk about their families, or how they could escape?

This day was so full of information that challenged our emotions. We were mentally drained after going over all of it as a family. Pa was able to discuss it with much more composure. Mom and Bee couldn't believe that Pa's uncle was actually sent here to work and die. It made the whole story so much more personal than it had been in the past. Pa brought an old photo to the table so we could see this relative and put a face to the name. He also had a tattered family photo and we saw Daniel's picture as well. There were consoling hugs throughout the conversation accompanied by compassionate tears. The girls would go down below with us tomorrow, and we would show them the cloth letter and the gold bar, as well as the ancient pick. The thought of a member of our family secretly crafting the primitive tool we found, again sent shivers down my spine. The feminine side of the family hadn't seen these items yet, and they were full of anticipation and eagerness. I must say, I was eager to look at the cloth and the drawings again, never mind the gold bar that still shone brightly in my mind.

We would speak with Mark regarding his lineage to one of the workers who died here in the tunnels. He already knew of our secret, and we were confident he would be able to remain secretive with the rest. Mark and I had so much in common, but now I felt like we could share more then we could have ever imagined. We would tell him at the appropriate time. Barry, our loyal friend and a police officer, said he would leave it to us to relay the results of this private investigation. It created a hunger in me to release more of the secrets of the tunnels and increase my knowledge about the descendants of the innocent prisoners. We hoped they would all be innocent.

The next morning, the smell of bacon served as an alarm clock, and we all ended up at the table shortly after its scent wafted up the stairs to our rooms. We ate quickly, anticipating the unveiling of our find.

There was a quick, loud knock at the door, then it opened as Mark walked in.

"Hey, what's for breakfast?" Mark inquired, smacking his lips.

"Mark, you're just in time. We are going down below today, and we have something to show you," I said. "Do you have time?"

"Sure do. I told my Mom I would be hanging out with you today," he replied.

"Then sit down and have some breakfast with us first," Mom insisted.

We ate as we enjoyed the conversation, not wanting to say too much about the details until we went below.

Pa told us a bit of information that grabbed my attention as well as Mark's. His brother Friedrich had lost two fingers at the second knuckle in an axe accident when he was very young. Thank goodness it was his left hand, and he was able to continue to use his right hand for most things, and did very well in spite of it.

CHAPTER 5

Mark Faces the Past

Mark was getting very anxious to go, and so were the girls. We cleaned up quickly, everyone doing their part, and locked the doors. We were on our way, entering the tunnels to go through the interior office room. Mark was so chatty, I had to tell him to keep it down.

As we closed the door to our underground living room and lit some lanterns, I went and got our new artifacts. First, I showed them the old pick, then the cloth, and, of course, the gold brick. There was utter silence. I think they were in shock. None of us had ever seen a bar of gold before.

Mark broke the silence with, "Where did this come from?"

We reviewed the facts as we experienced them, and, once again, Mark was mesmerized. This was a good time to tell him that his great-grandfather was also a prisoner and died here. Vinnie, unfortunately, was the only other known relative that had been traced to Mark. We told him he had a huge share in these tunnels, and we would make sure to give him what belonged to him. He didn't care so much at the time, but wondered how we found out about his grandfather.

We told him that the information was brought to light when Vinnie's past was revealed as a result of a private investigation. He wondered if he could tell his mom, and we thought maybe not right now. He could tell her that Vinnie was her relative. We would tell her the results of the research now and the rest in the future.

Pa and I were interested in the diagram Friedrich had drawn. It looked like it went into the tunnel under the graveyard. Dad went to talk to Pa regarding the fact that we could not follow this map, as there was water in the tunnel.

"Oh, I can remedy that!" was Pa's reply. "I will turn the water off again. It was only a protective measure I had installed."

We made plans to start first thing in the morning on another expedition. Pa would turn the water off at the graveyard so it could dry out a little. He said its base was hard rock, and he didn't think anyone could bury anything in that tunnel. We would check it regardless of the odds, as that is the place the map drawing led.

Mark and I were very excited, and Mark got permission to sleep over so we could get an early start. His mom experienced this regularly and had no problem with giving her permission. We got to sleep in the early hours of the morning, as our minds couldn't shut down. Finally, the waft of sausages entered our room, beckoning us to the table. We had slept in our clothes, so we were ready in a jiffy. To our surprise, Pa and Dad were already waiting, and Pa had made the breakfast. It was early, and the ladies of the house were sleeping in.

We decided to take a pick, shovel, and axe with us. The shirt-sleeve was an obvious necessity. I thought that we should photocopy the sleeve map, so we would have more copies. It would protect this fragile piece of material from any more wear. We would bring it back with us and make two copies, then store the remnant in a safe place.

We entered the tunnel from our underground living space, again passing over the place where we found the gold bar. We gave it another once-over with our lights. Dad looked inside the crevice again to see if we missed anything. As he shone the light in an expectant search, he noticed a rock that was out of place. It was a solid rock wall, but there was a piece that looked loose.

"Boys, come here and see this."

We all tried our best to look into the narrow crevice but decided one at a time would work better. Dad went first and tried to get close to the rock on the far side of the opening. He couldn't get to it. I was next, as I had maneuvered my body in as before. This time, I was not successful. Mark was anxious, and said he knew he could reach it. He slipped in one shoulder at a time and then his hips. On his knees, he pulled at the rock. Nothing moved.

"Give me the pick," he commanded.

It was grueling work, as he didn't have his body weight to help him. With the pick on the bottom to wedge the rock and pry it out, he almost knocked himself out as his body arched back to give it all he had. The rock moved, and he pulled it to the side.

"What is this?" he exclaimed.

There, in the small hollow, was a small box. Mark grasped it and tried to move backwards. What an ordeal, getting his body out of such an awkward confined space. Just as he seemed to be getting panicky in his stuck position, his body pulled free. He was so relieved that he forgot about the box still in his hand.

"What is it, Mark?" I asked.

"It's a metal box!" he replied, studying it.

"Well, let's open it," Dad ordered.

It was a very old pipe tobacco box. We lifted the lid closure and opened it. Inside were small drawings on pieces of cigarette paper, each with a name.

"Do you think there is one with my great-grandfather's name on it?" asked Mark.

"We will see," replied Dad.

"It would verify my research," Pa announced, very gratified.

"Let's put it here in the entrance of the crevice and pick it up on the way back." As much as our curiosity was aroused, we forced ourselves to take care of the task at hand. Especially since the graveyard entrance was made vulnerable due to the lack of water.

When we reached the water tunnel, there was just a trickle of water. I was amazed. There was the rope, one end hanging over the tunnel where the water had been. We climbed down and took out the map.

"Do you see this, Dad?" I said, pointing at a circle right across from the tunnel line.

We held our lights high, and Mark scanned with his flashlight. He found an irregularity in the formation of the wall. It was on the higher side of the wall and difficult to work at. We picked at it, then hit it, and nothing moved. My thoughts went to the day I was almost swept over the gorge to my death. I looked up at the rope with my flashlight and then looked down, wondering just how deep the water really was. I noticed a perfect square in the rock floor just in front of me.

"Look at this!" I shouted.

"Well, will you look at that!" said Pa.

"Let's try to wedge it out of there," Dad instructed.

Dad took the pick and I took the shovel as we worked tirelessly on the square rock. Eventually, it budged and started to come out of its tight stone encasement. It was difficult work and took great endurance, but we got the job done. The heavy stone plug was finally out and laying beside a matching square-shaped hole. What were we going to discover?

Our lights were all directed at this opening, our faces peering downward. To our disappointment, there was nothing but a nicely created square hole.

"What?" uttered Mark in disappointment.

I looked up at him. I not only saw him, but also the wall of the tunnel where the inconsistencies were. A rock was now jutting out, appearing like it was ready to be plucked away. The rock we dislodged must have somehow been connected and pushed it out. I pointed in its direction. In unison we moved towards it. Pa tried to move it, but Dad insisted to let him do the heavy work. Dad edged it out, being careful not to drop it. He placed it on the rock floor beside where he was standing. Pa peered in the opening first.

"Well, will you look at that!" were his only words.

"What Pa? Is there more gold?" I questioned.

CHAPTER 6

Proof

In the revealed rock hideaway, something lay rolled up. As we carefully lifted it from its years of refuge, we saw something else behind it. The first piece taken down was about a foot long and wrapped in a shirt with two sleeves missing. Behind it was another sleeve filled with many gold coins. This must have been Friedrich's money. The shirt and sleeve matched the sleeve we had found earlier. That rarely seen, fine hand-stitching could not be mistaken. The bottom of the cuff had been tied with a strip of the shirt so it would hold the coins like a bag. We would have to get a container, as the old shirt-sleeve would rip as soon as it was lifted. Mark and I would come back and carefully retrieve it. Friedrich's copied map was carefully wrapped again and made ready to carry back to our underground cavern. On our way back, we picked up the recently found small tin box. Its contents were still a mystery to us.

Pa and Dad were going to examine the new materials, and we would collect the coins and the other sleeve. We assumed that a few plastic bags and Mark's backpack would do the job.

Pa, with all the love and respect his fingers could portray, unwrapped his late uncle's shirt. What a devastating time for Friedrich, knowing he was not going to come out of this place alive. Pa wondered if he was able to look over the gorge and see daylight. It must have been blinding to his eyes. He unrolled the map very carefully. It was very fragile and starting to tear on the edges. Dad and Pa studied the map together, but only Pa could understand the script on it.

It showed tunnels going a great distance. A room full of explosives and the power station were marked, with only one tunnel leading to four others right under the plant. This was proof of the conspiracy. They would have to check these tunnels out and make sure the explosives were not there anymore. Dad and Pa were deep in conversation when Mark and I got back. After closing the door and putting furs and cabinet back, we asked what they found. They told us of the explosives and tunnels. The terrified look on our faces told the story.

"Could we blow up even now?" I asked.

Dad answered, "No, if we don't get fire near the explosives, we will be safe."

This place was so full of intricate devices that we wouldn't even know if we were doing that! Where was the next hidden room or tunnel? Where was the room full of explosives? We would have to be even more careful down here. We would not be using gunpowder in the tunnels again. That was made very clear.

"At least we don't have to use gunpowder for the cougar's sake, thank goodness for that!" exclaimed Mark, then refocused his attention. "What was in the box? Did you find my great-grandfather's name?"

Dad and Pa had not gotten that far yet. Dad took the box and opened it. He carefully took out the cigarette papers. They contained small primitive drawings. In the top right corner each had a name. Pa said he would compare them to his list. They seemed to be all last names. We didn't know, but we assumed each person had hidden their money and drew their own maps. They must have known they would be here until their death. It was going to be quite a job to follow each map and find the gold.

Pa took out his own list of names and addresses of descendants. He laid it on the table beside the lightweight papers. By now, he knew which name belonged to Mark's granddad. He searched for the name Schultz. His grandfather was Joseph Schultz. As he picked up the small remnant of a man's life, he was ever mindful that he was fulfilling a dying man's wishes in giving to his descendent all he had left in life as well as death.

Looking at Mark, Pa said, "This is your grandfather's, Mark."

He held it out so Mark could take a hold of this precious gem. Mark was overwhelmed with compassion for the one who had drawn this and had signed his name. He was a part of this person. Maybe he even looked like this person? Dad stepped over to Mark's side and put his arm around his shoulder, giving him a big squeeze. He was letting him know his support team was right here beside him.

"Joseph would have been so proud to know you, Mark. You are a fine young man, and your grandfather seemed to be a good man in standing up for freedom and not giving in to peer pressure, even if it would cost his life."

"Dad, can we look for Mark's money first?" I asked, trying to support in my own way.

"Of course, it all has to be taken care of and found, so why not," he replied.

We decided to bring the photocopier down below. It was too risky to bring these documents, proof of these lives, above ground yet.

We called it a day, and Mark seemed a little quiet as we returned. Quite understandable, considering that he hadn't known any living relative except for Vinnie, and had just discovered one was buried so close to where he lived. Mark had been starting to believe he had bad genes, until he found out about his great-grandfather, Joseph. It gave him more confidence about who he was.

We would meet tomorrow and follow Joseph's sketch to see what we could find. Pa and Dad were very interested in finding the tunnel to the power plant but made plans to have more provisions for that trip. It would not be a short one.

CHAPTER 7

A Change in Address

Mark came back the next morning with tragic news. Their land-lord farmer, Mr. Froese, wanted to retire, so he was giving his farm over to his sons. Mark and his mom would have to move. The cottage would be used for migrant workers. Mark was very upset, as he would not be here to help with the search, and his mom could not afford another place. We all tried to calm him down, but those brown eyes just couldn't be consoled. He went on and on about leaving the area and never coming back!

Mom and Dad were in the corner whispering when Dad finally spoke up.

"I have the perfect solution, Mark! You can move into the carriage house with your Mom. It will be rent-free. Just pay for your utilities. No one is in there now, and we would feel better if someone like you were living there. It is very special to us, as you know."

Dad winked, "What do you say?"

Mark just couldn't keep from smiling. He said he would talk to his mother right away and ran out the door. We were all smiling and thought it would be the perfect solution. These two needed a few good moments in their lives. The phone rang shortly after, and it was Angelica. She was worried about putting us out and abusing our friendship. She appreciated the offer, but just could not do that. We assured her it was very selfish on our part, and she would be doing us a huge favor. It was better to have someone in the carriage house than leave it vacant. She agreed, and we decided to move her in by the end of the month.

We looked forward to the day we could present Angelica with her and Mark's inheritance from Joseph. It would be enough money to provide a good life for them. How we would do that, we did not know, as it would have to be anonymous. There was always a chance that our family would be in danger if the wrong people discovered our secret.

This was going to be even better than we had imagined! Mark and I could get together any time to do more investigating. Mark returned with a smile as wide as his face.

We decided to take the copier down below, while our adrenaline was still pumping from the good news. There was a lot of copying and documenting of papers. We were ready to zero in on Mark's great-granddad's map. We would study that one well and try to find that treasure first. The wiring and Internet we put down below made life much easier. To think, Dad had been planning to have this place demolished! This would all have been gone!

We copied the small pieces of cigarette paper just as they were, then enlarged them so we could read them more easily. We made two larger copies and gently put the originals back in the tobacco box. We carefully copied the map for the power plant tunnels and wrapped it up again.

I enthusiastically studied the copy of paper Joseph had drawn. You could make out so many details, considering its rustic condition. Some of the drawings were just lines, while others were more meticulous. This little paper had some interesting markings on it. It looked like a full moon with beams down to earth. He had drawn a line, we presumed, representing a long tunnel, winding and ending with a moonbeam shining through an irregular oval, coming to a point at both the top and the bottom. Where could this be?

"Mark, this might be in the wet cougar tunnel. The first time I was in there, the moon shone into it the same way,"

"Do you think so?" Mark replied with excitement.

"There is one way to find out, isn't there?"

We were in the moment and nothing else mattered at this time. I grabbed my bag, and we grabbed our spare jackets that were kept in the storage room. We were off, flashlights in hand and each carrying a lantern. We knew these stairs as well as the back of our hands by now. It was an easy trek. Our haste into action caused us to forget the time. It was late evening when we had started to copy the papers, and by now it was after eleven. Upon reaching that dark opening, we were met by the cougar. She was lonely these days, as we didn't have too much time to spend in this area. It was good to see our friend and we gave her a hearty welcome. She seemed to want us to follow her, as she walked away and kept looking back at us.

I said, "Okay girl, we're coming."

CHAPTER 8

The Rescue

She seemed to be in a hurry. We ran behind her, out to the open grassy ledge where Mac and I sat that first night we discovered it. It looked like a body was lying close to the edge. We could see helicopters with searchlights further down the river, along with rescue boats on the river, scanning the rock ridge above. We had to think fast. They would see us and discover our tunnel, or see the cougar. We checked his pulse and, yes, he was alive.

"Mark, help me get him into the tunnel."

He was not heavy, and he was wearing minimal gear for rock climbing. He must have been hurt or something. We decided to take him up to the house to get him medical attention. It was definitely a long, difficult haul, although he seemed quite light. We woke up Mom and Dad, and soon almost everyone else was aroused with the commotion.

We laid him on the couch and Dad took a good look at him.

"This is a girl, and where did you find her?"

We were shocked at this discovery and started to explain, as dad shook his head in disbelief.

"Well, this time it is good you disobeyed and went down without signing in. You might have saved her life."

Dad saw her medical alert bracelet, which read, "Diabetic."

Mom ran for some orange juice.

"Can we get this into her?"

She stirred even before they tried.

"Can you sit a little with our help?" Dad asked.

It was a team effort between Dad and Mom as they plumped pillows behind her for support. Mom gave her the orange juice by spoon. Our newfound stranger seemed to be doing fine. She was even starting to get her color back. As I looked down at her, I wondered how she got to our secret ledge. Her hair was super short, and she had a slight frame. She was now looking startled at all of us, and we thought we had better tell her she was in good hands, and that we had found her outside near the edge of the cliff. She relaxed.

Dad asked, "Are you alone?"

She nodded yes, and we were relieved.

"Can you tell us what happened?" asked Pa.

She told us that she and her friends had made a bet regarding climbing the rock ledge. She was not going to go that far, but she got carried away with how well she was doing. At the end of the climb, she felt faint and made it to a ridge on a cliff, where she thought she would regenerate her strength. She didn't know if she was hallucinating, but she saw a cougar come towards her and she passed out. She said she knew her glucose was low before she reached the cliff. She quickly added she was an experienced climber and could take care of herself.

"Is that why you didn't have a safety rope?" asked Pa.

She looked guilty and said she knew it was protocol, but she got caught up in the moment.

Mark and I just gave each other that, "I know what that's like," kind of look.

Dad called the police to report our find, and Barry came over to get a report. I knew when Mac found out, she would want to know every detail of this night. Barry couldn't believe that she made it all the way up the cliff. That was impossible! We couldn't tell him what we knew at this point. He called the rescue teams and they stopped the search.

Our stranger, now revealed to us by the name of Alice, was taken to the hospital to make sure she was stable, and to meet her parents.

She saw a doctor and was given a clean bill of health by the morning. After hearing the story, her parents reminded her of how lucky she was, and that a man was clawed to death by a cougar in that same area. She knew she was fortunate to be alive, but was in awe that she had actually climbed that whole rock face to the top. Her parents made her promise not to do that ever again, and there was no hesitation on her part to agree.

We found ourselves feeling fortunate, as our secret was not discovered, nor had it taken another life. Mark and I were once more reminded to follow the rules. We had just been reminded that accidents can and do happen.

It was a long night and we were all lacking sleep, except for Bee, who had slept through all the commotion. When she arrived at the breakfast table in the morning, she informed us that she received a ridiculous text. Some girl had climbed the gorge last night, only to be rescued by someone at the crest where she'd passed out after seeing a cougar.

"Can you believe that, who would be so stupid to climb this gorge?"

We all spoke at once, "Alice!"

Bee looked startled at our response and we filled her in on our night. She was amazed.

Mark and I would try to follow Joseph's map tonight while the moon was at its brightest, as it was once again a full moon. It didn't take Mac long to arrive and demand to know what was going on. She needed to know every detail. We invited her to join us in our adventure if she could get away for the night. She made arrangements to sleep over with Bee, and we planned to start out after our dinner.

We could hardly wait, so we spent the day helping Mom clean the carriage house. It was in pretty good shape, but with mom being as moms are, it had to be done to perfection. We would store our unused furniture in the attic of the old mansion and go through it later, when we had time.

Pa was busy sorting the information and location of the ancestors he researched into groups. He was grouping them so we would be ready to visit their descendants, as soon as the money was found.

He knew that by now, they had migrated all over the world. It would take time and diligence to journey to their countries and locate them.

It was a simple dinner that night, barbecued sausage and sauerkraut on a bun. It was one of my favorites.

Pa and Dad looked at our enlarged copy of Joseph's map that we had retrieved from downstairs. They too, surmised that it looked like the crevasse opening high in the cave wall below. They wished us luck and reminded us to sign in and out when we got back. Dad wanted me to wake him and let him know when we returned. I agreed to do so. Pa sent a sausage for the cougar, his indebted friend.

We were finally down below again, and ready to make another discovery! We took a pick, axe, and shovel, not knowing what we would need for the job. With our tools, lanterns, and flashlights, our hands were full. It was a good thing Mac joined us, as it made the load a little lighter. We arrived at the dark shadow just ahead of us. We heard a loud growl.

"Yes, we are back," I yelled. "We have something for you."

CHAPTER 9

Meeting the New Addition

The cougar neared, a little more cautious than before. It was like she didn't want us to go any further. We gave her the sausage and she warmed up to our presence again.

"What's the matter, girl?" I asked.

"I think she's protecting something!" said Mac.

We took our time, letting her feel comfortable with us before we moved forward. I thought maybe the stranger last night had made her skittish. The cougar moved quickly to a dark corner, and it was rare for her to leave so quickly. We shone a flashlight over to her. We were shocked! It was the silhouette of a cub.

"Oh, look at that!" exclaimed Mac.

Mark added, "Can we go over?"

I thought we had better not. She was a wild animal, and protecting her young was a priority.

"We will be lucky to find what we are looking for tonight," I mused out loud.

We walked over to the opposite side of the cavern so the cougar would feel safe. It was where the moon shone in. We went to the exact spot where the beam hit the rock floor. Nothing was visible. We put all of our tools down and started to search intently with our flashlights. Suddenly, the cougar growled and startled us. We turned and got a glimpse of her carrying her cub off into the darkness. I guessed she just didn't want anyone around her right now.

We were left to continue our search.

"That crevasse couldn't have changed in all these years, could it?" Mark asked.

We widened our search. The wall wasn't far from where we were looking. I thought maybe it would give us a clue to where the money was. My eye caught something. It couldn't be another piece of material, could it? We decided that the men didn't have too many options in what to use for leaving their last thoughts on.

I was excited to zero in on something and shouted, "Hey, look at this!"

Mark and Mac's eyes focused on where I was pointing my flashlight.

"Hey, it does look like another piece of material!" exclaimed Mark.

"This is awesome," added Mac.

"Let's put the lanterns on, that will give us lots of light." It was near the base where the wall met the cave floor. Pulling my tweezers out, I got on my knees and bent low, trying to grasp just a bit of the material without ripping it. It was releasing a little at a time. I had to be careful, as it would hold important information for my friend, Mark. This would be cool, as I expected to find a letter from his great-grandfather. It was another map. No words, just another map. We studied it carefully. It was another moonbeam. It shone into a rounded, slightly irregular opening. The map had a line going to the opening, which was joined by another line close to the circular drawing.

"The only place I know of, that the daylight or moonlight could come in, is at the graveyard exit over the gorge," I said.

"Let's check it out, right, Mark?" said Mac.

We picked up all of our supplies and took them with us. It seemed like a long haul, and we talked about the cougar cub and what we would find at our next destination. Entering from our cozy cave, Mark and I were reminded of the sleepover we planned to have in this cave someday soon. Mac thought it very unfair that she couldn't join us.

CHAPTER 10

The Glow of Hope

The tunnel was familiar to us by now, and we moved along it quickly. As we neared the tunnel from the graveyard, which was now empty of water, we could see the moon's rays. We looked closely and took note of where it seemed to hit the wall. The opening was higher in the rock gorge than it had been in the previous one, and the glow spread higher on the wall in the tunnel. Upon close examination, we found a group of three rocks that seemed to be fit into a hole in the rock wall. We could hardly reach it, but we pulled them loose. We had to jump back, as the last tug caused them to tumble down to the ground. I held the lantern high, and Mark stretched to look inside. He felt with his hands, and in the back, as far as he could reach, was a brick.

"It's a brick," he shouted.

"Let's see it!" Mac returned.

He gave it to me and asked if it was also a brick of gold. I figured it was, but we wouldn't be able to tell until we washed a layer of mud off of it. I scratched it, and, sure enough, its beauty was revealed. Mark was feeling for something else when he shouted.

"There is a cloth, and what feels like coins!"

I thought it was too heavy to move.

"Leave it, Mark, and we will get a step stool and a pail to retrieve it. Then you can see if there is something else."

He could hardly pull himself away. He was hoping to get a message from his ancestor. We would have to come back later and see what we could find.

The gold bar was soaked and scrubbed. It glistened, just like the first one we found. Mac didn't know it would belong to Mark. We didn't make a big deal about it at the time.

"Well, let's go back with that step stool and a pail and get the rest," said Mac.

We took a couple of flashlights, a shovel, and a pail, hoping to retrieve some coins. Of course, it was Mark who stepped onto the stool and had a good look.

"Yes," he said, "I see it. It looks like a sleeve!"

I lifted the shovel up high while supporting the end with the rock ledge. He carefully rolled the aged sleeve to the edge, being careful not to compromise the fabric. Using both hands, he rolled it onto the shovel I was holding. We learned from last time that the coins were very heavy, and it took a lot to handle them, even a few at a time. Mark also supported the tool as we got it to the pail, then we carefully placed the coins inside. I reminded Mark to have another look around now that the cavity was empty. You could never be too thorough.

He agreed and took one more look around. He looked up and down in the opening and on each side. Nothing showed up, and he looked disappointed.

Mac said, "We've got lots, Mark!"

"Yes, I know," he replied.

We carried it all back and put the tools and step stool where they belonged. We needed to be diligent about this, as others might need to find them for another task. We carefully opened the sleeve, and, sure enough, the coins seemed the same as those of Josh's great-uncle. We emptied them into a separate container and marked it, "Joseph." Mac was examining the cloth, marveling at the workmanship of this old piece of clothing. The stitching was done by hand and was a work of art. She held it up to the light.

"Hey guys, look at this. There is a piece of something slipped inside the cuff of this thing. Do you think I should pull it out?"

CHAPTER 11

Uncle Vinnie!

We answered, "Yes!"

Our curiosity was aroused once more. What could it be? Another map perhaps? With the greatest attention to detail, trying not to rip the cuff any further, she pulled the material out. She revealed it with extreme care, so slowly, in a way that only a girl could do. She had that soft feminine touch, kind of like Mom's. She unfolded the torn cloth. Not to disappoint, it had some writing on it! We were elated! Mark couldn't stop staring at it. However, Pa wouldn't be translating it until morning. It would be a long night. Looking at my watch, I realized it was already twenty past two. Maybe it wouldn't be such a long night after all.

We photocopied the note and put it with all of our precious items. One copy was taken with us for Pa to translate. I checked in with Dad to let him know we were back.

It took us forever to settle down, and we must have only gotten a couple of hours of sleep. As usual, the aroma of breakfast made its way to our rooms and summoned us to the table. We didn't even wait until Pa had his first coffee to start talking over one another.

Pa said, "Hold on. Start at the beginning."

We did, and we couldn't wait to get to the good part, the letter from Joseph. Everyone was shocked at the addition of a cub. Bee wanted to go right down to see it, of course, but was deterred by

Mom. Pa was just as willing to see the new offspring of his tunnel companion. Dad surmised that, since the wage was the same for both workers, they must have all received equal amounts. It wouldn't have mattered how much the men were paid to the German commander, as he had thought they would take all the money back when the men died. Something must have allowed them to have time to hide their share before they were sent to their death. There was so much discussion, and, by the time we finally got to the end and showed Pa the copy of the letter, we were sitting at the edge of our seats.

Pa first read the letter to himself, and then, in a very quiet manner, he interpreted. "Well, this is a little bit of a surprise. It says Joseph already in his 50s, had a son by a woman before he was married and supported the child while in Germany. He married in his 60s, and his wife knew of his son. She agreed in supporting him and that they should stay in touch. During captivity, he secretly sent a letter out to his son, telling him about the money he was receiving. He had hoped the letter wasn't confiscated and that his son received it. He was asked to share the news with his daughter. She was born before Joseph was sent to prison."

"That means that Vinnie and your mom are a little closer related than you thought!" said Pa, looking at Mark.

He continued reading, and the letter asked if whoever found the money could make sure both descendants received it.

"Well, then, was Vinnie kind of like an uncle to me?" Mark inquired.

Dad affirmed it would be something like that, and he added that not everyone from the same gene pool was alike. He was insinuating that Mark and Vinnie had no resemblance in character. Pa had already done the research, and there were no more known surviving relatives in Mark's lineage.

"Well, how do I tell Mom that bit of news?" asked Mark.

Pa asked if he could wait until all the matters of the inheritance were sorted before telling her. Mark agreed, as it wasn't a plus to have Vinnie as a brother, even if he was only a step-brother. It wouldn't make her any happier right now, as she was just accepting and letting go of the fact that Vinnie would have killed Mark if given the opportunity. There were so many secrets, we wondered if we could keep them all.

Dad added, "This gives me insight into a little boy who was deprived of his father, so he clung to a piece of paper that would lead to his dad's money." He was referring to Vinnie, of course. "If he had found the money, he would have been validated as his son. Every child wants a father figure in his life. What a poor existence he must have had, with that hurt and longing to be a legitimate member of a family. It is too bad he couldn't turn all that energy and pain into a positive action, as many others have done."

This was another secret Mac would be in on. It created more pressure on her to keep it. She was very close to her family, and the respect they had for one another didn't allow for this kind of behavior. Although difficult, I knew she could do it, as she had never betrayed my trust in the past. Mac was so surprised regarding the lineage, and she couldn't believe both Josh and Mark had relatives who had worked down below at the same time.

"Do you think I had a relative down there, too?" she asked.

That was a natural question at this point.

"I don't think so. Mac, we have done a thorough investigation, especially since we found out about ours, and I have now traced all the names to their present families and where they live."

"We are hoping all the prisoners left some clues to confirm their names and lineage. That said, we never had Vinnie on our list of descendants. He was a surprise that introduced himself into the equation," Dad chuckled, rubbing his chin.

CHAPTER 12

Plans to Travel

The family decided that Dad and Mom would travel to Europe and follow up with a couple of families, without revealing what they knew. They would also use the time together and make it a holiday. Pa would hold down the fort, and we would keep looking for more treasure. We would follow the map to the hydro tunnel when Dad returned. Bee would keep the house and work at the lodge when she wasn't video chatting with Kelly. We promised to look out for one another, but Mom was still a little apprehensive, knowing full well that our intentions were always better than the reality.

Dad would try to get to know these people. We would figure out how to get the money to them. These actions would validate the men that lost their lives here on our property. We felt like we were giving them their final wishes. We could relate to the longing of wanting to know what had happened to their loved ones, and the concern of how they were, as we had thought of nothing else when Pa had disappeared. The feelings were mutual as Pa had hidden underground, not knowing what was happening to us. Although it was overwhelming, we were all ready to do our part to execute the next phase.

Pa got the only list of names, which was kept above ground in the safe. Our safe was an old monster, retrieved from the old Eaton's store in St. Catharines. It would not be moved easily and was truly a safe place to keep anything. It was large enough to house a shopping cart.

You could almost walk in while standing straight up. Pa had it built into the wall of his office using some of the space from the kitchen pantry. It was so well done that you couldn't even tell it was there. The paneling fit perfectly over it, concealing the safe from anyone's view.

CHAPTER 13

Still in Germany

"Here it is," he said, sitting down at the table with us. "These families are still living in Germany." There were three in this group. The first name was Schwartz. There was a map from him in the small tobacco tin. My investigation showed that his great-grandsons are still living in Hamburg, Germany. Mr. Schwartz had a son. The son continued to live in the same house where he grew up after the war. Mitchell III also had a son named Mitchell IV, as well as a younger son Dustin. They lived together in the modest home with their mother.

The Mr. Schwartz who had written this will, had apparently been imprisoned for hiding a valuable collection of books, among other items. He had not wanted to see them destroyed. He'd been taken from his home at gunpoint after a search of his residence. His wife and young son knew nothing of his activities, as it was too dangerous to tell them. The less they knew of his secret, the better. He was followed and reported after he rescued a painting from a massive pile of valuable art, which was ready to be burned. Those were the charges brought against him. He was dragged away, and the family never saw him again.

His son, Mitchell II, had a son and called him Mitchell III to honor his grandfather's memory. There were two boys, Dustin and Mitchell IV, known as the only survivors of Mr. Schwartz. The last generation alive, no matter how young, was to receive the money. The senior

Mr. Schwartz had made this very clear in his will. Compared to the other two wills, this was an uncommon request. There could be older relatives in most cases, like with Angelica. It was also a good reason to make each case personal and follow the wishes of each prisoner. Pa figured that the imprisoned Schwartz had probably thought that it would take generations to free his country and liberate art again.

Pa had eventually discovered that Fry had ancestors who lived in a small town in Germany named Buelstedt. Pa had not been able to find a living relative, so Dad would have to do some digging for information. We needed to know for certain whether there were any living relatives.

The next family was also difficult to trace. The Berlin Wall had separated them. One part of the family lived in free Germany, and the other on the communist side of the wall. While living on the communist side, it appears that this extension of the family had expired and could not be found. There was a member of the family still living in Berlin, but not much information was found on them. Their family name was Friezen. The war was a terrible time, causing immeasurable atrocities, and one of them was severing families, never to find each another again. Devastated, they left for other countries and new lives. The world had shrunk in so many ways, but it could still be endless when searching for the people you loved.

—⁂—

Mom and Dad had their work cut out for them. They would try to take only a couple of weeks to do this. Mom packed, and Dad compiled papers, as well as compiling files on his laptop. They would leave the next day. For today, Mark, Mac, and I would follow-up another copy of the cigarette paper will that had been carefully left in that tobacco tin.

CHAPTER 14

Unexpected

We were careful to sign in, as Pa and Bee would want to know our every step. It looked like the next three copies of the minute maps showed something located near the tunnel with the lake. I wondered if the men had worked together in small groups, as it appeared they had hidden something in the areas together. This one had a circle in the middle of it, and what looked like a sliver-like crevasse on the side. We figured it was the tunnel that led to the lake, and the crevasse where we'd found Pa's Bible. This would be a cinch to find. We grabbed our tools and were off. We wondered if we would see the cougar and her cub. Mac thought we should name them.

"I think Pa should have the honor of doing that," I said

"But what do you think are good names for them?" she persisted.

Mark said, "Give it up, Mac."

"How about Kitten," she replied, "for the young one?"

"Pa might go for that," I agreed.

We were now down at the bottom were the cougar lived. There was no sight of the two. She must have taken her cub to another location. We turned right, toward the tunnel to the lake. We walked along as if strolling on the sidewalk above ground. It was now familiar to us. We were relaxed and happy. We reached the lake and made a quick left towards the crevasse. We had done this before while snooping around down here. Being able to recognize the different areas sure was coming in handy. We wondered if there would be another letter written on cloth, or just the gold. We reached the place marked on the Schwartz map, we checked the rough face around the low slit of an entrance in the wall. It looked totally normal.

"Nothing unusual here," I said.

"Let's go inside!" Mark said.

"I think we should check the opening leading into the cave. We always get so busy that we miss checking the rock around us," I replied.

They were both in agreement. We bent as low as possible to make use of our flashlights. Mark took one side, and I took the other. Mac was there to pass us whatever we needed for our search. There was no room for her to fit inside with us, so she assisted by shinning a flashlight in our direction, also hitting the wall above us. There was silence as we concentrated on scanning the opening.

Suddenly, she let out a high-pitched scream of excitement, then said, "Hey, I see something!"

"Did you have to scare us to death?" I loudly replied.

"Look guys, up there, above you," she reported, pointing.

It was another crevice running parallel to the opening. Her flashlight revealed something brilliant inside.

Nearly five feet above the lake, we found a gold coin. It seemed to be wedged in between some rocks, as if left there to be found. As we peered down into the opening, we saw what looked like more. It appeared to be down a foot from the top of the crevasse in a narrow opening. How did they get the gold into this small sliver of an opening? We could imagine dropping the coins in one at a time, but we assumed the gold bar would also be hidden there. There was no way it would fit in the space.

Preoccupied, we did not notice the cougar's quiet, surprise reappearance. Mac gasped as their eyes met. She put her hands over her mouth, trying not to scream.

"Mac, what is the matter?" I asked, not realizing the cougar was behind me.

I turned and there she was. She looked beautiful in the warm glow of our lights, surrounded by the otherwise black tunnel. I spoke to her like Pa had said to do, and she responded. She came over to get a better scent and then approached Mac.

"Relax, Mac, it is okay," I encouraged.

She did, and the cougar even gave her a little nudge. She reached out her hand and gave the cougar a nice scratch on the head.

"Where is your little one?" She asked, when suddenly, she saw another pair of eyes.

The little one was following behind.

"Can I touch her?" Mac pleaded.

"I don't think you better, you know how the animal kingdom can be, very protective of their young," Mark added.

"Well, she brought it to us, didn't she? She must want us to get to know her."

We decided to stand still and see what the cougar had in mind. She turned around and picked up her young, then put the cub at Mac's feet.

"Is she giving it to me?" Mac whispered, trying to contain herself.

She slowly bent low to pet it. Her hands moved away quickly when she felt a wet gooey hole in its back.

"She is hurt," Mac gasped.

We put the light on its back and it revealed she was. The water created such a narrow pathway that we didn't have enough room to examine the cub. I thought we should try to get them into the cave.

"I will go in and call her to me," I said.

When I got inside, I called her, and she picked up her cub and disappeared. While I was still calling to her, she appeared inside the cave from another direction. Mac and Mark had already joined me with the lights. The cougar put her cub down in front of Mac, and she had a good look at the sore.

"It looks like an infection, but what caused it?"

I bent low to look, too. I shone my flashlight directly above the sore, and it caught the reflection of something inside the opening.

"Look, there is something in there?" I almost shouted.

The cougar became a little unsettled, and we decided that we needed to stay very calm, for her sake as well as ours.

I took my bag off my belt and dumped it onto the stone floor. I picked up my tweezers and told Mac to keep the cub still. I dug into the wound and got a hold of what felt like a bullet. I pulled it out, and the cub didn't even move. As the bullet dropped to the floor, it made a small clanging sound. Someone must have seen the two cougars and shot at them. People were very paranoid, as I would have been myself, if I didn't know better. We were fortunate that Pa had introduced us, as friends.

"I will have to clean the wound and maybe stitch it to keep it clean," I said.

"You can do that?" Mark asked in surprise.

I reminded him of his stitches, and that I had watched Dad. I would try my best to do the same. I had a needle and some thread, but first, I cleaned the inside of the wound. The little cougar was certainly compliant, as if it knew we were trying to help it. I finished up, and Mac let go. It made one quick move over to its parent, who did a quick check of our work by licking the area. I don't know how the antibacterial cream tasted, but I hoped she left enough on her cub to protect the area from further infection. As the parent took one more look our way as if to thank us, she picked up her youngster and they disappeared into the dark. We just stood frozen for a moment, thinking about what had happened. What an absolute privilege it was to interact with nature in this way. The cougar had displayed great trust in us.

"Did you see how the nameless cougar brought her cub to me?" Mac exclaimed. "What a sweetheart!"

"Which one?" Mark and I both replied.

"See, that's what I mean, they need to have names!" she insisted.

I suggested we call the baby Sweetheart. It was fitting, and it would remind us of this conversation. Mac was pleased and shone her light in my eyes to bug me.

"Oh my goodness!" she declared. "Look behind you, Josh."

Mark and I turned, and there on the wall above the opening crevasse, parallel just like the other side, was another opening. It didn't take long to look into it and discover a much wider opening. There inside were gold coins. It looked like they had been poured into the crevasse without being contained in anything. I put my hand in and moved the coins to reach the bottom. There it was. It felt like the gold bar. We filled our pail with the coins, being careful not to miss any. Then, Mark retrieved the gold bar. It was wedged quite well and took some maneuvering to release from the security of the rock after so many years. We searched but found no cloth. We only had the name on the map for identification.

Well, we had found another. This was so much fun and took such little effort on our parts. We talked about how much effort the men had put into finding their hiding places. The only one so far that had some technical difficulties attached was the one Friedrich had either used or designed. It made me wonder if it was designed for another reason, and, in the end, he decided to make it his own. He would not have had time to design something like that while being guarded. Considering the intricate workings of the storage room, I surmised this was one of the planned functions, and maybe it had been abandoned for some reason.

That went well. Mr. Fry's map looked very much the same as the Schwartz map did. There had to be a difference. What was it? They looked identical, as if they'd been traced.

Mac said, "Let's put one on top of another and see if they are the same."

"Good idea, girlfriend," said Mark, and Mac sneered back at him, not appreciating the expression.

The two small pieces of paper were laid on top of another. I held a light underneath them. To our surprise, they were identical, except one was lower than the other.

Mark almost shouted, "Do you think one portion is still in there?"

He was off to see if we had missed anything. It looked like a stone base, but it had a shadow around the edge.

"Maybe I can lift it out," he continued. "Give me something so I can pry it."

I handed him my small crowbar, and he started working with some success. I tried to help him by prying the other end with a pick. We slowly released it from its former hideaway. We were overcome with pride at finding our next treasure. The dirty, old, irregular piece of sack-like material lay there with the rounded shape of coins bulging at the sides. It was not a sleeve or sewn shape, but rather a rag, maybe found or stolen for this purpose. We unfolded the sides of material to expose the coins. The contents were loose but contained. Taking the coins out, we put them on the rock floor in a pile. Then we took the burlap cloth and put it on top of the coins that were already in our pail. We would separate the coins so both portions would go to the rightful families. We had found no instructions for the last two wills except for the names. In these cases, we would make sure the descendants got their inheritance. The bricks of gold would have to be carried separately. This was a heavy load, and we still had one more to find.

We decided to look further and try to find the next coins and bars of gold. It was in this area somewhere. We would leave our latest finds in the small cavern and resume our search.

We looked at the copy of the next piece of cigarette paper. It looked like the same map but had another smaller circle drawn inside the crevasse. We were inside the lengthy opening already, so we assumed that we should find a hole in the wall. We looked, starting at one side, up and down and all around. Then, it finally dawned on me.

"I think it's right where the drawing shows it is," I said. "Let me look at that paper again."

I pointed to the round circle inside the crevasse on the drawing.

"Let's look straight across, on the opposite wall of the rock entrance," I said, as my flashlight preceded my words.

You could not have seen it unless you were looking for it. It was an opening behind a rock wall that jutted out, hiding it. Could this be where the cougar had gotten in earlier? We were going to find out. We shone a flashlight into the opening, which was only about two feet high. We would have to crawl or lay on our backs to check it out. I took the first turn and lay on my back, with my pouch pulled to lie on top of me. It was an awkward space to maneuver in. How could anyone hide a brick of gold in here? Scanning the walls and the ceiling carefully, I moved my head, then my body forward while lying on my back. Inch by inch, until my feet were in too. I arrived at a crossroads in the tunnel. It was accompanied by a cool draft. Now what, which way do I go? I reported to the others on my findings.

They both asked, "Do you want us to come in?"

"Sure, and where do you think you will fit?" I replied.

I shone my flashlight to the right, then to the left. It was definitely much higher, and I figured I could stand in it. It made me wonder if the men had dug tunnels to the outside for fresh air? If so, the cougar would have direct access to the outdoors from a few locations. Looking at my surroundings, I felt that the map would have included this tunnel too, if it was the hiding spot. I informed my friends that I was coming back. It took some time to shuffle my way back, and I wondered if I should have turned myself around and crawled out instead. I was nearing the opening and was finally almost out.

Mac and Mark stepped back to give me room to stand and stretch. I told them there was nothing unusual in there. I had the thought that we had missed important clues in the past by overlooking them. We had focused on the opening so much that we did not examine the rock and small rock cave before it. I shone my light towards the small space where the two rocks met. It looked like one structure until you shone the light at just the right angle. Another crevasse was nicely hidden. It was beyond us how we had not seen it earlier. I put my hand into it and felt. You couldn't see inside due to the lack of light and because of the angle of the rock wall.

"Yup, I feel something," I said, adding, "This is different!"

"What is it?" asked Mac.

"It's a glass jar!" I replied.

"Bring it out, let's see it!" Mark commanded with a raised voice.

I tried to lift it with one hand, but it was too heavy. Using two hands in a very awkward position, I was able to retrieve the jar. It was one of two old specimens filled with shiny gold coins. I gave it to Mark and went for the other. Yes, there was another one. It was also filled with gold coins. Where was the gold bar? My hand made a thorough search and made sure there was no false bottom. That was puzzling. I guess this guy hadn't gotten paid what everyone else did. Or did he leave it somewhere else?

Mac checked the place out and reported, "This is too small to get a brick of gold into, on top of what we pulled out!"

She thought it would definitely be somewhere in the tunnel, and she pleaded for us to let her look. She figured she could get through with ease, as she had a smaller frame.

"Please let me try!" Mac pleaded.

We finally gave in to her persistent pleading. It somehow didn't feel right to put a girl in a position where she could get hurt or be in danger.

She put the headband flashlight on and crawled in. Since she was crawling, she could check the bottom of the tunnel more closely than I had. She was on her hands and knees, and about three feet in when she announced, "I found it!"

"You didn't," I replied.

"Yes, and you will kick yourself when you see just how easy it was."

She proceeded to back up out of the small cave, holding the brick of gold.

"Here you are!" she said, looking quite proud of herself.

When she stood up, we saw the brick of gold. She made a huge point of saying over and over how in the open it was. She found it at the side of the tunnel wall in a very slight crevasse. She figured I missed it by sliding on my back.

We were glad that we let Mac go back in there. I figured we probably would have gone back another time to investigate the tunnel, and then we would have found the gold bar.

"Give a girl credit when she deserves it," Mac encouraged.

We knew she was right, of course, and agreed that she did very well.

We realized we would have to make a couple of trips to get everything back to our safe underground place. Pa and Dad would be so proud of us. Mom and Dad were barely gone, and we had already found three more inheritances. It was going to feel great to report back to the senior family members, although it was too bad there had been no directions with our last discoveries. At least we had found the Friezen treasure. We would leave the rest for to Pa to figure out.

I did find a new tunnel to investigate, and I figured it joined with the outside, somewhere on the rock cliffs of the gorge. That took me back to when we found Alice, the rock climber. I hoped the opening wasn't too visible from outside.

We were tired by the time we got back up to our hideout. It felt like nap time. I gave out a big yawn, and the others followed suit. We each grabbed a cot and wrapped ourselves in our sleeping bags. We dozed off quickly, as it was cozy and warm. Our bodies were tired, and our minds filled with contentment after the job we had completed.

Terrified at a sound, Mac and Mark jumped to their feet. I couldn't figure out where I was, or what day it was. What was happening? Someone was shaking me and shouting.

"Wake up, Josh, wake up," Dad repeated. "Do you know how late it is?" He said in an anxious voice.

I stammered to stand up. I was fine, but in a bit of a shock and asked what time it was. Dad said it was well past three in the morning, and they were all worried about us. We apologized profusely and pleaded for forgiveness. What was supposed to be a little nap had turned into one of the best sleeps I had ever had. It quickly became the worst nightmare soon after I awoke. Mom and Dad had refused to leave with us missing. Once Dad, Pa, Mom, and Bee realized we were fine and what had happened, the whole party relaxed—including us. We were able to tell them and show them the rewards from what was now yesterday. Dad said he felt more motivated than ever about finding those to whom the legacy belonged. It would be more rewarding, knowing the gold was already found.

Mom looked upset and told Dad they would miss their plane. I felt terrible about what had happened. How could I have done this to them on the night before they were leaving? Their flight was leaving at 6 in the morning, and they would have to be in the international terminal three hours prior. It was already four thirty. Mom and Dad would not leave without knowing we were all safe, and after this episode, Mom didn't think she should leave at all. Pa tried to reassure her that we all make innocent mistakes, and that the family would be just fine. Dad added that we would be more conscientious next time. We promised with sincerity, and she reconsidered.

"Well, we had better see if we can get new tickets," Dad hastily added.

CHAPTER 15

The Hostage Situation

We all went upstairs through Pa's den and sat around the kitchen table. It ended up being an unexpected family time. Everyone was wide awake and hungry. The rest of the family had been panicked over our whereabouts, and we had missed dinner. Dad made a few calls and managed to secure a direct flight out at eleven o'clock. Their missed flight would have made a stop in Paris. The direct flight was okay, as the previous one didn't give time to do any sight-seeing in Paris anyway.

Mom was happy to assist Pa with preparing eggs, sausage, and pancakes. I made the coffee while Bee and Mac set the table. Mark was busy asking questions about the carriage house. He still wasn't sure what room he should keep for himself. He and his mother had shared a room until he put a makeshift wall up between their beds for privacy. The carriage house would give them much more space.

Pa couldn't let go of the fact that someone had shot Sweetheart. I figured Mac's suggestion for a name was going to stick with the cub. Pa had not even seen it yet, but he was grateful to us for taking care of the wound. He asked Mark questions about Sweetheart, and Mark fired back questions regarding their new home. It was comical to listen to.

So much had happened in one day. It always does, I thought to myself, wondering what tomorrow would bring. Mom gathered us together to sit at the old table, and Dad said grace. He prayed for our safety, the discovery of the money for the other families, the safety of the cougars and healing for Sweetheart, a safe journey, and the food we were about to eat. We enjoyed this impromptu breakfast together, and everything felt right again.

It was around two in the afternoon when we were alerted to a hostage situation at the Paris Airport. We all watched the TV intently. Barry called to see if our parents were on that plane. Pa had told him their flight number, but not that it was changed to eleven this morning, and that it was a direct flight. Angelica called to see if this was Mom and Dad's flight. We told her no, they were lucky not to be on that flight since their schedule was changed the last minute. We resumed watching to find out more. Someone had taken over the plane after it landed, and two passengers were shot and injured. He said he would blow up the plane if it was not refueled and made ready to fly again. We knew that wouldn't happen.

"Wait until Mom and Dad hear about their plane," Bee said, wearing that worried look she had inherited from Mom.

Pa reminded her that God was in control, and we asked God to protect them.

"Maybe we were supposed to make them late," I said, partially to console myself.

Bee said, "How about the people on the plane, does God care about them too?"

Pa said, "Yes, of course. Let's take a minute and pray for them too. God can protect them as well." Pa's prayer was so positive that we all believed those passengers would be fine. Later that night, Mom and Dad called to say they were at their hotel if we needed to get a hold of them. We relayed the news to them, and they were thankful for the change in their plans.

It was at the nine o'clock news that they announced the release of the hostages. They were finally over their ordeal. A sharp shooter had disabled the hijacker, who was found to be carrying a phony bomb. The injured were taken to the hospital and were in stable condition. We all sighed with relief. It was unnerving to think of Mom and Dad on that plane, not knowing what would happen next. I could only imagine how many lives were on hold that day, waiting for the hostages to be set free.

Our minds shifted, as we were all curious regarding what Dad would find out. Just how many Schwartz, Fry, and Friezen family members would he find, and what would they be like? We hoped not like Vinnie. The thought was terrifying. It was interesting how I zeroed in on Vinnie continually, even though the people we would find could be more like Angelica and Mark. I guessed that evil prevails in our minds if we chose to let it. I would try to choose the positive from now on.

Mark went home to do some chores for his mom, and Mac had a dentist appointment in the afternoon. We would have to check with each other later to set up another excursion below.

Bee came running into the room, laptop in hand. "Kelly is going to have his appendix out. I have to be there."

Pa looked up from his reading and raised an eyebrow. "Start again, and settle yourself," he demanded.

"I need to go to Lancaster," Bee urged, almost frantic.

Pa said he would see what he could do. He called Jake, who said the Amish driver was going today at five for another emergency run. It meant they would be driving into the night. Bee didn't care, as she was concerned about Kelly. I have never seen her move and pack that quickly. She was ready before Pa and I could make sandwiches and coffee for ourselves and for Bee to take on her journey. She spoke with Kelly, and he said he would be happy to see her smiling face again. He was going to be laid up for a while. Pa and I would drive Bee to Jake's, but this time, we could take a leisurely drive home. It was nice having Pa home, and I realized I would have him all to myself for a while. Maybe he and I could look for treasure together. That would be fun.

We started earlier than needed. Bee couldn't settle down, even to have a bite to eat. She would enjoy a sandwich better in the confines of the black car, knowing that she was on her way, and there was nothing more she could do.

The bridge traffic was heavy. Bee was biting her nails, and we were thankful for the earlier start today. We kept her busy by sending our best wishes and prayers for Kelly, amongst other topics. Bee hardly had time to say good-bye before she hopped into the dark automobile, next to another Amish teen dressed in traditional garb. As wound up as Bee was, we hoped this girl loved conversation. She would get it whether she did or not. We waved until they were out of sight and then left.

CHAPTER 16

Ride to Lancaster

Bee introduced herself and took out her notebook to log the day. She hadn't taken the time earlier as she'd been scurrying to get ready. She realized she had not even said hello to the teen beside her, so she put her pen down and did so. The girl was going back to her home town to see her mother, who was supposed to go to the hospital with complications having her seventh child. She refused. Bee's fellow passenger's name was Rachel. She was the third oldest and had the opportunity to further her education as long as she kept her faith. Her parents must have been of a liberal mindset to allow this. She had almost finished nursing college and was only eighteen. Bee thought she looked much younger. Rachel informed her that she would get her training and go back to Lancaster to work with her people. They would much rather go to someone of their religious persuasion than to a stranger who had a different morality and way of life.

Bee explained why she was going to Lancaster and how worried she was about Kelly's surgery. Rachel calmed her by saying that she had witnessed that surgery first hand, and it was going to be just fine. Bee asked how long she had been in training, as eighteen was when most kids graduated in Canada. She bashfully said she was gifted as a student and finished high school material when she was just fifteen.

"It must be nice," Bee said.

Rachel chuckled at Bee's surprised expression.

"I am going to start my last year of college, if it all works out with my mother," Rachel reported.

"What do you mean?" Bee asked.

She meant if her mom would be all right, and she did not have to help at home. Her oldest brother helped her dad on the farm, and her older sister was already doing so much to keep the house going. She baked, cleaned, took care of the younger ones, and so on. Her mother had been sick through the whole pregnancy and was told she might not have the strength to have this baby.

Bee interjected, "Why doesn't she have a caesarean?"

Rachel agreed, but added, "The midwife does not have the skills, but she has our families total trust."

Bee emphatically pushed, "You know better than that and could probably do it yourself!"

Rachel agreed and told Bee that if she got a chance, she would. She did not want her mother to die. Death was accepted as part of God's plan and taken with an unquestioning attitude. Her people were unique that way.

By the time their trip had finished, Bee had convinced Rachel of her skills, and Rachel was confident about doing this procedure. She was going to prepare herself for the surgery and get supplies from the hospital ahead of time. She would also get the drugs she needed, as she knew her mother would endure a lot of stress if she went into premature labor. It would be risky after the labor began. Rachel was putting in some hours at the local hospital so she could be home with the family. She asked for a three-month transfer, which her professors were glad to give to her. Her marks had been at the top of the class since she started school, and they were happy to oblige. The school was also trying to convince her to become a doctor. They felt she was a natural, and, with the right education, she could go places.

Rachel was dropped off first, so Bee knew where she lived. It was dark, so she wrote down the names of the roads and lanes. Bee said she would visit Rachel when she got a chance. They hugged and said good-bye. Bee could see Rachel's mom inside the dimly lit kitchen through the window. She looked too weak to get up from her chair, but she managed a wave to Rachel as she watched Rachel get out of the car. Bee hoped her new friend could convince her Mother to go to the hospital.

CHAPTER 17

At the Hospital

Kelly looked pale and was being medicated for his pain. The doctors would operate tonight. Bee had made it just in time. She was so glad.

She kissed him hello and said, "I am praying everything goes well. I will be here when you get out of surgery."

"Can you call my parents and let them know when I am out of surgery? My little brother is waiting for the call, at the phone booth outside of the house," he said.

"Of course, as soon as I see you," she responded and kissed him quickly, before they moved him to the operating room.

Bee felt alone. She knew that if she were home, her family would be there beside her. She was noticing the difference that Rachel had been talking about. The Amish kept on with their work and duties, and they accepted the outcome no matter what it was. Bee knew Kelly's family loved him, but this is how it was. She knew she could not live this way. She would have to live according to her convictions, like Grammy and Grammpy did. She hoped Rachel would live up to hers. It was nearing morning, and Kelly was wheeled back to his room. The bed was placed at the window. Bee was relieved, and she called the number she was given. The sweet voice of a young child answered after just one ring.

"Yes, Eli speaking."

Bee reported that Kelvin was doing just fine, and the surgery was over. He was in room 203. His family just knew him as Kelvin, so that was what she called him.

The phone went dead, and she assumed Eli ran off to give his report to his parents. He had been posted out there all night waiting for the call. She pictured a little boy, all alone in the dark behind the barn, in a little structure like an outhouse. It gave her the shivers.

She stroked Kelly's forehead and waited for him to come out of his drug-induced slumber. She was thankful to be here with him. Although they had not seen each other since her mom and her had to hide, she and Kelly had communicated using modern technology and they got to know each other very well. Her heart had ached in the past, as she wanted to see him again. Even though he was hurting right now, she was grateful that she could actually touch him.

Kelly came to slowly and started talking. He seemed happy she was there. After a couple of hours of visiting with him, he looked tired again.

Bee said, "I am going to go to Grammy's, but I will be back."

He gave her his car keys and asked her to take his car. She thanked him and gave him a peck on the cheek. He turned quickly and made it a proper kiss. Bee floated down the hall to the parking lot. It was all she could do not to run back upstairs for one more.

Bee would call Pa and Josh and fill them in on her trip. Mom and Dad would be anxious to hear how she was doing. It had been a long trip, and she looked forward to getting some sleep.

CHAPTER 18

A Better Farewell

On the way home, we acknowledged that it was a much more relaxed farewell than the previous one had been. So much had happened since then. It was a leisurely drive home, and Pa and I had many facts to review.

Pa was one of those people that liked to lay his plan out and follow it with no deviation. I, on the other hand, loved the fact that life put curves in the road, so I couldn't see what was around the corner. The unknown intrigued me, and confused Pa. Well, at least one of us would be enjoying the ride at any given time.

After unlocking the door and turning the alarm off, we had a quiet cup of "choffee," which was coffee mixed with chocolate. That was one of Pa's favorite drinks. Even his regular Tim Horton's waitress knew just how he liked it. I was sipping mine carefully when the phone rang. It was Mom and Dad. We informed them of Bee's trip and that she would contact Grammy and Grammpy from the hospital after seeing Kelly. They agreed it was the right thing to do, knowing she would be fine. We could call Mom and Dad anytime we needed to, sounded the last reminder. Mom sent us her expected, "I love you," and hung up the phone.

Pa and I decided to look at some of the will-maps from our safe. We would have dinner and make plans for tomorrow. When we were done, a good movie would do nicely to end our evening. I knew Pa would be sleeping in his chair soon after it started. That was fine, as I enjoyed just knowing he was there near me.

Mom and Dad had ventured out to see if they could find some of the Schwartz family. The phone book had quite a few, but not many with the names Mitchell and Dustin. They weren't your regular German names, like Laars or Dietmar. Dad promised he would log every detail on his computer for us to read.

CHAPTER 19

Dad's Account

It was a lovely drive, and we were heading just outside the city limits. It was amazing how close to the road the houses stood. There were small clusters of homes, separated by fields and other green spaces. The manure piles were right up against some homes along the side of the road. Some had barns attached to the homes, but they looked like one building. The barn door was on the opposite side of the building as the living area. This was how most rural families lived. The animals were directly on the other side of the wall. This provided warmth, and the setup was handy for a twenty-four seven, hands-on maintenance of their stock. This method of building was definitely a thing of the past. Even the houses built this way were not used for livestock these days. They were now garages or glorified workshops. Sheep and cows grazed in small pastures and lived in small barns on owner's properties.

The gardens could be described as works of art. Their straight rows of flowers and vegetables adorned the canvas, showing dominance. No blade of grass or weed could be seen in the garden. It reflected the owner of the property. The homes where all white and clean, most having red tile roofs. The odd century home still had a thatched straw roof. The windows were noticeably clean, showing off lace or sheer curtains. Almost every home had their lines full of laundry. Communities had laws that forbid laundry on weekends or other stipulated days. It all looked so tidy and uniform. We noticed many of the older homes had a name or a phrase over the doorway. It was something I thought would be neat to do, kind of like a coat of arms.

Every small community seemed to have their own bakery and butcher shop. Nerissa and I decided to stop at a bakery for lunch and see what it was like. The German breads, cakes, and pastries looked delicious, especially the tortes. There were no seats, but instead there were round tables to stand up against as a place to put your coffee cup and saucer. We did miss our mugs. The white-clad woman wearing a heavy net over her hair behind the counter couldn't speak English, so we pointed at the Gooseberry Torte and Bienenstich. The torte did not disappoint, and the Bienenstich was just like Omz used to make. The strong cup of coffee accented the sweets perfectly, making an incredible combination.

We were hoping to reach a town called Bremen. That was where the two boys were raised. It was the same town that many immigrants left from, after the war, hoping for freedom and the land of plenty. Pa's father and mother, with Pa as a child, were amongst them. The town had turned into a city, to our dismay.

The ride was pleasant, and we almost forgot our mission of the day. The GPS ended our daydreaming by announcing the address. We had arrived at the house we were looking for. It was an old home, but it was nicely kept, modest in size and surrounded with a white wooden fence. We walked through the gate and noticed that the old door had been brought into the 21st century with a bright red coat of paint. The heavy door knocker was oversized and prominent. It was there to be used, not just a decoration. The shiny surface where its handle came down to announce a visitor's presence was gleaming brass. We followed suit and thought to ourselves, it was louder than a doorbell.

We were greeted by an elderly lady. Wearing a big smile and an apron, she wiped her hands on her apron, bowing with an apology for her dirty hands. She summoned us to enter and we did. The house was spotless and full of old, neatly-placed knickknacks. She showed us to the kitchen, and we followed. She was baking apple strudel. Her apples and the dough were already prepared. She was going to fill the pastries and bake them on large cookie sheets. She motioned for us to sit down. All this was done through sign language, and we didn't know whether she could speak English or not.

"Now zat you ar sitting, I ken keep on vorking, vat ken I do fo you?" she said.

With shocked faces, we had to be careful not to let our jaws drop. We hardly remembered what to say.

"Pardon the intrusion, Ma'am, but we are looking for someone and think we could be lost," I said.

"Vel, tell me who ar you looking for unt maybe I ken help you?" she replied.

We looked at each other and wondered if this was going to work. "Well, I am looking for the descendants of a Mr. Schwartz. I am gathering information to write a story on war crimes committed against those that were arrested for reasons of moral conviction."

"Vat hev you herd?" she asked in her broken English.

"Well, I can say he tried to save books and works of art," I replied.

She replied quickly in her accent, yes, she was the wife of Mitchell III, and her sons lived with her.

"I hev gute boys," she went on.

The family had fallen on hard times during the war. The house was taken over by a Nazi family as their own.

"De fumily vas put on si street to find sheltar sumwhere," she stressed.

She said if it hadn't been for some kind people in town, the family would have died. After the war, her husband's grandmother had worked endless hours to keep food on the table and support her son and herself. She stayed close to the home her husband had been taken from. She hoped he would return to the house he loved, someday. She vowed she would one day buy it back for her son. This dream stayed with her son, even after his mother passed. She was not able to purchase it back in her lifetime. Her son also worked hard and saved until he could get a mortgage and buy back his father's house.

"De mortgage wus nut pait unt must be pait by generations ufter. It is like dis in hour cuntry. He hat a sun, my husbant, he pest away mit heart attic ven my boys vere smull," she said with a sigh. "It wus a jub keeping de haus, but ve did it."

The boys needed to go to school, so they increased their mortgage again. They hoped they would make a good life for themselves with their education in the trades.

"When will the boys come home?" I asked.

"If si jub goes vell, it vill be at fife turdy," she answered.

Her English was good. Through conversation, we found out she went to night school to learn English through a free Government sponsored program. We were in awe of her understanding of our native tongue. She informed us that the boys learned in school and were even better than she was.

The apple strudel had baked and cooled, and it was past coffee time. We were invited to have a piece with her. Our nostrils had been tantalized for an hour by this time, and we prepared for the delightful treat. We couldn't praise her enough, although she let us know that she made the best strudel in town. All we could do was nod in agreement as we ate.

There was a loud, "Hallo Mutti."

It came from the back door. Two fine looking young men appeared from around the corner. It was easy to see they had worked hard that day, as their clothes were torn and dirty, not to mention the sweat. Their skin was flawless, and one couldn't help noticing how good-looking they both were. The taller, who was also the youngest, had a thick head of auburn hair. They were both tall and on the lanky side, but it was clear that the older had worked on building extra muscle. He had blonde, fine hair in contrast to his brother. He looked like he really didn't need any at all to be a striking young man. Their blue eyes were stunning, mesmerizing. The light would make them transparent, like blue skies.

We introduced ourselves, and their mom took over. The talking was loud, and there was no doubt that the little lady ruled with an iron fist. We surmised that was why they had turned out so well.

—◊—

We were invited to dinner, and we looked at some old pictures of family members. It was nice to put a face to Mr. Schwartz. He had the same eyes the boys had, and it looked like Mitchell came by the name rightly, as he looked just like Mitchell I. Mrs. Schwartz told us that there was a birthmark passed down in the family, and her son, Dustin, carried it on his ear. Only one person in each generation ever had this birthmark. It was a small hole in the skin on the ear, near the temple area. We found this interesting and had a look.

The boys cleaned up for dinner, and the conversation was stimulating. They were in the plumbing and heating business, and they called their business MDS. We found Mitchell to be more hyper, and Dustin to be the silent type, although when he wanted to say something, it counted. We complimented the chef for the lovely home-style goulash that she had prepared in the summer kitchen behind the house, just around the hill in the yard.

We started talking about the stories passed down regarding their home. There were many. I asked what the large mound behind the house was for. They all looked at one another and explained that they did not know. It had been part of the property since back in the war days. It had been used as a point of interest, and a flagstone path led around it to the summer kitchen. Rose bushes and shrubs now adorned the hill, making it a feature. They showed us pictures of the house from the days of the war, and there was the hill. In one picture, it was bare. In the next, it was covered with grass and bushes.

CHAPTER 20

Another Link Exposed

Eventually, we felt so comfortable that Mitchell and Dustin volunteered to show us around their home. They wanted to show us something that was truly original to the house, something unchanged. We went into the small, low basement. It had walls of stone and mud, and it was painted with a coat of lime. Within the last year, Dustin had carefully installed the furnace. He had placed it strategically, as not to block the door. Mitchell told us about running the water lines, avoiding one wall. Did these boys know something they weren't saying?

We walked around the furnace, and there was the door. It was chipped and old, and had been made of a variety of woods. It was recessed. They had given it a coat of lime paint to blend it with the rest of the basement. They explained that this door was not exposed when they purchased it back from the previous owners. No one knew of it, as a layer of rock and mud covered it. Some rocks had fallen out, so they investigated by removing more and found a door. It was facing the back yard. They removed it at one point, but there was nothing but wall behind it.

I was getting very excited. Could it be that the Germans handpicked people from prison to send to the project in Niagara? Was this man already using his skills in the basement of his own home? It was a big chance I was taking, but I asked if we could investigate a little. They both agreed, saying they were waiting for the right person and time to do this. They carefully took the door off its hinges. There was just a stone wall blocking us from whatever lay behind it. I noticed the stones were nice and orderly, just as the rest of the wall had been built. There was one group of stones that looked smaller than all the rest. I touched them. They seemed to be in a straight line. Remembering our tunnels and different contraptions, I pushed on them. Nothing happened. The boys looked on as if I was mad. I noticed the rock right under the straight row. It had a much squarer shape to it.

"I bet that's it," I said, forgetting I was not alone. I pushed on it as hard as I could. Nothing seemed to happen!

"Okay, let me try this," I said in frustration.

I pulled the square stone down from the top, like I was flipping down a large switch. It moved, but we saw nothing.

"Was ist denn das?" we heard the boy's mother, Mary shout.

We turned to face her. The wall had opened on the opposite side. How exciting this was! The boys ran over and couldn't believe their eyes. They told their mother to stay back, and that we would check it out first. Both women looked on with amazement. The boys had flashlights hanging at the furnace and water heater in case the hydro went out. They gave me one, and we shone them into the dark entrance. A narrow hall led to a room, which had been dug out into the ground under the front yard. Rustic shelves built along the walls held old books. The collection of antique paintings was incredible. Along with them, we found a letter in an envelope, addressed to his family. The boys were moved to silence, and their mother was in utter shock. This is what their predecessor had died for. He had wanted to save these books and this valuable art. We couldn't stop ourselves from touching everything, appreciating the actions of this man. He had lived by his values and what he knew was right, not what others dictated to him.

We decided to go upstairs and let our hostess read her letter. I was careful to show them how to close the door and conceal this secret until they were ready and knew what to do with it. We all sat around, and Mary Schwartz read the letter, and the boys translated it.

It said, "Dear loved ones. If you find this letter, it must mean that

I have been taken, and the enemy or my loved ones have found this secret. I pray it will be my family. I hid books and art upstairs as a deterrent. The basement also housed some boxes of books, hidden under old dishes. I saved these artifacts and gave my life for them so future generations can enjoy and appreciate them. I hope they are still in good condition upon viewing by you. I am giving these to the last generation alive, hoping you are living in freedom and God's blessings. The cavern and tunnel were dug with my own hands, and I carried the earth to the back yard at night. This was before the war. God gave me a sense of things to come, and I obeyed, not knowing what the room would be used for. The work was done while my wife was away for the summer, visiting her family. When she returned, I had to explain the dirt. I couldn't, and asked her to just trust me, and she did. God blessed me with a good woman. When the war broke out, I tried my best to fill this room with valuables for the future. May this generation love them as much as I do.

Go with God before you, Mitchell Schwartz."

What a day it had been. We talked to Mitchell, Dustin, and Mary about how valuable this discovery would be, and we made sure they were prepared for the exposure and how it could change their lives. I suggested they should not talk to anyone about this, as the art would be in great danger of being stolen. I would get some contacts for them—if they trusted me to do this—and we would talk the next day. I knew very well that this art might be confiscated and put into a museum without them getting a cent. They could make money on showing tours through their place, but that would be unsettling for their mother unless they moved. I would have to do some homework tonight and get back to them tomorrow. We made arrangements to meet the next day for dinner, as Mary insisted we join them for some barbecued pig tails. Neither one of us had ever had them, so we thought we would give it a try and gladly accepted their invitation. We left in a shroud of uncertainty regarding all we had found. We could not imagine how our new friends were feeling.

I made some phone calls shortly after arriving at our hotel. One was to an art collector of rare and old finds. He confirmed that, if they did not belong to my friend, but he found them, they would either be returned to the rightful owner or the state would put them in a museum, depending on the value. I then called a lawyer friend, who was going to research this matter and get back to me. Pa was the next call, and he was elated that the search had gone so well. He was interested in every detail, and the conversation went on for an hour or more. Pa reminded me that the gold was theirs, and his proof substantiated that. The workers also made a will of sorts, which proved who they were. Their names were also on a list of prisoners that had been taken to work at a top-secret job. We knew the relatives would receive their rightful inheritance. Pa and I discussed whether I should confide in them. We decided that we would see what they decided to do with what they found.

CHAPTER 21

Big Choices

The next day, we couldn't wait to visit the Schwartz home. The aroma of dinner greeted us. Mary had decided to make a pork roast as well. She didn't want us to go home hungry if we didn't like the pigtails. It was a delicious meal, and we actually enjoyed the pigtails. It was like eating a barbecued chicken neck. We just couldn't dwell on the part of the body they came from. The boys looked tired from their hard day at work, but they were anxious to talk. They hadn't gotten much sleep, as their minds had taken them from their great-grandfather to present day and their priceless artifacts.

We sat in the small living room with a cup of good coffee. We were finding that the German people enjoyed their strong cup of coffee.

I gave the family my information and asked them what they thought. Mitchell, who was very sentimental, spoke first. He didn't want to hide the treasure, as his great-grandfather died to save it for everyone to enjoy. He would be willing to let a museum take them as long as people did not have to pay to see and enjoy the books and art. Dustin agreed, as they had talked about it earlier and came to a unanimous decision. All Mary could say was that she had such good, unselfish boys. She was so proud of them. They could have sold these items on the black market, and no one would have been the wiser. I told them it might come down to the next of kin to receive some of these items, if they were found and if they wanted them returned. They knew they would need assistance in getting this delicate job done. I told them I could help in that way, and we could keep their location and name a secret for now. This way, their lives would not be disrupted. I also told them our names had to stay out of their story for now. It was very important to their future. They would have to trust us.

The boys figured the coincidence was too great to have found these treasures together after one visit. We assured them that stranger things have happened. We also inquired about their neighbors and how curious they were regarding who visited. They let us know about Mrs. Semph two doors down, who liked to watch everything and everyone.

"Go on with your lives as if nothing has changed," I said. "When all the arrangements are made, I will call you, and we will discretely have the articles removed to a safe place."

"Now that business is done, can we go downstairs for one more peek?" I said as I rubbed my hands together.

The boys and Mary were anticipating another look as well. The door was engineered well, just like some of the ones in our tunnels.

"Do you know how clever this man was?" I asked.

Mary piped up a "yes" in agreement, but she added that her boys were just as clever and could figure out any obstacle and overcome it.

This was nice to hear, as I had noticed that my son had inherited many of his skills from his grandfather and myself.

"You boys are young to have made such a generous, wise decision." They were only twenty-three and twenty-one. "Your great-grandfather would be proud of you. He left all he had to you boys." They had no idea just how much he had left to them, as the wage was coming from Canada when all was settled.

It was like we had known each other for more than just two days. We had filled them in on my grandfather and grandmother coming to Canada with the family belongings after grandfather's brothers disappeared. We couldn't tell them everything, as there was too much at stake. It would just take one greedy person to find out about our secret, the gold, and the tunnels. Who knew what could happen? They knew I was an investigator, and they were trying to put a lot of things together in their minds.

We opened the door again. The boys asked how the door on the other side opened, as there must be a connection. I agreed and told them that if there wasn't a connection on the inside, it would be on the outside of the house.

"That is a lot of digging," Dustin replied.

I suggested we try to find the access point to the mechanical apparatus. With the boys high-powered battery lights they used for their work, we were able to give the tunnel a good going over. We could see all areas at the same time, placing one free standing light on each end of the tunnel. The walls were all quite uniform, except where the room entrance was cut in. We did the same search to this room. We moved every book onto some plywood raised off the floor, in the basement. This was done after taking endless amounts of photos from all angles. I couldn't wait to take my time and leisurely look at the treasures that had been saved so many years before. All the paintings, some still in their frames, were also taken to the now-cluttered basement. We had to force ourselves to ignore the captivating canvases to continue our search. The bookcases were moved away from the walls. There, behind the one on the end, was a nook where a stone had been removed. In it lay an old Bible from the eighteen-hundreds. I picked it up while the boys looked over my shoulders with curiosity. I recognized the name "Schwartz" in the inside, but that was all. In the back were names and dates. Mary would have to check this out. The Bible opened to a page where a small photo lay. There was writing on the back, which I could not read. The partial picture was of two men. Nerissa, being too curious to wait her turn, was peeking from behind me. She almost grabbed the photo from my hand, nearly shouting.

"Shawn, this is Mark! How did they a get a picture of Mark?" She was so taken aback that she forgot about the secrecy.

I, too, noticed the man in the photo. He looked just like Mark! What did this mean? There were more papers in the ancient book. I gave the Bible to Mary for further examination and focused on the small nook where I'd found it. There, in the back corner, was a metal pin. I pulled it.

The wall slid to the side like it had been made yesterday. Everyone looked my way! Dustin was quick to bring a light, and Mitchell supported with his. It was another living area. It was a nice sized room, about ten by ten. It had two cots, still covered with old blankets. A small, pitted mirror hung on the wall over the chipped washbasin. A small, very aged leather suitcase still sat on an old, unpainted bench.

"Is this a hiding place?" Mitchell asked.

"Who was hiding here?" questioned Dustin.

Mary added, "It vaz nut ourah families as ve know what happened to them. Maybe it vaz some of de Jewish people."

"But Mitchell the First would have hidden them," Dustin said.

"Yes, I belief he was vas dis kind of man," Mary replied.

Lifting the lid to the suitcase, our eyes regarded its contents, looking for clues as who was hidden in this room. There was a man's shirt. It looked hand-sewn, with the most intricate stitches on the cuffs. I had seen this kind of work before, on Joseph Schultz sleeve. It was the one with the note sewn into the cuff. Could they be connected? We found a woman's skirt, hardly worn. There was also a woman's undershirt. We were distressed at the fact that we found a little pair of red shoes, belonging to a child of approximately one year old. They were scuffed and looked worn, and still had the little red laces in them. You could tell they had been worn while crawling, then learning to walk. Beside them lay a hand-woven, natural wool child's sweater, edged in light green crocheting. It was definitely a feminine sweater, judging by its style. The small leotards were bearing the holes from crawling on her knees. A wide ribbon lay carefully rolled up, as not to get wrinkled. It was no doubt that it was for the little girls' hair. There were a few pictures loose in the bottom of the trunk. There was a photo of a man, woman, and child. No names. We wondered what happened to them, and, above all, if they made it to safety.

Dustin called to us, "Look over here."

We saw a crack in the wall from top to bottom. What could that mean? From past lexperience, I knew it was not there by chance. It seemed, these days, nothing was just chance. We were directed in a specific path, experiencing things that only God could ordain.

After examining the crack, I suggested that it was a decoy.

The boys gasped and said, "What?"

"I cannot tell you where, but I have seen this kind of thing before. We should look elsewhere, because the answer is not here. The decoy is here so we don't find the real thing."

We all took a wall and examined it carefully. Mitchell was the first to find something. It was another piece of metal stuck in the wall, but it had been flattened to make it inconspicuous. Upon a thorough investigation, we decided to pull it and see what happened. It was hard to do with our fingers, and Dustin ran to get a pair of pliers.

CHAPTER 22

Broken Hearts

I grabbed the pliers and with a firm grip and took a hold of the heavy metal with the pliers' teeth. I pulled with all my might, until there was a noise from behind the wall. We saw nothing, until the mortar started to come out in spots. The grinding from behind the wall was causing some smoke, and we hoped we were not going to blow the place up. I told everyone to stand back until we were sure it was safe. I kept on working the piece of steel. My pliers slipped, and the metal moved.

Another secret door opened to reveal its disclosure of the past. The boys led the pack this time. They were totally enthralled with all that was found. It was another passage, which led around the house to under the mound in the back yard. We wondered if it would lead to above the ground. I pointed the wiring in the tunnel out to the boys as we moved passed it.

"The last door must have malfunctioned," I said. "It was no wonder, as it was so old."

It would not have been designed to make noise and smoke when originally built.

The boys stood frozen. Before them, on the ground, lay something. They were shocked. Three skeletons huddled together in a collapsed fashion with their clothes still intact. Dustin and Mitchell had to leave for a moment to steady themselves. It was a traumatizing find. The ladies left too, holding both hands over their open mouths. I couldn't blame them. It was so overwhelming to look down upon this decayed trio. I checked out the skeletons and took special notice of the miniature one. It was the little girl. There was a big red ribbon, still tied into a bow, lying on the shoulder of the minute sweater on the child's skeleton. The child must have been sitting on the mothers' lap, as their skeletons were collapsed together, only separated by their clothing. The father had a short, broken-handled shovel in the skeleton of his hand. It looked like he had been trying to dig his way out to save his family. I took the shovel and started to poke the earth. It was an act of freedom for the family. I was compelled to do it. My heart sank as I thought about them sitting here, dying. It took no effort, and I felt fresh air. It was night, but I was sure I had reached the outside. We did not want to attract attention with a light beam appearing from the ground this late. I carefully closed it again. The boys came back, as well as Mary and Nerissa. We all bowed our heads to show our respect to this little family.

I suggested we go back up. We had our work cut out for us, as everything had to be hidden again. It was already early in the morning, but the sun had not come up yet. I asked Mary if she would mind if Nerissa and I stayed for the night. She was happy to comply with my request. What a kind, giving lady this was.

"Do you boys know where I could hide my car, so we don't draw attention to ourselves? After all, we are Canadians, and it is a rental," I questioned, looking at them.

Mitchell suggested that Dustin drive our car to their shop and keep it inside until we needed it. Tomorrow was Saturday, and they were not working this weekend. No one else would be there either. Mitchell would follow shortly after with his truck, and they would come home together again. It was not so uncommon to get called out at night to fix a broken water line in one of the ancient homes in this area. I would stay here and get started on restoring the concealed rooms. The ladies helped with carrying the books after I put the shelves up again. I had taken pictures of everything before we disturbed or even touched anything. We knew exactly where all the books and artwork should be put. I had not taken pictures of the family yet, but I planned to do that in the morning. I would be careful to put the shovel back in the skeletal hands exactly how I found it. The boys were back in good time and had locked our car up, safe and sound. Mary was careful to keep the Bible separate from all the other books. She was looking forward to reading the little notes.

We all flopped on the couches and recliners. Mary had two of each. The lights were off, as Mary didn't have full blinds, and anyone could see into the front room—although, the plants in the window tried their best to make a complete camouflage. The first thing I needed to address was the privacy of this home. We came up with a scheme to have the house interior painted. We could put sheets over the windows for this reason. Mary could tell her neighbors, in casual conversation, that the boys were going to hire a company to give the place a well-deserved facelift. She was also going to de-clutter the house, and these people would help with that. It was perfect. I would call the museum tomorrow and have them here as soon as possible. They would probably arrive on Monday morning. We would put everything in the basement as we found it, and they would take care of it from there on. No one would know about the tunnels until Mary and the boys were ready to tell them. With those decisions made, we all moved to the kitchen, where Mary would serve us some of her apple strudel. It seemed we needed the comfort of seeing each other as we spoke.

For now, all the talking would have to be done in the kitchen, where the lights were not noticed by passersby. As we sat around the kitchen table with a piece of her delicious baked goods, Mary read the letters to us, and the boys translated.

She read the inscription in the Bible. It belonged to the boy's great-grandfather. On its back pages, his spiritual journey and his marriage were documented. He had logged when he was born, converted, baptized, and the dates of his two children's birth. One died shortly after, a girl, and the second, a boy, was called Mitchell after himself. As I listened, I could visualize this man, so dedicated to the cause of saving life.

Mary read the back of the torn picture. She said it read, "Joseph and myself." She said she didn't know which one was which, and we assured her of which one was Joseph. One man looked like an older version of Mark, or, should I say, Mark was a carbon copy of Joseph. This proved Joseph and Schwartz were good friends. Mark was going to be elated with our findings.

Then, Mary went to a thin, fragile piece of paper in the Bible and unfolded it with care. It was so thin and permanently creased. It read, "To whomever finds this."

CHAPTER 23

Committed Friends

"I, Mr. Eisenhouwer, have written this as a last testament of my family's life here on this earth. We were hidden by our friend, Joseph, at the home of Mitchell Schwartz. The latter man has fed and hidden us for six months. We are so grateful for both of their sacrifices for us. My wife, Ramona, and our little girl, Natasha, are very ill and dying. There is no more food being delivered, and we are out of water. I tried to dig our way out the back as we had been directed, but the soldiers were camped right beside the hill. Mitchell told me, a human life is more important to save than art, and that my family and I were a priority. This is true, but we chose to stay in the tunnel and not disclose ourselves or the art to the enemy, as we know we would have been killed anyway. We pray generations to come will have the freedom to enjoy all that is hidden here.

In God we trust, Bernhardt Eisenhouwer."

We wiped the tears from our eyes as we relived those last days and moments with this brave man. He loved his family and, in the end, sacrificed all their lives for this secret. We couldn't imagine holding our sick child in our arms and watching it die. He had chosen starvation for his wife and himself, and it would not have been a quick death. If they had climbed out from their hiding place, it might have been a much quicker end. They would have been shot on the spot, but would have exposed the tunnels and all the hidden art. It was such a sad ending.

We were, once again, emotionally drained and needed to get some sleep. We said good night and were given Mitchell and Dustin's room. It had two single beds and was very comfortable. The boys didn't mind sleeping on the floor in sleeping bags. That blew my mind. They said they rather enjoyed it, and did it often, even when not needed. It made them feel young, like they were camping out.

The next morning came way too soon, but we were up and ready to get to work. We intended to box a lot of the books and wrap the paintings—after breakfast, of course. Mary made a lovely German breakfast of dark rye bread and crusty buns with her homemade preserve. She served sliced tomatoes fresh from her garden and soft-boiled eggs, accompanied by a lovely cheese and salami. They felt like our new family as we said grace together, acknowledging that our hearts were still heavy from our new discovery just hours before.

"You know what I was thinking?" I said. "You boys are making a lot of things right. Your great-grandfather tried, and you are getting it done." I added, "You're finishing the job he started decades ago."

I told them I had an idea regarding the family. The museum I had called was known to make exact replicas of such scenes for the people who found them, as a reminder of our past and future actions. I received permission from the family to call the museum again and see what they could do regarding our find. I would take pictures today and send them with my document. Knowing the museum's replicas were very precise, we decided to forgo the packing and leave all as we found it.

We were in deep conversation when a loud knock came to the door, and someone tried to open it. Mary went to answer it, but remembered to close the kitchen door first.

We could hear her say, *"Guten Tag Frau Semph."*

The nosey neighbor kept talking louder and louder. Mary finally told her to be quiet, as her boys had worked late last night. Mrs. Semph said she saw some commotion last night, but also wondered who had been here with the rental car. Mary said it was the painting company, giving her a price, and he was out with his sister, who was here from abroad, and had rented the car. They were going to do some sightseeing afterwards. As if Mrs. Semph found out all she wanted, she suddenly said good-bye, and that she would see Mary later.

We were glad she left, and once again confirmed that we could not be too cautious. The boys were very excited about the books and art, but even more about the family. They discussed that when the museum made their copies of the scenes and the skeletons, they were going to bury them in a proper cemetery, with a personalized headstone. They would use the picture of the family for the headstone, so all could see and remember this family. I thought to myself about how sentimental these boys were. One day, we would be able to give them all the information and belongings we had found from their great-grandfather. It would mean so much to them.

We would get a ride to our car and let the family have time to themselves. We also needed time to process and line up a few more details. When we called Pa and Josh, they couldn't believe how successful we had been. They relayed that Bee got to Lancaster safe and sound, and, after Kelly's surgery, she went to stay at Grammy's place. The elderly couple was doing very well and had adjusted to the inside phone quite nicely. Grammy used it to call her friends at least once a day. It gave us a chuckle. Kelly was recovering nicely and going to stay at Grammy's when he was ready to come home. Bee would use his car to pick him up.

We figured Bee would be a happy camper.

We told Pa and Josh that we might stay longer, as this project was getting so involved, and we couldn't just walk away from these nice people. We had met just a few days ago but felt responsible for the upheaval in their lives. Pa agreed and said his good-byes.

The museum sent someone down to have a look at our findings. They were amazed at the age and value of the books and the art. They would open a museum here in the city, as this is where they were found. Anyone could view them, free of charge, but they would have to make an appointment of sorts. To protect the books, they would let a regulated number of people in, one at a time. The public would wear gloves and then be able to carefully look at the books. Copies would be available to read, if so desired. It was a new concept in museums, and they were sure it would be a success. The plan was that they were going to make an exact replica of the tunnels and the two rooms. They would not give the address, location, or names of the owners. The story written on the fragile paper found was enough to explain it all.

The family would keep the Bible and the photos. It was all set into motion. The museum would come in on Monday to do some of the work. They used photography and laser to take exact measurements of the tunnels and the rooms. We had been notified to leave it all as it was, and it would be displayed in its original form in the museum. It was a job, getting the books back exactly as we found them. We were careful to use our photos to file and slant them as we had found them. People would pick a book off of the rustic shelf. There was a copy available for them to read later. It would be the original shelf from in this hiding place. What could be better? Imagine, touching a book that you know was rescued from destruction and knowing someone sacrificed his or her life for you to have that privilege.

Mary and the boys joined our excitement, even though there was no talk of money yet. They expected no money. The museum said they could get sponsors, who were also interested in preserving the past. If they liked the new concept, there might be some money in it for the family. There was a smile on all their faces. It was good to see. Of course, they had financial stresses, and any amount would make life easier for this German family.

We had to move on to our next destination, but we left our phone numbers, email, and address for them so they could contact us. We said we would be in contact in the near future and would have good news for them.

We hugged them, and we were off. As we pulled out, we spotted Mrs. Semph staring into the car windows, trying to see what she could see. It was a stroke of luck that the museum committee agreed to paint Mary's home and use a painter's truck, as Mrs. Semph wouldn't let that go without many nagging, unending questions.

We went back to the hotel and packed our clothes. It certainly didn't seem like a holiday so far, but it was exciting. We needed some normal days to enjoy being in Germany. This, after all, was where my family had lived so many years ago. This was the location of my roots, and I wanted to sense and appreciate this place, as well as experience first-hand some of the traditions that had been passed down to me. The next day, we would relax and take a ride past the old homestead. I was told it was still around.

We had a lovely dinner out and talked about our children, our experiences of the last days, what the next investigation would present, and once again about our children. Once you are a parent, your children become the center of your universe, and there was no changing that. This happens within a moment of an unconscious second, when your eyes behold this small, innocent being whose life depends on your untested parenting skills.

CHAPTER 24

The Old Family Estate

We woke early the next morning and started on our little road trip. The family home of my grandparents was in a little town on the other side of Bremen. My uncle's name was not immortalized on a list of names of those who had emigrated out of Germany. These names can still be found housed in Bremen, at the dock from where the migrants left. My Grandfather and Grandmother's names are amongst those that immigrated. My uncle was taken by force, imprisoned, and taken to a new land against his will. He did not even get to see this land and enjoy its beauty and potential. I wondered if I should put up a memorial for the prisoners that departed Germany under horrendous circumstances.

We were listening to our GPS, which was encouraging us to turn off just ahead. It did not look like a well-used road—as a matter of fact, grass had grown on parts of it. We hoped we were going in the right direction. The tree branches hung over the road. There were large bushes and shrubs on each side, closing the road into a narrow passageway. We could not see what was on either side of us past the thick over growth. We stopped the car at one point and struggled on foot through the brush to see what twas on the other side. There were only fields. There were no houses or animals. We noticed clumps of tall trees scattered over the landscape and figured they once held homes, now clearly demolished. As we neared the car again, I hoped it would not be all scratched up from the branches.

We continued our drive. At one point, Nerissa had to get out and hold a huge branch aside so I could pass with the car. She barely managed it, even though she could move wheel barrels of dirt and was no weakling. I had to maneuver over the huge hole while she held back the obstacle. Nerissa did not want to drive. We would hate to take this road in the dark. Pa had given us the latitude and longitude of the old homestead, and the GPS was still guiding our drive. The map showed that it would be up ahead, just a little way further. We were relieved that our ride was almost over.

"Did you happen to bring some food?" I asked, expecting a negative answer.

"Well, I wasn't going to tell you, but I ordered a nice picnic lunch from the hotel in case we found a romantic place to stop," she replied, adding, "I snuck it into the car earlier this morning."

I couldn't believe what I was hearing.

"We have food with us, never mind the romance," I said, just like a man.

The GPS announced that we had arrived at our destination. We would never have found it without the feminine voice coaching us on. The bushes and trees were hardly passable. I made a path of sorts, stepping down branches and breaking the higher ones for Nerissa to follow.

"Are there any snakes here?" she asked.

"If there are, they will run for their lives with all the noise we are making," I laughingly responded.

It didn't give much comfort, but it made for a lighter moment.

Nerissa took a second or two to look around instead of watching where she was going. She saw a face peering through the bush, and then it was gone. I asked where, but we couldn't see anyone. I consoled her by telling her it must have been her imagination. She stood still and had another look around.

"There," she whispered, "there!"

We could barely see part of a building through the wild growth. What we could see looked old. Now cautious, we kept our bodies lower and tried to be as quiet as possible. The old boarded house that was once home to my ancestors and Pa as a child was now protected by years of unmanaged gardens. It was still standing, and that was a huge surprise to us. We neared the door, and I checked the floorboards. We would have to be careful, but they could be walked on. I noticed the roof had been patched, and the work could be seen on the inside as the ceiling was missing, rafters exposed. I wondered who would patch such an old place. Though the ceiling was missing, the windows were all intact and the doors even closed. The inside walls stood in place with their original wallpaper.

"I will have to take lots of pictures. Pa will recognize this place," I blurted out with excitement.

"It sure is preserved well for its age," Nerissa added.

The kitchen had a pump fastened to the top of a floor cabinet. I tried it, and, after a while, water came out.

"It still works, Shawn, can you imagine that?" My wife was in awe of the antique.

We had stepped into the kitchen upon entering the door. There was an old oak table and four chairs to make a matching set. The kitchen cupboards created an "L" shape, including the pump. The counters were metal and, because of this, in very good condition. The small hutch standing against the other wall would have held all the dishes, as there were no upper cabinets.

"You know the dishes we use at our home? They would have been in this cupboard!" I spoke with the realization, putting the two different worlds together in my mind.

"I wished Pa could be here with us, it would bring back so many memories for him," I mused with my hand on my chin, contemplating.

Nerissa agreed and kept on looking in all the cupboards. There were a couple of odd cups and saucers, bowls, and pots. She found that to be strange. The small wood stove with its exposed pipe running through the ceiling had ashes and pieces of unburned wood inside.

We went through to the sitting room. It must have been cozy at one time. The large, flowered wall print still complimented the tattered burgundy velvet drapes, which had been hanging in an untouched fashion for so many years. The burgundy upholstered chaise still sat where it must have originally been placed, as there was no other area with enough room for its unusual length. Across from it, beside the fireplace, sat two wooden Victorian chairs. They still possessed the look of sophistication given to them by their craftsman's hands. The solid wood mantel on the fireplace told a story of years of use. It was nicked and scratched, but it remained a beautiful piece and accent for the room. We noticed the ashes still in the fireplace and wondered how long since a fire was made in this relic of days gone by. There were two doors off the living room. We knew neither led to a bathroom, as everyone had an outhouse in these areas back then. One door was easy to open, and it contained an old, painted iron double bed. The mattress was a piece for the museum and showed its age nicely but was otherwise in good shape. We wondered why the rodents hadn't taken the straw and demolished it from the inside. Besides a small wooden chair and a narrow chest of drawers, there wasn't much else in the room.

CHAPTER 25

Time to Give Back

The other door was difficult to open. It wouldn't push open like the previous one had. We pushed hard and heard a loud scraping sound. Finally, we managed to open it far enough to squeeze through.

"Look at that," I said. "This dresser was pushed in front of the door from the inside."

Someone must have used the window to escape, unseen. We tried the window, and it was still wedged open a crack. I looked out but saw no one. We wondered if someone was living here. Maybe it was a squatter. This would be the room to investigate carefully. We found tattered, but clean blankets on the bed with two decent looking pillows. Nerissa looked under the bed, only to find a large flat basket with a rattle and baby blanket in it. There were two cloth diapers rolled up at the sides.

"Do you think we scared them away? Maybe it is a single mom with her baby, where will they go?" she spoke, sounding worried.

"Maybe she will come back," I said.

It did not turn out the way we had planned, but I thought it would be a good idea to have our picnic lunch here in my grandfather's old house, just for the sake of nostalgia.

Nerissa reluctantly agreed to let me go get the basket the hotel had carefully packed for us. I told her that someone with a baby had to be harmless. I had forgotten that the instinct to protect one's young is one of the strongest known to man.

She would sit on the chest and wait for my return. I hurried along the rustic path we had made for ourselves and got back to the car. I could hear a baby crying in the distance. Someone had broken into our car and the door was tampered with.

I had no choice but to follow the weak cry. Silently, I crept up so I could see. It was a young mother trying to nurse her child. The child seemed slightly consoled but was not getting fed. I let my presence be known and stood up. The woman was startled and looked scared. Fright is a terrible thing to see in a face, never mind that of a mother holding a baby. I told her I was not going to hurt her, and she should come back to the house with me. She nodded like she understood and got up. I was bending to pick up our basket of food when she decided to try to run.

"No!" I shouted, grabbing her without hurting the baby.

"It is okay, I will not hurt you," I said again, hoping she would understand this time.

I took her by her free arm and grabbed the basket with the other. We passed the car, and she looked more upset than before. Again, with a kind smile, I reassured her that we were not going to hurt her and she calmed a little.

The baby was getting more restless and started to cry. We were almost at the house, and Nerissa came running out to see where the baby was. She ran over and started to admire the baby. She began talking so sweetly to the child, it stopped crying and listened to Nerissa's coaxing. The mom was taken aback by this natural outpouring of compassion and gave the baby to Nerissa after she pleaded to hold it. It was a little girl. She was so beautiful, with her dark eyes and dark hair. She looked like her mom. Her mother's clothes were worn and torn. We knew appearance was not a priority when you were trying to save your child's life. We guided them inside and sat her down. The baby looked well, except for being small and frail for her age. She was about nine months old.

"Are you here alone?" I asked, Nerissa still holding the baby.

She gave a frightened look over to the baby, and I assured her we were not going to hurt her, we wanted to help her. She lowered her head and did not know how to respond.

"Do you know English?" I asked.

She raised her fingers with an inch of space between them. I assumed that meant "a little bit." We asked again, and she let us know she had a husband, but he was not here. She said her name was Lovlyn, and the baby was Clara. Her eyes kept wandering over to the basket of food. Nerissa decided we should have our picnic lunch after all. She set the humble table.

The hotel had packed a nice, checked cloth that, when placed, transformed the table into an inviting place to sit. There were two place settings in the basket, which Nerissa used and took the other from the old cupboards. She mixed them all so no one would feel they got the old stuff. It looked rather eclectic and modern. There was a bottle of fine French Champagne with stemware and a thermos of good strong coffee. She had asked for a litre of milk and some cereal. She knew her man liked cereal for a snack. There was a platter of cheese and crackers, as well as a variety of meats, including salami. How much did they think we could eat? She pulled out some shrimp and sauce. The sauce was not like the one in Canada, but a white sauce, which was not as tangy as she was used to. She pulled out a long baguette, wrapped in a cloth matching the tablecloth. There was an easy to open can of tuna and a small jar of pickles she had also requested for me. Along with everything else, she pulled out a covered tray of pastries. They looked so delicious. The table was laden with goodies, and Nerissa asked us to sit down.

I motioned for Lovlyn to sit, and I pulled out her chair for her. She seemed shy about the special treatment. The baby had fallen asleep again and Lovlyn had a quiet moment to enjoy her food. I asked if she wanted a glass of Champagne, and she motioned "no," because she was nursing the baby.

"Of course, how could I be so foolish," I replied.

Nerissa gave her a nice full glass of milk and said, "Shawn does not want his cereal today, as we have so much other food to eat." She nodded and almost inhaled the milk. There was more, so I filled her glass again. We enjoyed our food while staying totally preoccupied with one another. There were so many questions on both sides of the table. We informed her why we were here, and that we were not going to stay long. They were welcome to stay here, as the land still belonged to my family. It was deeded back to us after the war, because we had always paid the taxes for it.

She looked shocked, then grateful. She conveyed in her broken English that they had escaped their town in Syria. ISIS slaughtered the ones left behind. They could hear their cries in the valley below as they moved up the mountain away from their homes. The only reason they continued on was the new life they carried in their arms. They promised their parents they would not turn back, but they would find freedom for their future. It took many weeks to get to civilization, and they could not trust anyone. They had to steal milk and food so she could continue to feed the baby. They ran into many people fleeing, and many riots against the hundreds entering small towns and over-running them. It was a terrifying journey. Her husband went to find food and should have been back a day ago. They had been without food for five days, and she couldn't feed the baby anymore.

We were thankful that we came along at the right time. We would, of course, leave all this food with them. We didn't indulge too much, as our appetite had diminished with the story we were hearing. Lovlyn was concerned about her husband. It had been a couple of hours since the baby fell asleep, and we quietly cleaned up. I put everything back on ice in our basket. Nerissa mused over something, looking at me with a smile. Now she could understand why this basket cost so much. I would, too, when I finally heard the price. She had no idea they were so efficient and even packed ice. It was the perfect choice for this special day. Except for the shrimp, the contents would keep a day or two.

As the baby crawled around barefoot, Nerissa thought of the red shoes Natasha left behind. She must have crawled on the cold stone floors, playing and doing what babies do at that age. She wondered how they kept her from crying. Natasha was the same age when she went into hiding with her parents, as Clara is now. The thought gripped Nerissa's heart, and tears welled up in her eyes. She decided she had to do more.

When she came to me to see what we could do, I had already been thinking along those lines. We discussed it in great length while Lovlyn and Clara slept in the next room. The next day, I would go to the closest town and get supplies. I would also make a call to Pa and see if we could sign over the land and house to these people. I realized I did not even know their last name. Maybe, as it was only a little over an hour away, I could have Mitchell and Dustin put in the plumbing and heating, and we could hire someone to run the wiring for the house. We would let them take care of the inside and fix it as they liked. I would see what necessities I could pick up in town. We agreed this would give them a very good start, and they would have a home.

We felt like, somehow, we were giving the little family that died in the tunnel a return on their death. We knew it wasn't them, but another family was benefiting in their memory. They were so much alike, and the baby girl was the same age.

CHAPTER 26

Knocked Senseless

We had fallen asleep on the old couch when Nerissa awoke to a loud thump. Shawn was slumped over, bleeding from his head. She looked up to see a man standing over her with a heavy piece of metal, ready to hit her too. She screamed, and Lovlyn came running to protect her. The man stopped and stood frozen. She started to shout at him and give him orders.

Nerissa looked at Shawn, who was still slumped beside her. She grabbed the tablecloth and put pressure on his head. The couple started to help. They laid him down and elevated his head with a pillow from Lovlyn's bed. She also brought a blanket and covered Shawn. Nerissa checked the wound, but she couldn't see because of the blood. Jervaih got some water from the pump and filled a pot. He set it on the floor beside Nerissa. With Lovlyn continuing to hold pressure on the wound, Nerissa started to clean the blood so she could assess the situation.

Nerissa kept calling, "Shawn, Shawn can you hear me?"

Finally, Shawn moaned and was coming to. He tried to get up, but they made him lay still. The bleeding was slowing down, and Nerissa was so thankful. Shawn's blonde hair became transparent, and she could only see a reddish scalp.

Lovlyn was winding up again and shouting in her native tongue. Nerissa could only imagine what she was saying. She knew what she would be saying if the people that were saving her and her child were attacked.

Nerissa could finally get a good look at the wound. It was deep, but not to the skull. She knew Jervaih was only protecting his family. She wished he would have asked questions first. Lovlyn came over with a needle and thread. She motioned if she could sew up the wound. She said she was the village nurse and had trained with a doctor that would show up once a month.

Nerissa made room for her, and she went to work like she knew what she was doing. By this time, Jervaih was very apologetic. Nerissa and Lovlyn accepted his apology. Lovlyn went and washed the tablecloth and pillowcase in cold water so the blood stains would not set. She did a marvelous job, and they totally disappeared.

Nerissa told them to take some time and be with the baby. She needed time alone with Shawn to make sure he really was okay. He had no concussion, but a severe headache. She stroked his head very gently, as it was one of his favorite things from childhood, and if there was ever a time to relax him, it was now.

"Well, I guess we never know what will happen next," she said quietly.

Was it only today since we arrived? She told Shawn to go to sleep, and that she would watch out for him.

Shawn dozed off, only to wake from a terrible nightmare.

"I dreamed that Josh got lost in the tunnels," he said. "I was frantically looking for him."

She assured him it was only a dream, and he went back to sleep. It left her with terrible thoughts of Josh somewhere below, lost and hurt. She told herself to stop that nonsense, and that all was well at home.

Morning came, and Nerissa made sure Lovlyn had her milk and something to eat. Jervaih checked on Shawn and thought he looked well. He apologized so much that I told him Nerissa and I would not hear it anymore. He bowed with apology instead of speaking the words. After we ate, we told them of our plan to give them the land and house. Although it wasn't much, it was a place to call home and start over. They both cried, and Lovlyn could not control herself. The baby woke, and Nerissa went to get her. She gave her to Lovlyn to feed, and she put on her smile for Clara. Parents can do anything for their children if they needed to, that was clear. Jervaih and Shawn would go to the nearest town this morning and get things rolling. Shawn made a couple of calls, and the schedule was arranged. The Schwartz boys, Mitchell and Dustin, were going to come that weekend and put in some heat and running water. They knew an electrician that could come out the next day. The lawyer would take care of the legal work.

Shawn was working off of his line of credit, as cash was short, but he knew there was money coming. He could not wait until he had more cash to get this family settled. They went to a grocery store and bought staples like flour, sugar, salt, oil, vinegar and so on. They also bought a set of inexpensive dishes. Detergents, broom, saw, screw-drivers, nails, and so on were next. Jervaih had already fixed the roof as it was raining in. It would need a new roof, but this would get them by for now. He also had the strictest of orders to buy a pack of cloth diapers, a baby blanket and a little pair of shoes for Clara. She would also soon need a baby bottle for juice and water. This was besides all the other non-perishable or canned groceries.

While loading the car with their goods, Shawn noticed a "for sale" sign on a post outside the store. Someone was selling a small mo-torbike. "That would be handy for Jervaih," he thought. Shawn took the ad, and they drove to the stipulated address. It was a farm closer to their property. While speaking with the man, they found out he was looking for a farm hand to do odds and ends. Shawn recommended Jervaih, and the farmer accepted the offer. He would make a fair wage and receive some meat when the farmer butchered. Now Shawn felt Jervaih could securely take care of his family. It would be a short ride to work each day.

The ladies could not believe everything we had purchased and ended up stuffing the cupboards. Nerissa was working under the pump in a not-so-pretty cupboard, as there was no more room to put anything away. She noticed an envelope. She took it from its roost. She sat a minute to open it, and noticed it was German. She couldn't read German. Lovlyn came over and looked at the paper. She said she could read it.

Nerissa called to the men, who were clearing a little land around the house. They came running, expecting a problem. "Nerissa found this letter," Lovlyn said in her native tongue.

Nerissa added, "She can read German."

"What luck," I said, sitting down.

Lovlyn read and Jervaih translated. It said it was written by Antonie Wittfoot. She hid it in this spot, which had been decided by the family for contacting each other in case of separation. She said she had not heard from her brothers-in-law. Her husband, herself and child were going to immigrate to Canada to the Niagara area, Queenston, where they'd secured a job as gardener and cook for a wealthy German family. She said they all knew where to look in the kitchen for correspondence. When they returned, they should let her know as soon as possible, as she would have all their belongings sent to Canada for them. She said they would try to keep the house until they heard from their loved ones. The letter said that they were well and hoped their son would have a better life in a new country. She was depending on her God to bring them together, even if not in this lifetime.

There was utter silence. No one spoke for a long time. It was like speaking with the past once more, and we knew our trip was ordained by God. This property was ready to be put into the hands of new owners. Our family had all been accounted for, as we knew what happened to everyone. It was time to let go of the past and give new life to this home. We told Jervaih and Lovlyn we were so happy they could experience this moment with us, as now they knew what this home meant to our family. We assured them it was a privilege for them to live here and start their new life. Shawn felt he should say a prayer of blessing over this home, and Jervaih agreed. We all held hands, and Shawn prayed with compassion and insight. Lovlyn had tears in her eyes, and Jervaih's countenance was solemn. They appreciated what they felt. They had experienced so much hate and violence, they were not ready for the feeling of warmth that only God could give.

We spent much time talking and we gave them our Bible. They needed to hear God for themselves, not just through others. We were leaving tomorrow, but we promised to stay in touch. We would provide the documentation that the property belonged to them within the month.

It was a tough good-bye, and it was difficult to let go of Clara. We prayed that she would have a good life in her new home and country.

We had a few hours of daylight to get back to a main road. We had not booked our hotel for the night, so we would look for one on the main road back to town. We remembered a couple places that looked like they would accommodate our needs. After a couple of hours, we decided to pull up at, "Das Gast Haus."

It was a quaint place with a Bavarian flair. It was a white building with wooden balconies displaying heart cutouts in the wood accents. The shutters were also designed with these heart shaped cutouts.

CHAPTER 27

Pa Remembers

After checking in, we were glad to shower and get ready for bed. I had a few phone calls on my agenda to make sure Jervaih was all set up. We left Nerissa's phone with them until they could buy one for themselves. This way, they could get in touch with us. Pa was informed once more regarding our day. He was so pleased that the small farm would serve the new immigrants well. It was fitting, and he expressed his gratitude at all we had done. He couldn't believe Nerissa had found the letter from his mother. Pa remembered her being so upset, her tears flowing freely. They were leaving the country, not even knowing where the family was. Pa said he had walked in the sitting room just as she was sealing an envelope. Only a young boy, he remembered putting his arms around his mom and encouraging her that every-thing would be just fine. She was consoled by the faith of her son, and she gave him a smile. Pa had forgotten about that incident until we jolted his memory by telling him about the letter and its contents. Pa remembered jokes made around their dinner table, regarding the secret hiding spot. This was because no one ever thought they would need to use it.

Dad said they were going to reorganize their schedule and take a couple of days off. He would touch base in a couple of days. Pa in-formed him that Bee was fine. Kelly was recuperating in the hospital. Bee was getting a chance to get to know his family better and was very content to just be there with him.

Pa and Josh were going to do some more searching and following of diagrams of the workers. I reminded them to follow the rules, and Pa laughed. He reminded me he was the man that invented rules, or had I forgotten my childhood. I liked Pa's sense of humor. It left me chuckling.

The fluffy feather pillows and comforter were calling to me. The bed was made up in bright, white, crisp sheets. Although the mattress was firm, everything that covered it was soft and cottony.

Nerissa re-bandaged my head after cleaning my wound. She commented again on how nice the five stitches looked. Lovlyn had done a good job. She should get some official training, if they could afford it one day down the road. Flopping into bed felt like laying in a cloud. We talked over our day with the light out and didn't realize when we actually fell asleep.

CHAPTER 28

Kelly is Discharged

Bee was ready to take Kelly over to Grammy's. She knew with all of those homemade soups and good food, he would be well in no time. The doctors were going to release him today. She was there early. As she opened the door, she was shocked to see Rachel. Rachel was on the job and said Kelly's vitals were all good. She was sure he would be released today.

"Can I ask how your mom is doing?" Bee asked.

"Of course, and thank you for asking," she answered in a confident, professional way.

She told Bee she had to do it soon, as her mom was due in a week. She was not sure her mom would go for it yet. Kelly looked on, wondering what they were talking about. The girls were oblivious to him, and Bee asked if she was ready. Rachel had done her homework and studied the subject some more, and had collected all the medical supplies she needed. She even had a doctor on call in case she needed assistance. He was willing to make a trip to see Rachel to save her mother's life. Bee said she could call her anytime and she would be over. Her mother's blood type was on order in case she would need a transfusion. She would have to consent, of course. She could have one before the baby was born to strengthen her, but she refused. Her mother had a severe hemorrhage of the bowel and did not get medical assistance. It went on throughout her pregnancy, and Rachel was concerned. She had lost a lot of blood, and no amount of beets could replace it as her parents had thought. It, of course, was an old wives' tale.

Bee said she would fill Kelly in later. It was all so complicated.

The doctor came in at mid-morning, and Bee and Kelly were on their way. Kelly was elated to see the blue sky and feel the wind on his face again. He was not used to lying in bed for so many days.

Grammy and Grammpy were sitting on the porch in their rockers waiting for Bee's arrival. It was a lovely day, and the lemonade was waiting for them. Bee helped Kelly up to the porch. He could feel the pull on his stitches.

"Let's sit outside," he pleaded.

"Okay, but tell me when you get tired," Bee demanded.

He sat down carefully with a big sigh.

"Thank you for taking such good care of me," he said with a wink.

Bee felt she hadn't done anything, so she shrugged it off with a, "You're welcome."

Grammy went inside to get some lunch, and Grammpy and Kelly chatted the time away. Bee had gotten a call and looked upset.

"I don't know what to do," she said after Rachel called. "When Rachel got home, she found her mom in labor. She asked me to come now, but Kelly has just gotten home."

Grammpy said, "We will take care of Kelly, don't you worry, go."

Kelly gave a stamp of approval with, "Go help your friend. I'll be here when you get back."

Bee ran for the car. What was going on at Rachel's place? Was she having problems so soon into the labor? Bee knew she just got off of her shift!

It took a few minutes to get there. There was already another black car in the yard. It must be the midwife's car. Bee ran inside without knocking. She was confronted with a horrible scene. Rachel's mom was laying on the floor, and the midwife was bending over her. Rachel was arguing with her dad to let her do caesarean, and he was refusing.

She yelled to Bee to call a number on a paper she threw at her. Bee did as she asked. It was the doctor, and Bee told him to get over to the address he had received from Rachel. She told him it was an emergency and was needed right away with the blood Rachel had ordered, and they needed to send an ambulance too. The midwife announced that the pulse was too low, and they were going to lose them both.

CHAPTER 29

Would Modern Medicine Prevail?

Rachel grabbed the huge bag that she had prepared. She put clean cloths on the large family table. "Help me put mom on the table," she ordered.

Everyone helped to lift her as she barely had energy to moan. Rachel hoped she wasn't too late. Her dad would never forgive her. She demanded the midwife help her. She cut the clothes and bared her mother's belly. After sanitizing the area, she made her first incision. She gave clamps to the midwife so she could assist her. After the second incision, it was only a few minutes until we heard a baby cry. It was a girl. This was an absolute miracle, and Bee was witness to it. The baby was put into Bee's arms, and the midwife cut the cord and took care of that end of things. Rachel was still working on getting ready to finish the surgery when her mom went into cardiac arrest. Rachel climbed on the table and, straddling her mom, did what she had been taught. She pumped her chest as the midwife gave mouth to mouth. They heard the ambulance, and the doctor came running in. He used the defibrillator on her instantly. The second time, they got results, and the monitor showed a pulse. The ambulance attendant hooked up the IV and the blood transfusion to keep her alive. Rachel stayed close to her mom and made sure her vitals where sufficiently improved before she moved away. The midwife had taken excellent care with the baby and in this situation had done everything right. She was a great asset in saving Rachel's mom's life. The doctor busied himself with closing up the incision, then cleaned up the patient and bandaged her.

Everyone breathed a sigh of relief. They were starting to get the patient ready for transport with the baby when Rachel stopped them. She looked to her dad, who was dumbfounded, and sitting with his head in his hands, weeping and rocking like a child. He still thought his wife had died. Rachel told him that she would be fine. She looked like a corpse because of the trauma and weakness, but she was going to be fine. He took his daughter into an embrace and cried on her shoulders. She knew it was a very tough day for him, and even though his rules had been broken, he witnessed his wife's life saved. He also saw how qualified his daughter had become as a medical professional. When he found the strength to stop his flood of emotion, he nodded "yes" to take her where she could be cared for. The midwife volunteered to go with the baby in the ambulance and make sure she was taken care of.

The doctor would need a ride to his car at the hospital. The ambulance was now full. Bee volunteered her services, and they left shortly after, but not before Rachel thanked Bee for making the phone call, as no one else would. She had been busy trying to save her mom, and her dad would not give her permission. They hugged, and Bee told her she was so happy it all worked out.

"It was because of your encouragement, Bee," Rachel said.

With a big, "thanks," Bee left. They made their way back to the hospital. Rachel would get a ride in with a neighbor as soon as she got cleaned up.

The doctor spoke of his concern for these beautiful people who had put themselves into a box and wouldn't let the new technology help them. He felt if they could hang onto their culture and embrace the present, they would have the best of both worlds. Bee knew it wasn't as easy, and every change came with a price. The doctor left her car and drove away in his Porsche. Bee sat quietly for a minute and said a prayer of thanks to God for saving these two lives tonight. She was on her way back to her grandparent's farm. She looked a mess and hoped Kelly wouldn't see her like that. As she drove up, there they were, all three were sitting on the porch. Kelly lay on the swing with blankets and pillows and looked as comfortable as ever. He was going to get up, but Bee told him to stay where he was. He looked tired, just how she felt. Everything was over now, and all would be fine, given the proper time.

When the porch light showed the blood on her arms and top, they wondered what had happened. She told them the whole story from beginning to end.

Grammpy said, "I understand how difficult a time Rachel has had. We have had to endure some of those ourselves."

"You must be so hungry, dear, I will make you something," Grammy said, going inside.

"I think I will shower before I eat," Bee added.

It felt good to shower. As she looked down, she could only see red as the blood mixed with the water. It was so nice that she had an inside bathroom to use. She was appreciating the little things in life. Her heart was full of thankfulness.

After her shower, she just sat in her robe and ate her supper outside on the porch. It was the nicest evening, knowing all was well.

"How are you feeling?"

Kelly thought he was doing very well and would help Grammpy with his chores tomorrow. Bee gasped and made sure he knew that was a, "no." He laughed and thought he could use a couple of days off first. He did say his dad and brothers were coming at four to help Grammpy put things in order. Bee thought that was nice, and Kelly reminded her it was the Amish way. Bee conceded that she was finding that out for herself. The Amish had their ways, some good and some not, but one thing was for sure: the people were kind, as far as giving of themselves.

For tonight, they would all feel better after a good night's sleep. They had all had a busy day.

CHAPTER 30

On the Road Again

We decided, after having a quiet breakfast and reading the news, that we would pack the car and set off to our next destination, a little town called Buelstedt. It was only an hour and a half from Hamburg. We had done the research, and if they were still there, we would find another a descendant. We hoped they would still be living there. We followed our GPS and were surprised just how quickly we arrived there. We turned onto a small country-like road. We passed a home with a stone walled courtyard in front of it. It was a well-maintained building, to say the least. There was a name and family emblem over the door to the home as well as the property gate.

We drove to the end of the road, and there stood a rustic, old home with a weathered straw thatched roof. It had the barn attached to it, in the fashion of the era it was built. An old school house, now remodeled into a home, stood at the corner across the road. We turned right onto the laneway. On the left stood a large, modernized farmhouse. We took the first road right, needing to find someone to talk to, as we had no leads regarding where a Fry ancestor lived. We drove slowly down this road, hoping to spot someone—otherwise, we would have to knock on doors. There was a man herding some sheep down the laneway towards a farm. As the windows rolled down, we were greeted with the fresh country aromas. We smelled grasses from the pastures mixed with sheep manure, and there was a faint wafting of something baking in one of the homes. We stopped and asked if we could talk to him. He motioned that he did not speak English. He pointed to the farmhouse on the corner that we had just passed. Thanking him, we turned around and hoped we were pointed in the right direction. We rang the doorbell, and the lady of the house answered. We asked if we could ask her a couple of questions. She was obliging and asked us in. She accompanied us to the bright front room with lace toppers over very large windows. We asked if she knew a family with the name of Fry. She thought for a moment, pondering. Her family had lived in this town since before the war, and they were very familiar with everyone. She thought maybe the oldest lady in the town could help us out. She had a very sharp mind, and could rattle off dates of deaths, births, and weddings. We asked where we could find her. She pointed and said, "Just over there." It was the oldest house in the town, the one with the thatched roof. She had been there all her life. We thanked her and asked if the senior resident of the house next door spoke English. The answer was negative. We took a chance and asked if she could come and interpret for us? She looked at her watch and said that she had an hour before her hair appointment. It would take her ten minutes to get there, so yes. We were delighted, and she drove next door with us. A beautiful, small meadow separated the two houses. She was curious about where we came from and why we needed this information. We had to be evasive and we found it so very unfair, as she was kind to us. She introduced herself as Carmela.

As she knocked on the door, she turned the doorknob and just walked in. Carmela seemed very much at home, and we figured she must look in on the elderly person quite often. We followed her in with anticipation. The room was full of antique furniture, adorned with white crocheted doilies and a plethora of nick-knacks crowding out any clear space there might be. The senior was sitting in her rocking chair in the front room, enthralled in her reading. Carmela spoke loudly to her. She explained who we were, and that we wanted to know if there was a family by the name of Fry living in this town. The time-worn hands shook as they raised to her chin, and she told us there was someone by the family name of Fry. After giving it some thought, she acknowledged it was Carmelita Fry. Our translator seemed shocked at the answer, as she did not know about this person. The elderly woman revealed that in the year 1947, a young widow and her daughter wandered into her village. They had nowhere to live, so Carmela's great-grandfather let them live in front of the pig-barn. They had a stove to cook on and the heat the pigs provided. The beds were on the same wall, which divided the living quarters from the pig stall. It was what they did back then, she explained. They slept on mattresses of straw and worked on the farm for food and lodging. The little girl would follow her mom while she worked on the farm, and often fell asleep under the apple tree across the street. We looked out the window as she leaned forward and moved the curtains so we could see it. The tree was massive and looked older than the senior we were speaking to.

She said that they loved this little girl. They picked her up from under the tree every day to bring her in the house, and they would put her into the clean white sheets of a bed they had provided, just for her. They would give her baths, comb her hair, and feed her. It was such a joy to have this little one on the farm.

I asked what happened to the little girl. Her face became troubled, and her eyes glazed as she spoke again with sadness. "There was a fire and they both died. We did not have a fire department, and the stable burned down before we could get them out."

We were sorry to hear of their death, and condolences seemed natural, given her emotional state.

She paused after long deliberation and said, "No, I must tell the truth. I am over one hundred years old, and must make a wrong, right. I will not have many more years left to tell the facts."

The three of us were shocked. What was she going to divulge to us? She sat quietly, contemplating what she was about to do.

When she started again, her voice was even quieter than before. We strained to hear, although we did not understand a word she was saying.

Our translator seemed upset. We realized she was the grand-daughter of this woman, now frantically calling her Omie. The elderly lady's daughter was not married and had no children, so she went to speak with Carmelita at her humble home, the pig barn. It was regarding giving her daughter up, so her childless daughter could raise her as her own. Carmelita Fry was very angry, and she said she would never give up her child as long as she lived. The century-old lady said, "She tried to argue with her, giving her reasons why it would be advantageous for the girl. Mrs. Fry was so angry that she accidently knocked over a gas lantern that stood very near to the bed. It toppled over when Carmelita threw a plate in frustration. The flames exploded, and the room was ablaze in seconds. I grabbed the child and ran out of the room in time to save our lives. The roof collapsed behind us. Carmelita Fry perished that day. No one knew we were arguing, nor what we argued about." She added, "I was looked on like a hero saving the child from the flames, and I gave her to my daughter to raise as her own."

"Omie, are you saying I am actually the daughter of Mrs. Fry? Not your granddaughter?"

"Yes, you are actually Mrs. Fry's daughter," she said, her voice breaking and her body slumped. "You will always be my granddaughter," the elderly woman added, "We have always loved you dearly."

As our translator, Carmela conceded that she had always been loved. She hugged the elderly woman with a genuine embrace and kissed her cheek. She told us her mother had passed away fifteen years earlier and never gave her a hint of the truth. She always wondered why her mother looked like a carbon copy of her grandmother, and yet she looked nothing like either one of them. It all made sense now. This was why she did not have an original birth certificate and so on. The elderly woman had finally let the truth be known. Now Carmela couldn't wait to tell her own granddaughter what her real history was. Carmela's daughter had died in a car crash ten years before. She left her one granddaughter to look after. Other than that, she and Omie were alone. Carmela had also never married and had her daughter as a single mom. It was strange, how history repeated itself. Her granddaughter was a good girl but, as she did herself, felt like a lost soul. Losing a mother and father at a young age was not an easy thing to overcome. Carmela knew of this kind of loss first hand,

and the struggles that she had within herself to overcome her need, although she didn't know where they came from.

Carmela herself had issues with separation anxiety, and now it was clear where these feelings came from. She had blocked all of those painful memories. She could now suddenly even recall the smell of the fire and hear the screaming. She had a fear of fire all her life, and now it all fell into place. To think the screaming sound in her mind was her mom's, caused her to break down and sob. When she was able to compose herself, she continued with her search for answers.

Carmela questioned her tiring grandmother regarding her father. Did she know what happened to her father?

"He was much older than his wife. Carmelita told me he was arrested during the war and never returned. This is why she moved away for safety."

We had all the information we needed. Of course, we had a lot of emotional supporting to do before we left. It was such a shock for Carmela, finding out who her mother really was. She and her granddaughter, Hannah, would be the heirs to Carmela's father's wages. They would work through their feelings and emotions and find peace with the facts as they happened. The elderly grandmother would also have peace, going to her grave knowing she righted a wrong in her old age. She now had a clear conscience as well as honest relationship with her granddaughter.

We drove, not talking, as we thought of the secrets people keep and how it haunts them all their lives. The truth sets a person free, and when a secret is exposed, freedom prevails.

We were going to check into a hotel as soon as possible. It had been another long day. We were in Buelstedt longer than we expected, although it was a productive trip. We would stay in touch with Carmela, though we had to come up with a good reason for wanting to know about the Fry family. She was too upset to even think of it at the time, but when her head cleared, she would ask the question. We would have to be ready with our answers.

We stopped at a nice little place in Willstedt, about half an hour from Buelstedt. It was a quaint town, also on the small side. We drove past a cemetery and decided to take a walk. It was quiet and peaceful, and a walk would clear our minds. It reminded us of our little family cemetery plot. We wondered what Pa and Josh were doing right now. What would they be up to? We talked about appreciating the normality of our family, and simultaneously started to laugh. What were we thinking? This was not normal! We had these secrets that we could tell no one. We were in Europe looking for people and couldn't tell them why, when we found them. Our life was not normal, although we thought of it as so. Our family is a regular one, who loves each other in the common ways.

We spoke again of the terrible things war does to people. Some are going through it right now, due to turmoil in the world. We decided we would pray every day for peace in the world and for good to prevail over evil.

We noticed a large family tombstone. It was the name Pilser. That was Carmela's last name. We checked the dates and names closely, and, sure enough, it was her mother's. There was a very large headstone for the senior member of the family, and the date of birth of Carmela's grandmother. Others had smaller stones in rows. We noticed Carmela's mother's head stone. Then we saw one with the name Fry. It was Carmela's biological mother's head stone. It had been included in the family plot. How fitting was that? It made me wonder why Carmela didn't see it before and take notice of it. We knew she would in the future. People didn't seem to take note of cemeteries and what was in them. But to be fair, when Carmela had need to visit the cemetery, her focus was on people she loved, and her heart was breaking with pain of their absence in her life. She had endured many hardships and lost many loved ones in her lifetime. Everyone around her had died, except for her grandmother and granddaughter. How could she notice the small details of this cemetery, when the object of her arrival was like a huge boulder she couldn't look over or around?

We gave our families a call when we checked into the hotel. Bee was excited about what she had experienced with Rachel, and Kelly was on the mend. Pa and Josh told us of their plans for the day, and we hoped they would be successful. We were kind of looking forward to a normal life, if we even knew how to live one anymore. We missed our family and looked forward to the normal routine, with the odd diversion, of course. For now, I would have my lovely wife by my side and appreciate everything about her. I had learned that it was about appreciating every moment with the person you loved. The stories of the people we were following up showed us, you never knew if you would have that chance tomorrow.

CHAPTER 31

Going to See the Baby

Bee, Grammy, Grammpy, and Kelly were on their way to see the new baby. Rachel was visiting her mom and welcomed them. Her mom was still weak and not out of the woods yet. The baby was in a bassinet beside the bed. Bee peeked at her and couldn't believe how her skin looked today, compared to yesterday. She had been ruddy and swollen when Bee had held her just after birth. Her skin was pink and smooth today. Her hair was brushed, and she smelled so fresh. That baby scent was intoxicating. She just couldn't get enough of it. This was a special baby, as Bee took part in her debut entering life.

Grammy asked if she could do anything, like cook or do some wash for the family. Rachel relayed that her sister was doing her usual chores and keeping up with it all. This was amazing, since Bee knew of moms that had a difficult time keeping up with a family of four. Grammy and Grammpy congratulated Rachel for the good job she did, and her mother nodded her head in agreement. She understood that her life had been on the line, and Rachel had saved both her and the baby.

"What is the baby's name?" Bee asked.

"Well, you will never guess. It is Chelbee," announced Rachel. She added, "Do you get it?"

"No," Bee said with a puzzled look.

Grammpy was already smiling and realized what was coming. He knew the combination and its purpose already.

Rachel proclaimed that it was a combination of Rachel and Bee: "Chelbee."

"Really? It is our names put together?" Bee exclaimed.

Everyone joined in with surprise, and Kelly gave her a big hug. She again reaffirmed she had not done anything, and Rachel strongly asserted how valuable she was in making the calls. Bee was delighted, of course, and thought of herself like a Godmother of sorts. She was sure the Amish did not know what that was, but Chelbee had a special place in Bee's heart. They did not want to over tax Marion Lutz, so they said their good-byes and left quietly. Bee was taking Grammy and Grammpy to get some groceries, and Kelly was going to wait in the car. He had had enough exercise for one day. Bee would run into the store next door to pick up a gift for Chelbee.

She knew she couldn't buy a frilly little dress, a sweater set, or cute little shoes. She would have to be creative with this gift. Grammy said to pick up a little patchwork quilt for her and Grammpy to give the baby. Bee hoped she wouldn't be too long, as Kelly would be in the car waiting alone. She saw just the right sized quilt as a gift from Grammy. She had walked around the store three times when the nice Amish girl behind the counter asked what she was looking for. Bee told her she didn't know, but it was for a special baby. The sales clerk said she had something behind the counter and to follow her. Bee did, and the sales girl pulled out a nice burgundy Bible. Bee thought that to be a perfect gift. The Amish believed in the Bible, and, at Grammpy's, they read it all the time. She picked up some special wrapping paper, not too fancy, but it was pink. She would write something nice in it for Chelbee. Bee was excited that she found a gift that she was happy with. When she got to the car, Kelly's eyes were closed, and he was having a catnap. Her grandparents were just coming out with their groceries. She helped them put the groceries in the trunk, and they were headed home. She would drop the gift by later and let Kelly rest until she got back. The senior couple usually napped in the afternoon, and it would make for a restful time for all three.

CHAPTER 32

Something to Make the Job Easier

Pa and I were having our breakfast and talking about the day ahead. I was cooking today and had learned how to fry eggs perfectly along with the sausages. Pa was studying some maps when I brought his plate over to him.

He looked up and said, "Josh, I have a surprise for you today."

"What is it, Pa?"

Pa replied, "I have ordered a metal detector."

"Wow, that will be awesome," I said. "It will be fun."

He agreed with me, and I asked him if it would tell us what we would find. He said it advertised that it signaled according to the metal it detected. He handed me the instructions he had in his pocket, figuring that I should familiarize myself with it. He pointed to the box in the corner of the closet, and I ran to retrieve it. I was in no mood for breakfast, but Pa insisted. We had a lot to do, and I would need my energy. Pa also knew I could eat every hour these days.

Suddenly, there was a knock at the door. We both yelled, "Come on in!" at the same time. To our surprise, it was Barry. We looked kind of shocked, and he asked what was wrong. We both answered, "nothing," and asked if he wanted to have some breakfast. It was the polite thing to do.

Pa got up and put the maps in the next room, then laid the metal detector right on the table. "Look at what I bought for the kids to have some fun with."

Barry examined it and said it was a good one, then asked what we were looking for.

"You know, whatever is lurking under the grass, waiting for us to expose it after years of captivity," said Pa.

"Well I should join you, but I came to tell you something. Mac has caught some kind of bug, and she has a high temperature. She wanted me to check on both of you and let you know. She thought you might be sick too, since she was over just a day or so ago. Are you sure you both feel all right?" he asked again.

"Yes, yes, we promise, we are just fine," Pa reaffirmed.

Barry didn't want breakfast, and, after he finished his coffee, he left. I shouted after him that I would come and see Mac later, but he yelled back that I better not for a couple of days. Pa and I decided we would be more careful with our plans, as you never knew who would show up. The phone rang, and we answered it. It was Barry, and he thought he should inform us that the law stated that if someone found an object of a certain age in Niagara on the Lake, it had to be turned in. In fact, it was against the law to even use a metal detector in Niagara on the Lake, unless on private property. He didn't know if that applied to the Queenston area. Pa said he would check that out before we left our property and thanked him for keeping us on the right side of the law.

I cleaned up the dishes after checking all the features of the metal detector.

"Pa, did you know it can detect metal under water, too?" I asked him.

He had read the instructions and was well aware of its features. The maps were put in the safe, as we had other copies in the underground living space, which we would use. Today, our plan was to find a couple more spots of buried treasure that had been earned by some poor prisoners. The doors were locked, and we were off. After signing our ledger and closing the secret doors, we were almost there. I carried the metal detector, hoping Pa would let me be the one to use it.

It was nice, having the lights when we needed them, and I found myself wishing we had hydro everywhere down below. In all the tunnels, not just our living area and storage room. We wouldn't have to drag all this equipment with us every time. I was getting lazy with my thoughts to modernize everything around me. I was too young and foolish at the time to realize that it was all so intriguing because it had been left as it was so many years before.

There were five maps of the lake area. We would take them with us and see what we could discover. It looked like the men had definitely been in groups. We still mused about the fact that the men could have met each other at some point, maybe against their captor's wishes. We hoped that to be true.

On the way down, Pa and I anticipated running into Sweetheart. I asked Pa why he didn't name Sweetheart's mom. Pa answered that he didn't need to. He had one friend, and when he spoke, it was to her. Otherwise, he did not need to speak.

Well, that made sense, I thought to myself. His friend, unlike Wilson in the movie we watched, was real, and she came in and out of his life. He did not have to name her to make her real. How interesting, although I thought I would have named a friend like this cougar.

Pa added, "Maybe, in a sense, I did name the cougar, as I always called her girl."

"Maybe we should name her, 'Girl,'" he said.

I concluded it was a unique name and would work, as she responded to it already. At the bottom of the cave where the cougar den was, Pa called out to her.

"Hey girl, where are you. Come on girl, let's see that kitten of yours," Pa spoke out loud.

He jokingly suggested that the cougar wouldn't know it was him, as he never spoke to her while she wasn't in sight.

"So, you think she read your lips?" I laughed, nodding my head.

We kept on walking, as they were not in sight. Pa and I discussed the fact that some of the treasure maps looked like they were marked right inside the lake. How were we going to retrieve them?

"That is why I got this new gadget," he said.

I guessed it would be very useful in our search. We made it as far as where the tunnel met the cavern with the lake. I told Pa that

I should have been using the scanner on the way down, so we didn't miss anything. He thought it was a good idea, and I started it up. Scanning as I walked put a spring to my step. I just couldn't wait to get my first hit! Pa went ahead, and I followed.

The marking was at the edge of the lake where we had found the crevasse that led to Pa's small hideout. It was right in the water. We shone our flashlights down to where we thought it should be. We saw black and the reflection of the light.

CHAPTER 33

In the Underground Lake

I put the metal detector down into the water and you should have heard the noise. It was similar when I tested the instrument upstairs on the coins.

"I guess they are in there somewhere," Pa said.

I tried to touch them with my shovel but couldn't. How did they get them in there? Maybe there had been less water in this lake back then. It would have been difficult. We pondered over what to do next. We decided to look at the map once more. The five clues hidden in this lake all contained the same name, Ritmeir. Pa said he found nothing on them, except their names on a list of prisoners. It didn't even say what they were arrested for.

"Pa, look at this little line. What do you think it means?" I questioned.

It was fascinating, how a small line on one of these pieces of paper could look like nothing. Instantly, it could take on its own life and come into focus with such importance. I had never considered it to mean anything before.

"Look, Pa, it comes right from the edge of the lake, toward the small square on the drawing."

We got on our knees and felt in the water along the edge of the lake. There was a rope! It was fastened to the rock and was still attached to something under the water. We could not budge it.

"What are we going to do, Pa?" I questioned.

He said nothing, rubbing his chin.

After a long silence he spoke, "We would be able to manage the weight until it reaches the top of the water. Then, we would need help."

I wondered if there was a place to tie it off, so we could pull it up. I could get that huge rope we had used to tie Vinnie's friend, the "suit guy." Pa thought it would be good to have, so I ran to retrieve it. It was more than I bargained for. I dragged the heavy rope behind me and finally got back, already tired. The light was now in the small cave.

"Pa, what are you doing in there?"

"Come on in with the rope," he ordered.

He had found the right spot to tie the rope off.

We attached it tightly. We took the rope through the cave opening and to the water's edge.

Pa figured the rock would act like a pulley and help us to support the weight. We both started to pull. It was quite easy and light at first, until the large box neared the top of the water. It was still too low, and we could not lift it over the edge.

"Josh, can you hold the rope while I see what the problem is?"

I nodded, and he carefully and slowly let go, giving me the full weight. I pulled with all my might. I decided to wrap the rope around the rock and tie it.

Pa was strained, "It is right there. I can see the box right near the top." He pulled on the rope, but he could not lift it.

I hurried to his side to see what the problem was.

"Let me loop this around the box, and maybe we can get the job done." He fashioned a large lasso loop on the end of the rope. As it was pulled on, it would get tighter. He managed to get it around the box without falling in. Only his arms were wet, but that didn't matter.

We were ready to pull, and I used the rock for leverage. It was coming. Suddenly, with a thump, it lay on the floor of the cavern. I shouted with joy.

Pa said his usual, "Well, will you look at that."

"Let's open it now." I got my crow bar and started at the box. It was a German Gun Powder box, and it was well preserved. We worked, and the lid finally came off. There were five portions in separate sacks, just like the others. We would have to recruit Mark and Mac to help us carry this stuff.

"Maybe a wagon or something will help, Pa?"

That was why it was so heavy. All we had were names for these men. They were all the same.

"One name, one box, one find," I said.

The name shown on the maps were Ritmeir. We decided they must have been family, and they were very strong to let their box down into the water that way. Pa would look at his notes to see what he could find on them when we got back.

CHAPTER 34

The Body

We would forge ahead and try to locate the treasure at the other dry lake. It was marked with the circle and filled with small circles, piling up. There was a small line, and now we knew better than to ignore it.

When we got there, we would look at the map again. We did not understand why it had a line going up from the circle. Maybe it would be clearer when we saw the place again. It took a while to get there with all our stuff. I used the metal detector as we moved through the tunnels. Finally, I heard a noise. It was something like metal, but not precious. I found the spot and bent over. There was a small crack, and in that crack was something dark and round. I used my tweezers to retrieve it. It was a button from a uniform. Pa said it was from a German soldier's uniform.

"That is a keeper," I said, putting it into my bag.

We kept on going until we got to the lake of rubble. Shining our lights, we carefully scanned the edge before doing anything else. We looked under the first layer of rubble as far as we could see to catch a glimpse of something, anything. We were almost halfway around before the metal detector made a sound. It was the same sound that the button had made, but louder. We looked carefully into the crevasses of the rocks piled on top of each other. My flashlight exposed something. I called Pa over, and the metal detector got louder and louder as I moved. We looked under the first layer of rock and saw a uniform. Then, we saw the skeleton wearing the uniform. That was gross. I had never thought I would see a skeleton with a uniform still on him.

Pa figured that, if the money was here too, the guard probably surprised them and they had to kill him. He wasn't sure until we saw the uniform and skeleton closer up. We would try to retrieve the skeleton. We had our work cut out for us. Pa and I knew enough to take pictures of all our findings with our phones. We were moving the layer of rocks and threw them over to another area. We tossed them nearer to the middle, out of our way. The map showed that the gold was near to the circumference. We had the body cleared, and Pa decided to climb down to retrieve it. He took one look at it and saw the skull had a gunshot hole in it. It was in the center of the forehead. He would leave the body where it was for now. He noticed the uniform front was missing a button. Pa surmised that a superior officer had shot him. They were all to be killed before the secret got out. The prisoners didn't have guns. Hopefully, we would find out what happened

We still needed to find that gold. We decided to leave the body and look where the line showed on the wall. Our lights exposed a rustic, hand-chiseled line in the rock on the wall, which continued along the floor to the side of the dry lake. We followed it from the edge and carefully examined where it led. It went down the wall of the dry lake in the direction of the skeleton.

"I guess I will have to move that body after all," Pa stated.

I stepped up to the plate, as Pa was older and would have a more difficult time climbing the rocks. The soldier's skeleton wouldn't weigh a lot, so I could retrieve it. Pa asked if I was sure I could do it. I was sure, so I made my way over the edge and down into the basin. The rocks were difficult to maneuver on. I pulled at the jacket, and, of course, the bones were displaced. For now, I would fold the hands and arms in and fold legs up. The skull was put in the middle, and I wrapped up the jacket part of the uniform. I carefully carried the remains of the soldier to the side where the rock floor was flat. I placed him at Pa's feet and quickly went back to see what I missed. There was nothing in that location but a few misplaced bones and more rocks. I turned to go back, and my eyes caught sight of where the chiseled line ran down from the wall. It ended a foot down from the floor above. I had a close look, but nothing struck me as unusual. I ran my flashlight along the hand-hewn crack. A coin was stuck in the crack. I pulled it out, as it wasn't difficult to get at. Behind it was a small roll of paper. I retrieved it and passed it to Pa. It was a folded up five-by-seven piece of paper, folded in half and neatly rolled.

Pa took a moment to look at the paper. It contained orders to kill all the prisoners and a reprimand that he would be killed if he did not obey orders this time.

"I guess he didn't kill the prisoners after all," said Pa.

While Pa was reading the official order, I noticed some writing on the back.

"Pa, there is something on the other side!" I shouted.

"Well, let's look at that too," he continued.

He studied it for a moment and reported. The men had used the soldier's order form for paper to write their last thoughts on.

CHAPTER 35

A Good Man, the German

"The soldier did not obey orders to kill us. He was killed by his commanding officer when it was discovered that we were still alive. We left my money just before the tunnel at the top, where we were going to be taken in the morning. We were interrupted from putting it under the rubble. We did not believe our lives would be spared, and we knew the end was imminent. The guards were rounding up all the prisoners into one area for the night. This soldier was to guard us. He had helped us to collect all the maps and gave them to a man named Friedrich Wittfoot, who hid them. Friedrich knew how to get into all the passages, tunnels and rooms, as he was one of the masterminds. The soldier assisted in covering for us as we hid our money. The five Ritmeir brothers have no remaining family. They witnessed their family's murder by firing squad before being taken to prison. I have a wife and two sons. My brother, Rudy Kempt, is not married and has no children. The soldier's family shall get my brother's share, as Rudy specified. The man's name is Herman Wolfgang. He has a wife and family. We found his body in the tunnel and gave him a quick burial under the rocks. It was the best we could do under the circumstances.

Tell my family I love them, Eckhart Kempt."

"Pa, I needed some good news. This is starting to get me down," I said.

"Yes, reality is harsh, but when the families start receiving their money, you will have so much joy and will know that you are doing the right thing," Pa replied.

I knew he was right, and we would check out one more area, which was at the entrance of the tunnel to the coach house. We didn't use it as much and were not as familiar with it. We stood at the entrance where it led up. There was nothing.

"Didn't he say before the entrance, Pa?"

"Yes, he did."

We backtracked a little. There, under a pile of sacks, was the money. It was put inside two sacks, and then covered with empty sacks. How could we not have found it earlier? At this point, we just worried about how far this would be to carry. We would leave it right here until another day. At least the job was done.

We were on our way back through the tunnels, chatting over the information we had found. It was riveting to know this German soldier was so kind and followed his heart, even unto death. I remembered his remains were still lying by the rubble lake. We would treat the remains with respect when we went back for them.

"If everyone acted according to their conscience, this would be a better world, wouldn't it, Pa?"

"I would like to believe so, but some people have no conscience."

"I didn't think about that. We are all so dissimilar and think differently," I added.

There she was: Pa's Girl and her Sweetheart. She came to Pa out of nowhere. Pa was so delighted to see the kitten. I was shocked that she had grown so much. Pa checked the stitches I had administered, and he thought it all looked good. He asked if I had the bullet. I said yes, I had put it in my exploration bag, where it should still be. He would look at it later. He was enjoying watching his friend be a nurturing cougar.

He said a few times, "What a delight."

Her visit was over, and she left as quickly as she had appeared. Pa reminded me again that he owed his life to this cat. Pa was always encouraging everyone, so he didn't hesitate to let me know that I would make a good doctor. He thought I had what it took. Of course, I thanked him for his confidence, but I still wasn't sure which direction I should go with my studies.

He understood and said, "Yes, time will show you and sort that all out, and God will direct your path."

We would have so much to clean up tomorrow, as we had left quite a trail behind us. The body needed to be respectfully hidden, the money in the ammunition crates would need hiding, and the gold under the sacks should be hidden. We knew we would need some more muscle for the job. For today, we would report to Mom and Dad on our findings, then give them another name to investigate and contact.

CHAPTER 36

Berlin - Dad's Account

We were on our way to Berlin, waiting to see what the day would bring. I remembered being there just after the wall came down. Back then, the difference between the east and west side was like night and day. Pa and I had rented a hotel room on the communist side, and we had no idea what we were in for when we booked it. It had been reasonably priced and in the area we would be working.

Pa and I had climbed four flights of stairs with our luggage. A lonely light bulb hung by an old cord in the middle of the room. There were two old iron beds with the mattress covered and only one blanket. It had two small pillows with embroidered pillowcases. I will never forget having to pull the dirty string adjacent to the light on the high ceiling. It was covered with grease and grit of many years of use. There were no chairs, no dressers, nor paintings on the walls. It looked absolutely bare. Pa and I put our luggage on the floor and lived out of our suitcases. We were investigating a company that had sold illegal products in Canada, and a private client wanted to sue. They wanted to have all their ducks in a row before they began such an undertaking. It would take time to develop the case and get all the information. I remembered we had a difficult time, as people were so untrusting that they would not speak to just anyone. We won that case, and we were handsomely rewarded for a job well done.

I hoped our stay this time would lean a little more to the side of convenience. I was not into climbing all those stairs with luggage this time, as Nerissa packed much heavier than Pa.

Berlin showed itself to be a modern city boasting skyscrapers, modern highways, and stores advertising the absolute latest trendy styles in their gigantic storefront windows. We looked for a moderately priced hotel downtown but found only the best for the most prices. I would be working in this area. The government buildings were a block away, so we splurged. Nerissa could go shopping while I searched the registries for our last family, by the name of Friezen. I hoped it would go well. I knew the shopping end of the trip would.

The hotel was lovely and had all the modern amenities we would want or need. The glass exterior made it feel even roomier. As you entered the suite, your focus was on the wall-to-wall glass, as well as ceiling to floor. It would draw you in, so you could look through the astonishing piece of glass, and the vast city of Berlin would impress you even more. It was quite captivating, taking our breath away with all the tall, modern buildings and the metropolitan aesthetic. The kind bellhop quickly showed us where the button was to have privacy. I took it that past guests had been taken aback at the lack of it as they first walked into the suite. When he pushed the button, it turned the glass into a solid white glass wall. We did enjoy the feature, though you couldn't just peek out when you wanted to. It was closed or open.

We settled in, and Nerissa called me to see the lavish bathroom. It, too, had the same glass wall as the bedroom, only it was the wall between the bedroom and bath. There was a huge air tub and modern square waterfall faucets. The toilet was separated from the bath and had its own enclosure. The room was overstated with a top-of-the-line bidet. The bidet had all the gadgets you could need and more. Two lovely, soft white robes with matching slippers lay in a basket near the tub. A gift card was placed on top of the basket, on the speculation that it would be added to, by our extending the spa treatments. It was for a free hour at the hotel spa. Nerissa thought that would be such a treat. I knew she would have way too much fun while I was out working. She might not want to leave.

Beside the coffee and alcohol bar sat a delicious looking basket of fresh fruits, accompanied with some biscotti, muffins, and chocolates. A chaise was nestled in the corner with a companion chair beside it and a low table to complete the trio. The room was done in multi textures of warm white to complete that spa feeling. It was sophisticated and comfortable. Just perfectly put together, even to the vase of white roses and a novel to read beside them. Not omitting the man's touch, it displayed a beautiful fifty-five-inch television screen, cleverly disguised as a fireplace. I thought we were going to enjoy this place.

Checked in and unpacked, we called home and Grammy's. Pa and Josh gave us the latest updates regarding their finds. We were flabbergasted at how much they got done. We didn't even want to know any more names until the first list was completed. We now had one more name to follow up. It was the name Friezen. Pa was going to send me all the info he had on the new names. We did not know if we would stay in Europe for a while or go home first. Time would tell.

Bee couldn't stop talking about Chelbee and how cute she was. She told us what she bought for her, and I told her to find a meaningful scripture for her future. Something that she desired for her as well as something God would want to give her. Bee said she would give it some thought and find just the right one. Kelly was doing very well, and so was Grammy and Grammpy. I always appreciated hearing from my family. We were blessed to have a good, loving family.

The next day, after a lovely—but costly—breakfast at the hotel, I made my way to the Registry Office. Nerissa was going to take advantage of her free spa pass and read a book.

I entered the building and had to give them not one but three pieces of identification. It looked like they took security seriously. I went to the fifth floor, where the files of the deceased were kept. I would start in 1939 and look for a Mr. Friezen from this area. I would see what I could find. He had been arrested in 1941. Pa found this on a list of prisoners taken from Berlin. There was no reason given for their arrest. I moved from the elevator to a room full of computers. This kind of work used to be done with books and papers. Times certainly had changed. Hopefully, it would make my job easier.

I sat in front of a computer and put in the password the staff had given to me. I filled in the name and place of last known location. The computer searched for about a minute and gave me some information to read. It just said he was arrested, and his first name was Fritz. The information stated he had no family. There was nothing new. I looked up his birth certificate and those of his parents. His mother was Italian, and his father was a German man. They married in Venice, Italy. I was surprised to find out his father's vocation was as a gondolier in Venice. I wondered why he ended up going to Germany.

We would take a drive to the last known address of Fritz tomorrow. For now, I thought I would go back to the hotel and have a few leisurely hours of luxury. Nerissa was at the spa for a massage and had left me a note that she would return by two this afternoon. I sat and went over my notes while I waited for her. There was only this one loose end, and then we could go home. I hoped we could find a relative. It gave credence to the lives of these imprisoned laborers, to give their descendants the wage paid for by giving their lives.

Nerissa was very relaxed when she arrived back at our room. She had enjoyed a hot stone massage and reminded me that it was free. She showed me the price list and I was dumbfounded. That was an outrageous price. We were definitely in a high-end hotel, and the prices certainly reflected it.

Instead of waiting for tomorrow, we thought we would take a drive through Berlin and look for the neighborhood where Fritz had lived. It would also give me a good visual of how the city had changed. We made our way to the outskirts of town, as the GPS commanded. The homes were more modern than the rest of Germany.

"They have certainly done an incredible rebuild of this city," I remarked.

Sitting contemplatively beside me, Nerissa agreed. She was wondering what we would find this time. As we neared our destination, we could see it was an area not yet rebuilt. The homes were to be torn down, as they were now a hazard to the community. The large machinery looked eerie in the dusk of the day. It was parked there, and it looked like they would start within days. We stopped where the GPS directed and parked the car on the side of the mud-laden road. I wanted to go inside and see if I could find anything of interest to us. It was not roped off yet, so I felt it was safe. Nerissa wanted to see the building from the inside too, and, against my better judgment, she accompanied me. We would have to hurry before we lost the sunlight.

The door opened easily and we walked into a tiny room. The original wallpaper, now old and stained, still hung on the walls. There were noticeable outlined areas where pictures had once hung, and the accompanying nails were still firmly implanted. Through the front room, we entered the kitchen. It was shabby-looking, with grease blotches, many varieties of paint chipping, and peeling walls. The sink was streaked brown from age and minerals. We walked into the bedroom. It had been made smaller by dividing it to make a bathroom. The bedroom had nothing in it, except a calendar on the wall. This one piece was so eye catching, we had to have a closer look. It demanded that we look at it, being the only thing left in the house. It was a piece of personal property belonging to the previous inhabitants. Gazing at the past year of the calendar, we read many meticulously written notes. Appointments and so on were marked in red. We looked at today's date, and it had a red circle. Why did they not take this calendar if they still used it? The note on the schedule for one week from now was also in red. The calendar was from Italy and had lovely pictures of Venice, especially of Gondoliers. There was an address handwritten on the top of it, as well as a postal code. The address appeared to be in Venice. I would try to call the number that corresponded with this address from the hotel and start my search. We found nothing else in the house, but we took the calendar.

There were some teens playing ball on the street outside. Their English was very good, like most of the inhabitants of Germany. We asked if they knew who lived here.

They answered, "Yes, of course."

"What were their names?" I questioned.

CHAPTER 37

Venice

"Their names were Mr. Friezen and Fritz," they said, and my jaw dropped.

That name was certainly a name we were looking for connection to.

"When did they move?" I inquired.

"Oh, our friend Fritz left a week ago and would arrive in Venice today. They were going to be gondoliers, starting a week from today! Why do you want to know?" the lad added in his broken, yet understandable English.

"We have some news for them," I answered.

"I hope it is good news, they were so happy to get the last news," the young man replied.

"Do you know what the news was?" I asked in passing.

"Sure, Fritz was our friend and told us it was regarding the old family business. They could resume it, or they could sell it. They decided it would be a good start, and that they would try it."

"Thank you very much boys, have a good evening," I said as we left, and they carried on kicking their ball down the littered street.

We went straight to the hotel, as I was anxious to call the address we had found. We didn't think there were any living relatives, but here we were with the names of two people to follow up.

Nerissa was getting excited, as she thought we would be going to Venice. The number for the address had not been connected yet.

That made sense, if they just moved there. We would have to make a trip to Venice to get this settled. I notified the hotel of our checkout in the morning. I set my GPS as well and got some maps printed by the hotel for the return of the rental car. We wouldn't need a car in Venice, so we decided to take the train there. It was quicker than driving taking only 16 hours, and we could sleep during the night. The cost was $300 Canadian for both of us, and it would be an enjoyable relaxing experience.

We returned the rental car early in the morning, in order to make our departure smooth. It was lovely to see the countryside and the mountains while traveling through some long rail tunnels. We were getting closer, and I noticed the homes had lost their pristine white looks and turned to that natural sun bleached, neutral tanned color. They blended into the landscape more instead of popping out against the canopy, like they did in Germany and Switzerland. The vineyards and olive groves climbed the hills, creating unbroken views of serenity. The estates looked like they had been there for centuries. Eventually, we were seeing more water and knew Venice was near. After gathering up our belongings, we were ready to leave the train. I left the calendar in my outside suitcase pocket for easy access.

The taxi left us at a parking lot right across the waterway from a hotel. We crossed over on a lovely brick bridge and went inside. They had a room facing the canal. That was perfect. Breakfast would be included. Going to the third floor was not easy, even though there was an elevator. Nerissa and I and two carry-ons barely fit into it. We arrived in a narrow hall and opened our door with a large key on a big wooden block. The key would never be misplaced or forgotten in a purse or pant pocket. It was a quaint room, with upholstered walls done in a medium gold color. The headboard was painted white with blue accents. On each side of the bed, over the nightstands, hung beautiful Murano glass fixtures in a pale blue. Looking out of the window, we could see the bridge and boats and gondolas passing by. A plumber's boat went by, loaded up with pipe and other materials, ready for a day's work. It reminded me of our new friends Mitchell and Dustin. Then, a carpenter's boat went by. He had his wood, saws and many wood crafting tools. We would leave our belongings, except for the calendar, which Nerissa placed into her large travelling purse.

We were on our way to find the Friezen family. There couldn't be too many names like that in Venice! We caught a gondola at the corner, where the next bridge intersected with another canal. I couldn't get over the wet, musty smell of the city, although it didn't stop Nerissa from thinking this was the most romantic city she had ever been in. We gave the address to the gondolier, then asked if he knew a Mr. Friezen. He started to get angry and shout and speak with his hands, throwing them around in all directions. I interrupted and let him know we could not understand. In his broken English, he told us about the newcomer who had caused problems for him and a lot of others. He took his gondola out and almost crashed every gondolier in Venice. He would take me to him. His black and white striped, long-sleeved sweater looked crisp against the red vest he was wearing. His gondola was special to him, as he said it was in his family for many generations. It was black, with worn red velvet seats and lining. He said it looked this way when his grandfather had taught him how to be a gondolier. He was very proud to carry on his ancestor's business. He said it had to be born into, and a person could not easily attain a boat by buying one outright. It would be difficult to start as a gondolier today.

He took us through some narrow canals. There were old doors that looked like they could fall off at any moment, if not for the oversized heavy hinges and metal hardware. The wood was old and rotted at the bottom, and the windows were old glass, and difficult to see through. He said this was the oldest part of Venice, and the poorest. Many people had left this area for better homes. He stopped at a huge door. He said it was to park a gondola in. Beside it, the tilted threshold of a door clung to the old bricks, looking as unsafe as anything we had ever seen. We were told to climb out onto this dangerous-looking landing. We asked if he could wait, and we would pay him for his time. He agreed. We loudly knocked on the door. Then I knocked again. Finally, a young man answered the door.

I said, "Fritz?"

"Yes," he answered.

"May we come in?" I asked.

He showed us inside and closed the heavy door. The water was also on the inside of the door. There was a gondola parked beside an old, worn wooden walkway. He led us up some stairs to a brighter hall and into a living area. We arrived at what could only be described as an enchanting kitchen. It was all brick, with one large, open window that you could step outside from. There was a narrow platform used to hang out laundry. An old window box containing flowers adorned the slip of a balcony. I had the thought that it might be too dangerous to use. The bricks set off the old, black wood stove in the kitchen. The eating area had been shaped by cutting up an old gondola's seating and putting a table in the middle. It had a rather unique, quaint look. He motioned for us to follow him into the sitting room. Another large window and more old furniture, although very tidy, made this room showcase its wall-to-wall bookcases. They were filled with books and other interesting items, like unique pieces of glass. The smartly-dressed man came over to shake our hands. He motioned for us to have a seat. Speaking German, he told his son to make a cup of tea.

"Do you understand or speak English?" I asked.

He did, and we started our conversation.

"We were in Berlin looking for a Mr. Friezen and found this," I pulled the calendar out, and he was shocked at the sight of it.

"Yes, I forgot to take it. Thank you for bringing it to me," he said as he grabbed for it.

I had copied all the pages, so I was glad to return it to him.

"Can you tell me where your parents are from, and why you ended up here?" I inquired.

He stammered and stumbled over his words while Fritz came in with the tea.

Mr. Friezen asked how we got there and after telling him, he said we could dismiss the gondola and they would make sure we got back to our hotel safely. I went to pay the gondolier and thanked him for waiting. He said, in his broken English, to tell the man to get out of this business. He did not know how to maneuver the gondola. He left, waving his arms and hands and very loudly talking to himself.

I found Mr. Friezen studying the calendar. I asked him what he had done to the gondolier.

He replied that Fritz and himself were so excited about being gondoliers that they took out the long boat as soon as they were unpacked. It proved to be a great error. Not only did they go on the wrong side, they also went in the wrong direction. What had he been thinking? He should have known they had rules, just as all other boaters. This was true, especially in such small canals with so much traffic. He also relayed to us how he actually crashed into many of the gondolas while trying to get back home. He was well known in Venice because of one outing. It was a close-knit family, the boat owners, and they protected one another. They met early for their morning coffee and discussed the latest news. They had known that he was coming to Venice to take over his great-grandfather's gondola.

I directly asked if he had proof of who he was. He said no, in a suspicious way. I thought to myself, "What is he hiding?"

Something didn't sit right with this guy. I asked if he had his son's birth certificate. He replied that everything had been lost a year ago. I found this to be strange and kept on prodding, even though Nerissa was becoming uncomfortable with the whole thing. Fritz looked nervous, as everyone got more intense and voices became strained.

Finally, he came out with the truth. He said they had been down to their last dollar when they were sent a beautiful gift.

"We had a chance to have a wonderful life. We received a letter which said that my supposed grandfather in Venice left us the gift of a home and a gondola in the heart of Venice. We were losing our home of many years. My father lived there, and he said his grandfather lived there. It was so old, but we could not renovate it because of lack of finances. The city bought the property for next to nothing and we were forced to move. I know I should not have pretended to be the rightful owner of the gondola, but I had nowhere to turn. I needed to provide a new home for us. I thought it would be easy and no one would be the wiser. When we got here, we liked the home and its charm and personality. I found out it was not easy to be a gondolier. Not only to maneuver one, but to own one. The rights are passed down from generation to generation. I told him I knew that. He asked why we had come to locate him? Of course, I couldn't say, but said I was looking up records of families and understood the family of Fritz Friezen was dead."

"No, they are not!" the father shouted.

"You cannot take that away from us, we are Friezen and we have proof. Fritz, get our papers," he commanded.

Fritz came back into the room with an old metal box.

"Here they are, Papa," he said.

Mr. Friezen pulled out a neatly bound stack of papers. "Here are Fritz's birth certificates and mine. I also have the bill of sale for my property."

I looked at the amount and said, "Yes, you did not get much for your property."

He said that it had been just enough to pay the medical expenses for his wife. She passed away three months ago. We gave our condolences to them both.

CHAPTER 38

Two in One

"Let me look at the birth certificates," I urged.

He reluctantly passed them to me and maintained that he meant no harm in what he had done. The name was correct, and he had been born to Carl Friezen in 1970. He had his father's papers too, and he'd been born to Fritz Friezen and Maria Friezen ne De'Marco in 1940.

"Did you know you are both these people?" I suggested.

"What do you mean?" he insisted, still angry.

"I mean you are the man we are looking for, being Mr. Stephan Friezen, the grandson of Fritz Friezen. You are the rightful owner of this place. As the grandson in-law of Stephano De'Marco, the grandfather on your grandmother's side, left you this place. He had no more heirs to leave it to, and it was important to keep a family business going. He must have found the same lead we did, and that was the old address of your grandparents. How marvelous that you lived there, all this time!" In Europe, families lived in homes for generations. I could now see the advantage of that.

He was ecstatic. Fritz could not hide his joy and ran to hug his dad, saying, "Pa, Pa, we are going to be fine! We can stay here!"

I looked at his legal documents regarding his inheritance. Sure enough, it was from a Stephano De'Marco to his last living relative. No name mentioned. It said he had a daughter, Maria, who married a German man.

"Well you have the proof that this is you as you were born to Maria. Although your name is not mentioned, you can prove this belongs to you. It looks like the lawyer had already done his research and knew it was you. You have legal entitlement to everything you have here."

Stephan was so relieved. "*Danke, danke,*" he repeated, meaning, "Thank you, thank you."

He still thought we were here getting information regarding his inheritance, so we left it at that. I encouraged him to make friends with the other gondoliers, as they could help him with the business and teach him and Fritz how to handle the long boat. I would speak to the fellow that gave us a ride tomorrow. For now, they had a lot to consider and we would call it a day.

"Now, how do we get home? There was water right outside their door!" I expressed concern regarding our departure.

Stephan took out a map to show us. They would walk us to the hotel, but he wanted to show us how easy it was to find our way. We came in on the back side of the building. The other side had a narrow walkway, which joined many others and eventually some wider sidewalks that crossed those beautiful Venetian bridges. The walkways were all running alongside the canals. The Friezen home was indeed in the old section and was one of a few that could put their gondolas inside their home at night. It is what everyone did in days gone by.

"Our gondola is special," Fritz said. "It was my grandfather's and great-grandfather's," he added, taking ownership of his family inheritance.

Nerissa pleaded, "May we see it, please?"

"We are proud of our ancestors and how they maintained this piece of art. Come with me," Stephan insisted.

They were definitely taking on the role of pride in their heritage. We went back down to the narrow hall and into the boat dock. We hadn't seen anything special when we came in this way. We walked along the old boardwalk towards what we learned was the front of the house. There, in the water, was the most beautiful piece of art, in exquisite form. There wasn't a scratch or nick on it. It was painted with gold leaf and finished with red velvet seats and backrests. Its front was embossed with the carving of the name, "De'Marco" and also painted with gold leaf. We asked if this was the gondola that they took out that day. They would have been noticed, even if they did nothing wrong.

"Oh no," was their simultaneous reply. "We would never do that. We have two old ones, too. We left one tied up where we were when we crashed into the other gondolas, but we managed to get one home together. We were not allowed to bring the other one back yet."

We laughed at that story but greatly appreciated the fact that they could see the value in this exquisite piece of history. Stephan was quick to add that it was like money in his pocket. I reckoned this might be their way into the circle of gondoliers. I figured if the townspeople could get over their jealousy, they would love this for its history and value, and they'd give the owners another chance at a new life. We didn't know too much about this kind of thing, but we could see that it was valuable.

They walked us past the spectacular specimen to an outside door. It led to the front walkway. The lights on the buildings shimmered on the water as the moon perfectly placed, hung overhead. If we were not in a party of four, it would have been a romantic walk back; that is, if we could have found our way. We talked as they led the way through town. Stephan still used a map since he hadn't been here for very long himself. Every once in a while, we would stop under a street light or on top of a lit-up bridge to find out where to go next. It was lovely, taking all these back streets, as this was the real Venice.

We stopped in at Harry's Bar. A step or two down off the walkway, it was in a cozy part of town, close to a well-lit bridge. The soft lights and lively music beckoned one in, as well as the sound of laughter breaking the silence of the narrow walkway. Stephan suggested that we were not far from our hotel, and we should get something to eat. It sounded like a good idea. As we walked in, it seemed like everyone was familiar with Stephan. He must have visited this place often but without Fritz. He introduced his son and his visitors. Fritz looked disturbed but said nothing. We sat down to order a small meal, and Stephan was going to order his drink.

The waiter commented, "I know, Stephan, just keep it coming."

Stephan was a little embarrassed but laughed it off. We were starting to think there was more to this story than we knew.

Fritz said, "Papa, you promised you wouldn't!"

The light went on in our minds, and we soon realized this was why they lived in such poverty and didn't have money.

CHAPTER 39

A Grim Reality

"Is the money all gone?" Fritz asked.

"No, of course not," his dad replied, looking sheepish.

When the waiter came over, Fritz was bold and clever enough to ask how much Stephan's tab was.

He looked at Stephan not wanting trouble, and said, "The manager keeps track of that."

Fritz quickly spoke, "May I see the manager please?"

He had all the traits of the child of an alcoholic. He took charge, playing the role of the caregiver and taking responsibility.

The waiter said he would send the manager over. After he left, Fritz told Stephan he should be honest, as he would find out anyway.

His dad said he had used up all the money and was in the red. Fritz got so angry. We were caught in the middle of a family argument, and it felt rather awkward. We agreed with Fritz, of course, and we couldn't just leave him to fend for himself. He was still a boy, not even as old as our Josh. I suggested we eat our snack and talk further on the subject. Fritz would have no part of it. He conceded that they had no money, and he could not pay for this meal, and neither could his dad. I volunteered to pay for their meal, and we could talk and figure out what to do. He settled down a little, as he felt he had nowhere to turn.

I directed my attention to Stephan.

"Do you think you have a problem?" I boldly prodded.

"Yes, I do," he divulged. "When we moved here I thought it would get better and I could stop, but as you see, I haven't. Fritz has suffered so much because of my drinking. What can I do?"

"We cannot leave Fritz here with you if you continue on this path," I informed him.

I thought it might scare him enough to come to his senses.

He started to cry and pleaded, "Please don't take my boy from me, he is all I have left!"

We had to stay strong and show no mercy. I let him know he left us no alternative, as Fritz was a minor and had to be properly cared for. I would be negligent to leave him in this situation.

The manager came over just then and Stephan told him that this establishment should not serve him any more alcohol. His son could check up on him any time. Fritz asked what the tab was and was shocked that it had added up to two hundred Euros in this short time. I told the manager I would pay the tab if he sold no more alcohol to Stephan. He agreed, and imparted that he did not know there was a problem. Stephan thanked us profusely, then was quiet.

"What are you thinking?" I inquired.

He started slowly, and I sensed his apprehension. He didn't know if he could do it. He had tried before and failed. We would set up a game plan for him. First, we would look for some connection or support for him. An AA group would help tremendously. Fritz would come with us to the hotel for the night. It was not protocol, but I figured it would put enough fear into Stephan to make sure he would stay sober for the night. It was a huge test. Tomorrow, we would inquire as to what else was in the city. We were grateful to be able to help them both. At this rate, Stephan would have sold that beautiful old gondola to pay off his unending debts, and, putting two and two together, I gathered he alluded to the fact earlier while we were looking at their well-preserved gondola.

We said we would check in with him in the morning. By then, we would have more information on the local Alcoholics Anonymous and laws regarding minors living with alcoholics. Fritz hated to leave his dad, as he felt so responsible for watching over him. We told him it would show how serious he was regarding his drinking. The worst that could happen was that he would be drunk in the morning.

Stephan went home alone and had all night to think. I asked Fritz why his dad looked so clean and well-groomed all the while an alcoholic. He divulged that his dad was once a successful businessman and kept up the appearance of his past, trying to hide his alcoholism. He hardly remembered his dad working, as it had been quite a few years since then. When his mother became ill, his dad started drinking more heavily. When she died, it just became worse, and he was sober long enough to shower, get cleaned up, and go back to drinking. He remembered taking care of things for his mom since he was eight years of age. His dad had worked back then, but he'd had frequent binges. Fritz hoped it would be different after they moved.

We encouraged him and told him that we would help him. He was grateful. We set up a cot for him in our room, and I inquired at the desk about a group for alcoholics. The night manager said that he thought they had a group in the city, but he didn't know much about it. We had the rest of the evening to talk, and Fritz expressed many fears and thoughts.

In the morning, Fritz's first thought was to go home and get breakfast for his dad. We encouraged him to let his dad fend for himself, and he could enjoy a breakfast with us. We would take him back afterwards.

We caught a gondola at the same place as the day before. Of course, it happened to be the same gondolier too. We started talking and asked if he could teach Fritz the ins and outs of the city, and how to maneuver a gondola successfully through the canal. He was delighted that we would ask such a thing. He called Fritz to the back of the boat where he stood and gave him the oar. Fritz was glad to oblige. The gondolier also held the oar lightly to guide it.

"Can you feel the rhythm?" prodded the gondolier.

"Yes, I can!" announced Fritz with excitement.

"The boy's a natural," divulged the teacher.

While still teaching, he asked where Fritz's father was this morning. Fritz replied that he was at home.

Oddly, the man asked, "Too early for the alcoholic, eh?"

We were all surprised at this comment, so I asked him how he knew. He replied that one drunk recognizes another. I questioned to find out if he was saying he was also an alcoholic. He said yes, but that he does not drink anymore. He quit many years ago for his family's sake. I asked if there was an AA organization in the city of Venice.

"Yes, and I lead it," the man announced.

"Stephan is ready to accept help. Can you help him?" I prodded.

"If he is ready, we can help him," he replied with a heavy accent. He added, looking at Fritz, "This boy needs a father. And, he needs to learn to be a gondolier. He has a natural talent."

Fritz was now handling the gondola alone. It was nice to see a gleam in his eyes, as a sense of pride took hold of him. He was going to learn how to be a gondolier. His dad would be sober, and they would be together here in Venice. He was delighted.

"This boy can work with me anytime, and I will teach him what I know," reaffirmed the man.

We had a chance to talk with Mel, the gondolier, as he took his time and a few extra canals for Fritz to practice. He had been sober for many years, but remembered what it was like. He volunteered to come in with us and speak to Stephan. We saw such kindness and willingness on his part to share and impart courage to another person.

Stephan was up and had his breakfast, as well as cleaned up after himself. He was startled to see the face of the angry gondolier again and expected trouble. We introduced them properly, and he relaxed a little. Mel explained where he had come from and how he hoped to help Stephan get through this difficult time. He also added his son, Fritz, was a natural with the gondola, and he would teach him more. Of course, he would teach Stephan too, if he wanted. They talked and made plans to connect. Phone numbers were exchanged as well as emails. The phone was being connected today. The first meeting for Stephan at the AA was to be tonight. Mel asked if he could make it.

"Yes, I will be there, I promise," confirmed Stephan.

CHAPTER 40

New Hope

"I will count on seeing you there," Mel said. "Also, I will introduce you to my family tomorrow. My daughter is about the same age as Fritz and can show him around Venice. You have the summer to get to know where everything is."

Stephan was overwhelmed at the kindness of this once-hard exterior. The man had given him hope and extended a hand of friendship, an ingredient so badly needed at this time. He would make a point to honor it and not drink another drop. Fritz was important to him, and he wanted to be a good father and raise him as a sober man, able to be in the moment and remember everything. He would do his best. They discussed the withdrawal process and what that would mean to Fritz. He would stay with Mel's family. Mel would be here with Stephan, helping him over the bad times.

We left for the day, sure that father and son had a lot to talk about. We would take a boat ride out to the islands off of Venice. One island is where the Murano glass factory has been manufacturing precious collectables for hundreds of years. Another island reminded me of a miniature Venice, complete with waterways and colorful houses. They specialized in fine linens, hand embroidered goods, and hand-crafted lace. It was nice to see beyond the Grand Canal and Marco Polo Square. These are magnificent features of Venice, worth visiting over and over again, but we wanted to do something different today. We travelled by a larger boat to the islands where we could look around and come back at our leisure. It was a lovely day and seemed far away from all our concerns regarding Stephan and Fritz.

When we arrived back at our hotel, we called home. No one answered at home. Even Grammy and Grammpy were out. We would try again later, after we checked in with our new friends.

We walked over to Stephan and Fritz's place. It was still light, and we had familiarized ourselves with the route. Venice was fairly easy to get around in, if you knew the small walkways and which way to turn on them. This time, we arrived at the front door. It was a magnificent wooden entrance, curved, with the brickwork around it also forming a striking grand arch. A corner stone visible to the right side read, "1780." The whole exterior of the building was done in brick and plastered over the top. It displayed its Venice charm, as the plaster was aged and chipped off in variously shapes and areas. The large windows on either side of the front door, on the second floor above, were also characteristic of Venice. They were dressed with window boxes and old shutters, which were painted to match the door. Large, heavy iron fasteners were used to mount the shutters as well as the door. The door was an aged, deep green, which gave a lovely contrasting visual to the old building.

"Nerissa, I'll bet you would like to take this door home, wouldn't you?" I asked with presumption.

She surprised me by saying that it looked stunningly romantic here but would not have the same influence at our home in Canada. Our doors where more suited to our homes. I studied it again and could easily agree that it was true.

We used the humongous door knocker and waited, as we now knew it would take a minute to get down the stairs, walk down the ramp, and answer the door. Fritz, a little out of breath, answered with a cheerful countenance. It was nice to see. This visit would give us a sense of what they were going to do in the near future.

Stephan was happy to see us, too, and offered us coffee. We declined, as we were going out for a nice dinner later. They proceeded to tell us of their plans. Fritz announced that his dad was going to start

AA tonight, and Mel would keep him accountable. Mel was going to hire Fritz to help him for the summer, until school started in the fall. He could make some money and learn the trade at the same time. Stephan was going to resume his accounting. He was licensed and felt he could make the most money doing what he loved best. He promised not to juggle the financial figures of their home anymore.

"I am sorry, but I must leave," Stephan announced anxiously.

"Of course," I said, knowing where he was going.

He explained it was his first AA meeting and he did not want to be late. We understood and said we would see him before we left the city.

"That is a sad thought," he spoke with genuine affection and gratitude.

Fritz kept us busy talking a while longer, and we enjoyed getting to know him better. He was an interesting boy, with many dreams and aspirations. One, of course, was becoming the best gondolier and having the best gondola. He already had the best gondola, we were sure of that, and saw promise in him to be one of the best gondoliers. It was a unique city to live in and especially to be a part of, with its unique personality working on the waterways. He would be fulfilled in his job, meeting tourists from all over the world. He told us that his dad played the accordion. We suggested that Stephan play for Fritz while he takes the people on their tours. Maybe the evening tours would fill his dad's time, as well as fulfilling the need for a job. He thought that was a great idea.

Fritz had a future, and so did his father. We were happy for them and planned to stay in touch.

We left that evening feeling good about the family. We left Fritz before he was expected at Mel's house, as he was to stay with the family overnight. This was just until Stephan battled his withdrawal. He would be feeling the horrible symptoms by tonight.

The evening was now ours, and we strolled the narrow streets of Venice under the dim streetlights and once again passed the Murano glass store with its sparkling display of precious glass. We had dinner at a cozy restaurant with a glass-enclosure on the Grand Canal. It couldn't have been more romantic. The waiter gave us a cup and saucer from the restaurant, "The Casanova Nero Caffe," after finding out that we were from Canada. It was a lovely token on his part, and it made a great souvenir for Nerissa. We would wrap it carefully for our trip home. We were missing our family and wondered what they were all doing tonight. I took pictures of the moonlit bridges and illuminated store-fronts. As we walked through St. Marco Square one more time, we noticed that it lacked the cooing and flutter of the pigeons. It presented us with a quiet, peaceful experience, as there were a few couples strolling, but otherwise it was now deserted.

Walking back to the hotel was not a chore. It was delightful to be in this ancient city. I marveled at its architecture, illuminated with enhancing lights. The home of Marco Polo still stood as it had so many years ago. It was marked with his name in the stonework of the building, near the top for all to see, especially the ships of his days that were sailing into Venice. The city must have had a kind of magic and energy back then, as a valuable port known throughout the world for its trade. It was frequented by prominent visitors. For now, I thought our visit was done, and, after saying goodbye to our new friends, we would be leaving.

We would get more information from Pa tonight. After talking to Pa, Josh, and Bee, as well as Kelly, Grammy, and Grammpy, we were pretty much talked out. Telling the same information so many times is draining. Pa gave us the run down on the Kempt brothers and the information he had on their ancestors. Since Pa had just found out about the guard Herman Wolfgang, he would have to research the name and let us know more later.

He didn't know what our plans were, but he said the Kempt family moved to South America after the war. They journeyed with many others to Paraguay, then moved again to Santiago. Should we go to South America now, or home first? That was the question. We would have to let him know after discussing it. We had much to consider. We wanted to get home for a bit. It was decided, and I called Pa to tell him the news. He was delighted. We would catch a plane home by tomorrow evening.

"I was thinking about South America," I said to Nerissa, adding, "I think after we find the tunnels under the hydro plant, we will send

Pa and Josh on a trip to South America. As a matter of fact, Bee can go, too, if she wants."

"That sounds like a lovely idea, but then we will be home, and they will be away!" Nerissa grumbled.

"That is true, but it will only be for a short time, and then they will all be back in the nest." I chuckled.

She conceded with apprehension. Mothers being mothers, she felt she needed to touch base with her children. She needed to know what Bee's thoughts were these days, as well as Josh's. Mark and his mom were moving in any day now, and she was not there to help.

"Pa told me he and Josh were already taking boxes over with Mark. They will be in as quickly as Angelica can pack," I said.

"That is not the point," she retorted. "I should be there to greet her."

I understood and encouraged her that all would work out, and she would still get a chance to welcome her to our property. Mark was a staple around our place, so he would just need a, "Welcome back home."

"I guess so," was the last I heard about the subject.

Tomorrow, we would head for home, and Europe was done for now. Soon, it would be a matter of designating the money to these families properly.

Nerissa had a good thought. "Can we tell them we found their ancestors' notes dictating their wills for the money? We could say the documentation stated that they were in the wills that were found. We could continue to keep the location of the wills a secret."

"We can be truthful with most of what you said, but we can't have it connected to us. We cannot be connected, as someone might want to find out more and snoop around our place. They might think there is more money, and I don't want my family in danger again," I added

"Yes, you are right, of course, we could have another Vinnie at our doorstep," she agreed.

"We also have to see what to do with the bricks of gold. It would be better to turn them into cash or bank notes. I can just imagine trying to give someone a brick of gold," I laughed. "There is so much to do."

"I hope we will all be safe when this comes to an end," she said.

For now, there was nothing we could do but go home. I was looking forward to going down into the tunnels again to discover more old secrets. It was immensely rewarding, turning old deeds of wrong-doing into calculated closure by helping others receive their inheritance in the process.

—⁓—

Our tickets were ordered, and we would fly out tonight. It gave us a leisurely morning and a long afternoon at the airport. We had connecting flights in Germany and then back to Toronto Pearson Airport. It would be 1am by the time we arrived in Canada. It was going be a long day, or maybe I should say, night! We ordered an airbus to take us home. It was an unearthly hour to ask family or anyone else to come and pick us up.

Pa was told of our plans and hesitated just a little, then quickly continued to say how nice it would be to have us home again. Noticing his hesitation, I pondered for a moment, but quickly regrouped my thoughts, as we had to pack and get our papers in order. Nerissa's joy was transparent, as she was singing one of her favorite songs and dancing with each piece of clothing before it made it to the suitcase. As much as travel excited her, family gave her the energy that nothing else could.

CHAPTER 41

Going Home

It was a long day and night as we arrived at the airbus stop outside the Toronto airport. A gentle breeze blew warm, humid air, relieving the clammy feeling on our skin. We had forgotten how humid our summers were. Nerissa texted to say we were on our way, but we hoped everyone at home was sleeping. She had promised Pa that she would. The shuttle ride home was a quiet one, and our thoughts raced from one person to another.

We were enjoying the cool of the air-conditioned vehicle when Nerissa asked, "Do you think Clara will be okay?"

"Yes, I do. Her parents love her, and they have a place to call home. Jervaih has a job, and we saw what a good mother Lovlyn is."

She replied, "Yes, I know, but I would love to see them again."

"It was so nice that Mitchell and Dustin could install the water and heat for them. They are nice young men."

"I could sure use some of that great home cooking that Mary sent over to Lovlyn with her boys!"

Nerissa agreed, but then sighed, still looking puzzled.

"Do you think Hannah will feel more fulfilled, knowing about her family tree?"

"I know I would, if the missing pieces were all put together. Look at our family history, and how knowing about the surmise of Pa's uncles has put the family at rest," I replied.

I quickly added that I was sure Stephan would be able to deny alcohol out of respect for Fritz and the promise of a good life together, knowing that would be her next question.

"We certainly have made a lot of new friends, haven't we? It is very handy that we have social media for communication. Maybe someday Jervaih and Lovlyn will be able to have a computer too. For now, they have my phone with limited Internet." Nerissa added, "I can't wait to see our family, and I hope Bee will be back soon!"

It was an easy ride, as we were on the road before the Toronto traffic, and the QEW was not yet backed up. We were both quiet until fleeting thoughts of, "what will be," needed to be spoken. We arrived at our laneway! There stood the pillars that could have killed Bee the night of the accident! The horrible recall stirred up many forgotten emotions, and we involuntarily gripped each other's hands.

The house looked peaceful this time of the morning, and a coyote ran along the ridge, back to its lair. The car stopped and as we opened the doors, the fresh morning breeze filled our nostrils. It could always be counted on. Life was good, and we were in the best place in the world: home! As quietly as possible, we took our luggage inside the porch doors. Everything was still, and we were a little disappointed that no one was up to greet us. Leaving all the luggage at the door, we crept up the stairs and flopped quietly into bed. It felt so good to lay our tired bodies down, and we drifted off quickly. Awaking with a start, we couldn't remember where we were! I checked the time. We had slept for hours, so we jumped to our feet. Where was everybody? We needed a coffee to get our bearings. We put on our casual clothes to go down to the kitchen.

CHAPTER 42

Not Only One Surprise

Pa and I were busy in kitchen, as we knew Mom and Dad would need a coffee and a good breakfast after their long trip. The plan was to let them get some sleep, then surprise them. We could hardly contain ourselves until we heard them coming down the stairs, at which point we acted nonchalant. We had the coffee made but held off on making the bacon. That would have woken the whole household. Mom and Dad were shocked to see us in the kitchen. After lots of hugs and kisses, mostly from Mom, of course, we sat down to enjoy coffee and conversation. Pa continued to fry the bacon as he talked.

Mom exclaimed, "That is enough bacon to feed an army!"

Pa just laughed.

"What smells so good?" Bee inquired, half asleep.

"Bee, you are home!" Mom shouted as she jumped to her feet to welcome Bee with kisses.

"What a nice surprise!" Dad added, then finished with one of his amazing hugs.

Mom and Dad hadn't even had time to fire questions at Bee when the door opened again. All eyes were on the slowly opening door to find Grammy and Grammpy appearing. My parents could not believe their eyes. What a welcome home! The whole family was united under one roof. The kitchen became a loud buzz of chatter, with questions and answers flying across the room, accompanied by loud laughs and agreeing gestures. It was Christmas Eve, but in July.

Finally, Pa shouted, "I hate to break this up, but we need to sit down for breakfast!"

All was silent, but just for a second. We took our seats at the table, and the talking resumed. Pa served bacon and eggs. We had made French toast earlier and kept it warm in the warming oven. Grammy had brought some homemade preserves and her homemade bread and pastries. What a treat. Suddenly, there was a knock at the inside kitchen door. We all turned around, and there stood a young man that Mom and Dad had never met. Bee jumped up, took him by the hand, and introduced him as Kelly. Mom and Dad were delighted to meet the man who had captured their daughter's heart. They welcomed him whole-heartedly, and Kelly sat down beside Bee. I caught Mom and Dad happily looking around the huge table. Under the table, they were holding each other's hands, their faces beaming with immense approval. Dad's prayer was one of gratitude and love as he blessed the food. He told us afterwards that a thought of the starving Eisenhouwer family came to his mind while he was thanking God for the food.

Mom asked where everyone was sleeping. We filled her in on the situation: Grammy and Grammpy had taken the spare room, and Kelly was staying with Josh in his room. She was delighted that everyone was settled.

Kelly had taken the bags at the door upstairs but left them outside of Mom and Dad's room in the hall.

"How considerate, Kelly, thank you very much," Mom said. Her love language was good deeds, and she took note of his action.

"I can see why Bee has taken to you," Dad added.

Bee looked pleased that Kelly had made a good impression, although that had never been a worry.

Grammy looked well, and so did Grammpy. They said that, when there was time, they had some big news to tell us. Everyone was instantly quiet, which created the right time.

"Go ahead and tell us," Mom coaxed.

Grammy started, then paused, so Grammpy took over. "We are going to sell our farm. We have decided it is too hard a life for us to keep up. You know we only lived there for the simple lifestyle, and that suited us for quite some time. We feel that we would like to be closer to family. We loved having Bee with us, and of course Kelly. Kelly has looked up some senior homes in this area, and a few of them look like they would suit us. We would not be a burden to you at all, except to see you more."

Mom and Dad looked at each other with a question in their eyes and nodded slightly.

"We would like you to stay with us," Dad invited.

"Yes, that would be wonderful," Mom added.

"Do you think our way of life will be a hardship on you, Grammpy?" I questioned.

"I think we have changed our lives, as we knew God wanted us to, and we can do this now. Family is more important than the way we chose to use the conveniences of the world."

We all congratulated them on their decision and were pleased that they would soon be with us.

They were going back in a few days to take care of the sale of the farm and sell their belongings. Kelly had agreed to help them in the process, and Bee volunteered to go and give Grammy a helping hand.

Mom wasn't sure about Bee, as she thought maybe she herself should go, but would consider it. They had a lot of change thrown at them in one sitting, but they never wavered from the thought that it was going to work out. Breakfast wasn't even over when another knock came from the outside door.

The family called out in unison, "Come in, Mark."

He sheepishly poked his head in and said, "Just thought I would see what you were up to today?"

He was invited to breakfast and joined the conversation, having met Grammy and Grammpy and Kelly prior to this morning. They had arrived three days before but wanted to surprise Mom and Dad.

He did not know about the news of Grammy and Grammpy moving down to Ontario. His face looked stunned, and he didn't know what to do with himself.

Dad noticed the awkward behavior and asked him, "Is something bothering you, son?"

He tried to be casual without success and answered, "I guess you will be needing the carriage house, then."

"Oh no, Mark, we will have them stay with us!" Dad affirmed. "You will be fine in the carriage house."

"By the way, how are you and your mother doing? Are you settled in, and can I do something for you?" Mom asked, feeling the guilt of not helping them.

"Pa and Josh got us settled with no problem, but thank you. Josh and I had most of the boxes moved and unpacked in no time, didn't we, Josh?" he added. "It is a big place, and we would have room for someone if you needed it. Mom would love the company, and cooking would not be a problem for her!"

"You are so kind to give us that option, Mark. We think we are fine, but we would feel free to ask if we needed to," Dad responded.

It was like real family time. Many conversations were going at one time, and I was wishing I could hear all of them. My thoughts went down to the tunnels. I wondered if we would be able to keep our secret from the newcomers. When would we talk about the new things we would find?

After breakfast, Bee and Kelly cleaned everything off the table, and Grammy and Grammpy did the rest of it. They seemed to have a system going already. Pa, Mark, and I went to our rooms to meet and discuss how we should liquidate some of the gold. Mom and Dad retreated to their room to unpack and discuss the events of the morning.

Dad figured they should add an in-law suite to the old mansion. The elderly couple would be no problem to have around, but he wanted to give them quiet and serenity if they needed it. After all, they were so accustomed to a quiet way of life. Where would they put the extension, as there were so many tunnels under the house? Did they even know if they had found them all? After much discussion, it was decided that towards the ridge and the gazebo was not good, and neither was the area towards the carriage house.

Towards the gorge certainly was not good, and towards the graveyard was definitely a no go. The only place left was to build onto the front left corner of the house. This put the addition right in the driveway, which would be an awkward placement unless designed to make sense. We had such a huge property, and yet because of our secret tunnels, it was unusable for the build. We had our job cut out for us. Nerissa had a very rough sketch drawn in no time. It would be attractive and add to the architecture of the home. We would need to finance it until we liquidated some money. It was a good plan, and we would have an architect draw it up. There would be no basement. Dad hoped the tunnels and all within them would not be compromised by our project.

We would have to meet with Mom and Dad privately to discuss what Pa had learned regarding the gold. Each bar weighed ten pounds. That alone would be a wonderful amount of money to help the descendants of those who died in the tunnels, never mind the coins on top of it. Pa told me that he had a buyer for the gold bars. So far, we had found twelve bars of gold. All were the same size and weight. We wondered if there were any more. Mark was in awe of the amount and couldn't keep his jaw from dropping.

"How are you going to give this money to them?" he inquired.

"That is the big question," replied Pa.

There was a quiet knock on the door, and it was Kelly, who had finished the kitchen chores with Bee. They were going to meet with Carly and show Kelly around the area, then they would go out to eat on Clifton Hill in Niagara Falls.

"I am sorry to interrupt. I just need my wallet and jacket," Kelly apologized.

"Come on in," I said, and we made a point to look casual. "No problem," I added, as it seemed to be quiet and felt strange.

He grabbed his jacket and off he went, meeting Bee in the hall at her door. We could hear them running down the stairs, laughing. Bee had worked hard to graduate from college this year even with the many interruptions.

Pa had just begun to explain how we should go about it when there was another knock on the door. It was Dad, and we welcomed his presence and input into our conversation.

The first thing Dad said was, "We cannot let anyone know that we are asking about the gold. We will have to be very discrete in our search."

We all nodded in agreement.

Mark broadsided the conversation by blurting out, "Oh, no, Mom wanted me to help her today!"

"I think you will be fine. Nerissa went over to see if she needed anything and to help. She was feeling guilty about not being here for the move. She will help her, Mark, don't worry. Maybe send her a text that you are with us."

Relieved, Mark did that and returned to his relaxed mode.

"Pa has researched and found a buyer who is interested in buying the gold bars," I said. "How did you contact them, Pa?"

Pa knew better than to give us away. He had done it under a false name at the library in Buffalo. He also researched the buyer, and they proved to be a legitimate buyer of gold. He did not tell them where or who he was. We were satisfied that we were still safe.

Dad referred to family life becoming complicated, especially the communication aspect regarding the tunnels. He suggested that it was not that any of the family wasn't trustworthy, but he did not want to put an unnecessary burden on anyone else.

He told us of the planned extension to the house for Grammy and Grammpy and his concerns for the tunnel structures. We decided that we would gather all that we had found and put it into one very safe place, which we could get to if the tunnel system failed. We decided it would be near the secret door of the carriage house. It would not be compromised, as it was far enough away from the building project. Mark living there made it safer, as no one would be snooping around unawares.

Grammy and Grammpy were going back to Lancaster to settle the sale of their home and farm equipment, and then would return to move into their new home, of which they knew nothing yet. He made a note to tell them soon.

He added we would need to follow up on the Kempt family and the Wolfgang family, and, as far as we knew, that would take care of all the descendants. He wanted to finish the search during the summer while us kids were out of school. He could take care of the distribution afterwards.

I could tell Dad was overwhelmed with all that was supposed to take place. He added that we had to find the tunnel to the hydro access and make sure there were no explosives left down there. That could be an astronomic disaster, which would cause so much destruction.

We were done for now and would continue with our plans as soon as our guests had left for home.

CHAPTER 43

The New Home

Mom and I had taken some homemade cherry tarts from her freezer and a jar of Grammy's homemade preserves as a little spur-of-the-moment housewarming gift. She rapped on the door, remembering the good times the family had experienced, as well as the tense experiences living in unknown danger. Her body shuddered as she recalled Bee's accident when Angela answered the door. She wanted to make her name more North Americanized so she dropped a few letters. She had the biggest smile and welcomed Mom with a hug.

"Come in, come in," she insisted. "My home is always open to you."

"Thank you," Mom replied.

"I thought you were that strange, nosey man back again," she resounded with disgust.

"What did he want?" Mom inquired.

"First of all, I did not trust his looks! He wanted to see the place, and almost forced his way past the door that I was hanging on to. I was angry at him and told him no, and that I would speak to him right here."

"Were you scared?" Mom questioned. "You should have called for help."

"No, just annoyed with him. Bee and Kelly drove by, and I waved at them. I could have stopped them, but I was fine."

"What else did he say?" Mom continued.

"He wanted to know if I bought the property, and who I was! Can you imagine, he wanted to know who I was!"

She told Mom that he had no business knowing anything, especially since he came to her door. She would not tell him anything, as he was a rude person. She said he looked past her into the house and it had given her an extremely uncomfortable feeling. Mom was glad she had taken a moment to come by. They had a cup of coffee and discussed the stranger at length. She reaffirmed that the house did have a good alarm system, as they were robbed the night of Bee's accident. Angela remembered the terrible night and Mark's escape from Vinnie, near death after the beating.

"Do you think we are in danger?" Angela realized.

"No, I do not think so, but we will check this man out. What did he look like? Can you remember anything unusual?"

While sipping her coffee, Angela tried to remember. "He was pointed!"

I laughed to break our mood. "What do you mean, pointed?"

"Well, his nose was thin and pointed, his chin was pointed, his ears were pointed, and he wore his hair combed to the middle and up about 3 inches in the air, so his narrow head looked pointed. Even his shoes were pointed. He wore very tight black jeans and a tight, dark brown sweater, which accented his skinny frame."

Mom started to laugh as her mind drew the picture, and Angela joined her.

"Now, I know that does sound funny, but that is how he looked," she continued.

Trying to move on to another subject, although quite concerned, Mom asked if there was something she could help with. Angela, finishing her coffee, pointed to the stack of pictures sitting on the floor. She needed help hanging them, and Mark seemed to have lost track of time in the mansion.

Mom and I were glad to help hold up pictures, one after another until the right frame and canvas was found for every location. It only took a couple of hours. As they were putting up some family photos, Nerissa remembered the photo of Joseph she had copied to give to Mark. He looked so much like his ancestor and had inherited Joseph's humanitarian nature. He had been on many mission trips with our church. Our family was happy to sponsor him. He and his mother did not have the means to fund them.

"Is there anything else that I can do for you?" Mom asked.

"That is all I planned for today, thank you. This was very helpful. It is a good job for two women who have patience, yes?" Looking at me, she said, "Men are not so good at this kind of thing, as I remember," she finished, deep in thought.

Mom assured her that she would look into this "pointed stranger," and chuckled as she thought of the description she heard from Angela.

"If you need anything, please, let me know, and keep your alarm on!" Mom insisted.

Angela waved good-bye at the door and watched as we walked home along the driveway. I was relieved to think someone was living in the carriage house, and it was not left vulnerable and vacant. The incident seemed to stir up something inside of me.

At home, Grammy and Grammpy were having their lunch, and offered us a sandwich as well. Mom was behind in her plans for the day, but accepted the kind offer and sat down. They talked about their health and how they felt about the move. Mom wanted to know how Bee and Kelly were getting along and how Kelly's studies were going.

Kelly's dedication to his education was driving him to work hard and put many hours into his studies. He was already working on the next year's work and had passed with honors into his third year of college. Mom couldn't wait to get Bee alone and see what was going on in her heart and mind. Mom realized that her parents were a great influence on Bee and Kelly. The time spent with them was not wasted, in more ways than one.

Grammy asked if Bee could return with them and assist her in sorting and packing up what they planned to bring. Mom would have to discuss it with Dad but would let them know. It was a good time to fill her parents in on the new addition. It was a project, and Nerissa loved projects of all kinds.

"We do not want to bother the family this way. We can get an apartment at a seniors' home. There is a lovely home, 'Pleasant Manor,' right in Virgil. It is close to banks, groceries, doctors, and stores. I understand there are quite a few Mennonite families in the area."

"Of course, we would never stop you from doing as you wanted, but we would be honored for you to live with us and yet have your own space," Nerissa intently added.

"Only if you let us pay for the build," Grammpy said. He added, "We will have quite a bit of money from the farm, and we insist. I am keeping a corner of the farm over by the creek, in case someone would like to build a house on it one day. The rest will provide more than enough to retire on."

"I don't think Shawn will like that, but I will run it by him and let you know," was her reply.

Mom showed the elderly couple around, and they were stunned at the size of the rooms and the house in general. They loved the old, grand porch, and Grammpy thought he should fix up that gazebo so it could be enjoyed. They loved the breeze coming from the river, over the crest of the deep gorge. They visited the cemetery plot and discussed the foundations of the gardener's house. Mom hoped Grammpy wouldn't start straightening out the water faucet on the headstone. He was a very particular man, and he could fix anything.

Mom explained who the neighbors were, and that Barry was a law enforcement officer. She also explained that Mac, a very good friend of Josh lived there. They had met her the day after they arrived, and it seemed she wanted to tell Josh something, but hesitated as she came running onto the porch before she saw us.

"You know kids, they love drama and always seem to find some. Please, don't take it personally," Nerissa assured them.

The four guys—Pa, Dad, Mark, and I—went down below from the gazebo to avoid being seen. It was the long way around, but going through the office with so many people in the house was not an option. Dad was amused at the lived-in look of the tunnels. There were a couple of wheelbarrows, shovels, a box of large freezer size bags, three high powered flashlights, and some pieces of wooden planks. Pa and I quickly said that we intended on coming back down here to retrieve the gold, which was heavy, when Bee called to say that she was coming home with guests. Pa said he understood, realizing how difficult it was to get down here today. We would clean it all up soon.

We made our way up the stairs to the supply room, through the underground living space to the tunnel leading to the upstairs, and towards Pa's office. At this point, Dad told us to be mindful of the angle upwards and reminded us how close to the surface he thought we were. He also thought we might need a transom for support, to do the job correctly. The tunnel was comfortable, yet it took energy to travel as it angled upward. We reached the stairs below the office. There were twenty-four steps. That would mean at least sixteen feet below the surface of the ground.

"No, Dad, I think there are another eight feet of dirt above that!" I said confidently.

"Why is that, Josh?" asked Dad.

"When we come down from Pa's office, in that little space entrance, we go down another set of stairs when that hidden wall opens. Isn't that right?" I questioned.

Pa spontaneously uttered, "Well, will you look at that, the boy is right. This tunnel is at least twenty-four feet underground."

We looked at the wood structure of the bottom at the stairs and the stairs themselves. They looked very solid.

"Pa, did you reinforce any of these?" Dad questioned.

"I built some and reinforced others to my satisfaction," he stated.

We went up as far as we could, undetected. The wooden structures were all very solid. We decided that the plan would work, and the build was a go. Pa was going to take charge of the building above, as he had the most experience with it. Dad had the rough sketch in his pocket, and we studied it in the underground living room. Pa studied it a while and thought it was good, but he wondered what would happen with the garage in the back. It also needed a poured footing below the frost line. He wondered about pulling the building forward a car length, then it wouldn't encroach on the ground above the tunnels. We agreed that it might work. We would still have to be very careful with heavy machinery and so on.

CHAPTER 44

Another Discovery

Pa and Dad left and went above ground, making sure they were not seen. They joined Mom and her parents, who were sitting on the large porch at the front of the house. What a grand place it was. Pa loved sitting there as memories of his childhood flooded his mind. We had the original wicker swing repaired and re-hung, as it was everyone's favorite place to sit. It was good to see the senior couple enjoying our home. We were going to hear many interesting stories from the seniors in this family, and I was looking forward to learning from them.

Since we were already below, Mark and I decided to look around a little. We grabbed a couple of flashlights and I made sure I had my bag by my side. The lights were shut off, and off we went to check on our gold that hadn't been put away. I wanted to check out the air draft coming in through the tunnel that Mac had found the gold in. It had to go somewhere to the outside. It didn't take us long to get there, as we were very familiar with the tunnels by now.

"I am going to crawl in head first. I will get to the taller tunnel, which adjoins this one at the end, and will let you know when to do the same. Okay?" I said.

Mark nodded, and I was in. It was tight but manageable. I was sliding the flashlight ahead of me into the taller tunnel when I suddenly lost it.

"Mark, I can't see anything! Shine your flashlight in!" I yelled.

Mark did, but there wasn't much room between the wall and my body for the light to shine through. It was a job. I caught my breath and gathered my strength before I shimmied my way back out of the tunnel.

"What happened, Josh?"

"I pushed my flashlight forward, and, all of a sudden, it disappeared."

"Wow, are you saying there's no floor?" exclaimed Mark.

Mark was quick to give me his headband flashlight to use. I couldn't lose it. Mark had one more flashlight in his hand. He reassured me that he would be fine.

"Here I go again," I said nervously.

Crawling like I did before, I got to the same point and looked down.

"Okay!" I shouted.

"What? Tell me what you see!" Mark demanded.

"Well, I don't know how we would get across this opening!" I exclaimed.

"Can you see your flashlight?" questioned Mark. "Or the bottom?"

"Negative on both accounts," I answered. "This tunnel ends and runs into another taller tunnel. Where they join there is an endless shaft downward."

"I am going to take a good look around, just hang on," I ordered.

It was a tall, crevasse-like tunnel, and I wondered if it was a natural one that had been enhanced for a purpose. You couldn't crawl ahead to stand up because of the shaft ahead of you. It would be too dangerous. I looked to the right, then to the left. Both sides seemed to be safe and were made of stone. They looked like they went on for as far as my light would illuminate. Suddenly, an idea came to me.

"Mark, you know those pieces of wood we saw near to the wheelbarrows?"

"Yup," he replied.

"When I get out of here, we will go get them and put them across the opening."

I backed out once more, and we took off to retrieve the wood. I knew the plank couldn't be too long, as I would not be able to get it from the first tunnel into the other and across the opening. It also couldn't be too short and had to be safe to crawl over and back. We found five pieces, and I suggested we take all of them. They weren't very long, but I hoped they'd be long enough. They were four inches wide and an inch thick.

"Do you think we can do this safely?" questioned Mark.

"I think so," was my hesitant answer.

We lay the boards beside one another to see their lengths. One was way too long, and the other seemed too short. I grabbed the two mid-length ones and pushed them ahead of me until we reached the opening. I had to maneuver the end of the board out of my tunnel over the shaft in the tall tunnel.

"I did it!" I exclaimed. "It is resting on each side by about six inches," I added.

"Is one enough?" asked Mark.

"No, I will try the other one too," I answered.

I worked and wiggled until I freed the other board from under myself. It was longer, and I would have to work harder to get it out of the tunnel. I repeated my actions until the board was in the next tunnel, lying on the rock floor beside the other one. This one straddled the opening with an overlay of twelve inches on either side. I felt good about that. I thought that would hold us.

"I am going to try it, Mark."

"I don't know if you should, Josh."

I started to move forward, inching my way out of my safe tunnel and onto the boards. I had to be careful to put my weight on them without sliding them. How was I going to move forward to stand straight? I put weight on my left knee and started to crawl forward moving my right leg onto the board too. I moved forward cautiously. I was finally on solid rock.

"I made it, Mark!" I yelled.

"Nice work!" he shouted back, relieved.

I told Mark to stay where he was. I would take a quick look around, following the tunnel to the left.

He disagreed but promised to stay where he was and wait for me.

I ventured on, as I could feel that draft once again. I must have been too preoccupied to notice it before. I was careful to take my time, looking up and down and all around before each step. I did not want to miss anything. I walked for about twenty minutes before coming to a crossroads. What now? Which way should I go?

I decided to go to the right. It still seemed like a natural crevasse in the rock, except for small areas where hammer and chisel marks were visible. It looked like the tunnel had been widened in a few areas. There were pieces of rock strewn throughout the tunnel. I came to a wider area and noticed a long pile of sacks, just like the ones we saw in the upper tunnel. I kicked them gently to make sure they were not hiding something. We had been fooled before. It didn't feel like sacks, but like a pile of sticks. I started to pull the sacks apart one by one and made another pile. I was startled by the appearance of a soldiers' uniform. All that was left was the skeleton. Who was this? I looked closer, holding my light near the skeleton. The skull had no markings, and the uniform was intact, with no visible bullet holes. The uniform looked too high to be on the ground, so I looked under it. I know what Pa would have said, and I thought it: "Well, will you look at that." I couldn't believe my eyes; here was more gold. I moved the uniform over with the skeleton inside. I jumped and screamed as a snake slithered from the cozy home it had made in the uniform. It took a minute to regain my thoughts, and my heart was pounding. There were twelve more bars of gold. Were they supposed to go to the workers, and the soldier had held them back for himself? I wondered, because, so far, we had found exactly twelve bars of gold. Now, we had double. There was nothing else, except the soldier's rifle and a stick of gunpowder with no fuse on it. They both lay right beside the soldier. What a find! I couldn't wait to tell Mark and the others.

Somehow, I caught a breeze. It smelled like grass and something mossy and wet. I moved forward to check it out. It was getting stronger and stronger. I had reached the end and found myself behind a huge boulder. There was room to see past it. I thought I was down in the gully somewhere. I recognized the old pump house, across the gully on the other side, now abandoned. We had played there many times as kids. I had found another way into the tunnels. I felt proud of myself. I also noticed that the sun was getting low. I checked my watch. It was already 7:30, and we had missed our supper. I had been away from Mark for at least two or more hours. I couldn't believe it was so late, but I know I walked very slowly, looking around after every step. I pushed on the huge boulder, but it would not budge. Maybe that is what happened to the soldier. He stole the money and thought he would escape, but instead he couldn't get out and couldn't give up the money.

As I passed the soldier on my way back, I had a thought. There might be a clue or note or something in his pockets. I carefully picked up his uniform jacket and shook it first, then checked all the pockets for a clue. There was nothing unusual. He carried a pocketknife and a handkerchief. Next were his pants. It was odd, shaking the bones out of them before checking the pockets. I found nothing. Where would someone hide something important on his body? We found many pieces of shirt, but this solder's shirt was in good condition. It had two pockets with nothing in them. I saw the shoes lying there and thought maybe it was in his shoes, but nothing. I picked up the socks and realized there was a letter size paper in it.

Carefully extracting it from the sock and opening it up, I realized I could not read it. This was irritating. It was once again carefully folded and put into a safe pocket for Pa to read later. I made my way back much quicker, as I knew it was safe until I got to the shaft and boards. There it was up ahead, but one thing was missing: the boards.

What was I going to do?

CHAPTER 45

The Rescue

Mark was waiting as he promised, but it was taking so long for me to return. He called to me, but I didn't answer. He thought he would follow and try to find me. He entered the tunnel and arrived at the high tunnel where the boards were. He leaned onto one with the upper part of his body. He mistakenly hooked the other with his belt, and it went flying. It was gone down the hole. He became terrified and backed up into the tunnel he came from. The board he was leaning on slipped as he moved back. His body weight kept him in the tunnel, even though his balance was thrown off. He shuffled backwards to get out. How would I get out? He had to find another board and get help. He ran up the tunnel stairs and toward Pa's office. He almost ran into Pa and Dad coming down. They had excused themselves from the dinner table after looking at each other and their watches. Mom had looked a little worried, as Mark and I hadn't shown up and Mark's mom had already called to see if he was eating over. Bee and Kelly were in their own world and didn't notice my absence. Grammy and Grammpy had asked about me, and excuses had been made. Pa and Dad hurried away and quietly left through the office entrance to the tunnels, where they ran into Mark.

"Where is Josh?" Dad demanded.

"In a tunnel. I need some boards, so he can get back out!" Mark was frantic.

Pa spoke softly. "Take your time, son, what kind of board do we need? Where is the tunnel?"

Mark replied in a more coherent fashion, "Down where your room was, further back."

"I know the size of board we need, Mark, and where the tunnel is," Pa moved as he spoke.

Pa grabbed a wide board from the storage room and two six-inch wide boards. They looked about as long as the ones we had taken. Dad and Mark shared the load. They walked as quickly as they could and arrived just as I was calling for Mark. Pa and Dad replied to my call, and I was glad to hear it.

Pa said, "Stay there, Josh, I have some boards here."

"I don't know what happened to Mark. I think he fell down this hole, and we have to help him. Do you have a long rope?" I exclaimed with fright.

Mark answered, "Josh, I am okay, I really am!"

"Oh, buddy, I thought you were a goner. Thank you for being alive!"

"Okay, enough sentiment. We have got to get you out of there," Dad said.

"I know the opening," Pa said. "You can slide on your stomach all the way to the end, pushing the wide board ahead of you. It should fit across the opening and not slide. I put two boards underneath for that exact reason. I was going to check this out some day."

Dad slid the board to the end and over the shaft.

"I can help you, Dad." I lay down on my stomach so I could support the board.

It was a wonderful fit, as if made to measure. I was able to slide right over top and into the low tunnel. I had to wait for Dad's slow, backwards-going pace. It was good to see Mark. I had to give him a big hug.

"Hey, your hugs are almost like your Dad's and Pa's," Mark exclaimed in shock.

"Boys, what were you doing down here?" asked Dad. "Do you know how worried we all were?"

We told them about the airflow in the tunnel, and that we wanted to know where it went. Pa added he did too.

"What did you find?" Pa asked.

"Wait till I tell you, you won't believe it! I found a soldier in uniform, with a rifle and a stick of gunpowder with no fuse, and twelve more bars of gold! All under a huge pile of sacks, so you couldn't even see any of it. Oh, and a snake! It was in the jacket of the uniform and freaked me out! This was in his socks," I said as I pulled out the folded paper and held it up.

"Wow," Mark said. "You found all that!"

"I also found another way out to the gully. There is a huge boulder in front of the opening. It is right across from the old pump house down there. The one we used to play around, Mark. I can't wait for you to read this piece of paper, Pa. My bet is that the soldier stole all the gold from the captives. You will see when you read the paper."

"First, we need to get word to your mother, Josh, and yours, Mark. They will be worried sick about the two of you," Dad reminded us forcefully.

Pa asked to keep the paper while we ate our dinner, and we would meet later on in the office, where Pa would be doing his reading. We knew Grammy and Grammpy would be going to bed soon, as they were used to going to bed early, soon after sunset. The Amish lived their lives around the sunrise and sunset, so they got very accustomed to this routine. Kelly would be out with Bee, and we didn't have to consider his whereabouts.

CHAPTER 46

The Paper

Mark and I snuck from the office to the front porch. We made some noise as we came in and headed straight for the kitchen. Mom looked puzzled and relieved at the sight of us.

"Mark, please text your mom, she is worried about you!" ordered Mom.

"I already have, but thank you for reminding me, just in case," Mark replied. "She said it was okay to eat over and stay for a while, as long as she knew where I was."

Mom looked at me, questioning where I was with her eyes. I wondered how a person could communicate so clearly with only their eyes. I answered Mom, without her even uttering a word.

"Mom, you will have to trust me for now, but I will tell you soon. Okay?" I spoke softly.

She nodded her head and silently warmed our dinner. By now, we were hungry, and we attacked our plates as soon as they hit the table. Mom reminded us that no one was going to take them away before we had enough to eat. We laughed and kept eating, knowing that Pa and Dad would be reading the paper I had found. Grammy and Grammpy came in to say good night. They said they couldn't have gone to bed without knowing where we were. I apologized for making them worry and made excuses for us. They were so loving and non-judgmental. I would have to get to know them better when they moved in. They were off to bed, and Grammpy was going to read the book he was carrying.

"Mom, do you mind if we see Dad and Pa in the office?" I asked, my voice almost a whisper. She nodded and asked if she could join us.

"Sure, I think you will find it interesting, Mom," I replied as I got up to clean off the table.

Mark helped load the dishwasher, and we made a quick job of it. Mom said she would be along in a few minutes, and we should go ahead.

Keeping secrecy a priority, we snuck into the office via our secret hall entrance.

We startled Dad, as he was sitting in front of us as we appeared. Pa was sitting at his desk with the letter laid out in front of him. I noticed two pieces of paper.

"Were there two pieces of paper?" I asked. "No wonder it felt so thick."

Just then, Mom came in to see what was happening.

"Well, I guess we are all here," Pa announced, ready to relay what he had read.

He translated as best he could what was on the first paper. It was an order to kill the prisoners within a day. The guards could take their money as payment for a job successfully done. There was to be no evidence of the prisoners or the money.

"I told you, the soldier stole the gold from the prisoners," I interjected.

Pa continued with a, "Now, just wait."

He picked up the second piece of paper. This was a hand-written letter from the prisoners, including their names. It stated that this soldier would try to get out another way. He was given one bar of gold and one portion of coins from each prisoner and promised to give it to their families as soon as possible. This soldier, as well as one other, had become a friend after spending so much time in these tunnels with the prisoners. This was why they had such good fellowship with each other. They made it possible. They were also blindfolded and did not know where they were located. They got their orders from soldiers stationed below the ground, but part of the way up. The soldiers were kept here with the prisoners the whole time, becoming captives themselves, but making the prisoners lives much improved. They knew they were going up the day after the letter was written, and these soldiers decided to help the prisoners. One was helping them hide their wills, and this soldier was given a brick of gold from each of the prisoners for their families. The Ritmeir brothers, not having any other family, decided to give their gold to the other prisoners, who'd become family. This soldier volunteered to give his life for this cause. He said he did not know how long he had left, as he was coughing up blood already. He would gather the twelve gold bars and coins into the small cave near a place that he could escape. He had found two exits. He would try one and if that didn't work then blow the boulder of the other away. We gathered sacks, so he could cover himself and wait for days to make sure no one was around.

"Can you imagine if he'd gotten out, Pa? Your parents could have helped him," I gasped, tense from the reality of the image before me.

Pa continued on, nodding his head in agreement. "It ends with, 'In the morning, we will be taken upstairs, and we do not know what will happen. Helmut will already be hiding with our gold and coins and Herman will be staying with us to help us hide our wages. We are all in agreement.' Then they signed their last names."

We were all silent, once more reminded of how difficult those days had been for our relative and the others. The soldier must have died while waiting to escape. What other explanation would there be? I was wrong again and had judged a man on how he looked without knowing all the facts. I felt bad for accusing him wrongly. I wondered where the coins were hidden?

The kitchen doorbell rang, startling us. Mark and I went to answer it. It was Mac.

"How come you rang the doorbell?" I asked.

"Are you kidding me?!" she exclaimed. "I've been knocking forever but didn't get an answer. Finally, I decided to ring the doorbell!"

"I'm sorry, but we were having a family meeting, if you know what I mean," I said, giving her a wink.

"Okay, I get it," she replied, adding, "I need to tell you something."

We sat down at the kitchen table and she started with a whisper.

We strained to hear her.

"Speak a little louder, we can't hear you," commanded Mark.

She started again, but it wasn't much better. She continued that she had been very ill with a virus and developed a high temperature.

"I swear I was hallucinating," she said two times.

"We believe you, we believe you," we spoke in unison.

"What did you do?" I asked.

"Well, while I was very ill and out of my mind, I talked about the tunnels. Mom and Dad had to almost tie me up to keep me from escaping, because I wanted to be safe in the tunnels. That made it worse, because they were always with me, and they heard me babble on and on. When I got well, they questioned me intently about the tunnels that I was in with Josh and Mark. Oh, I am so sorry. Dad asked me about the gazebo, and if I hang out there. Can you imagine?"

"It will be alright, but we have to know what you told them," I reassured her.

"I promise, I acted very casual, as if it was funny, and asked them what else I was dreaming. They said I had a friend, a wild cat, and I helped her kitten. I laughed and said that would be neat, and that it was too bad it wasn't true. Oh man, I hope I was convincing!" She stopped to take a breath.

"The story is too bizarre to believe, unless you told them how to get into the tunnel and they check it out. I am glad you told us, so we have a heads up. We will tell Pa, Dad, Mom and Bee so they are aware of this." I added, "Please don't get sick anymore."

Just then, Pa and Dad came in to get an evening coffee and overheard the end of our conversation.

"Are you ill, Mac?" asked Pa.

"Not now, but I was!" she replied.

We told them all about it, and everyone reassured Mac that it was too crazy for anyone to believe.

"Thank goodness you told us, so we are informed. We will tell Bee and Nerissa."

She said she needed to get back home, as she didn't tell her parents she was coming over. Mark and I would walk her home and come right back. Pa said good night, as he was tired, and Dad would wait up for Bee to get home. Mom had turned in early. They had just gotten home from Europe, and it had been such a stressful day. Luckily, they did not have to fill us in on their trip. The results were communicated to us every day from Dad's journal, and by phone. Dad loved writing down his thoughts and the details of his days. We told him he should write a book, but this would not be the one to start with. There were too many secrets. Maybe someday we could reveal all we knew, but not now. Mark said good night, and that he would be sleeping at home, as his bed here was taken. We all chuckled, then Mark and I left with Mac.

We filled Mac in on all the findings of the day.

"It's unbelievable that your parents have only been home for one day," she said.

I agreed and said they probably wished they were still away.

"No, I know your Mom, Josh, she would never want to be away from her family unless it was necessary," Mac spoke, showing her respect for Mom.

"You're right, of course, I was kidding. You know that," I directed at Mac.

We walked down the gorge path to her house, but we stayed in the dark. We whispered, "Good night," and Mac snuck back into the house.

Mark wanted to borrow a new game that I had, so he accompanied me back home and waited in the house for me to get it from my room. Dad stopped me as I passed his bedroom door. He was talking to Mom, and she told him about this strange man at Mark's house. He came down the stairs with me, so he could tell Mark and myself the details. We entered the kitchen where Mark was waiting and having some more dessert, and he could tell something was up.

With his mouth still full, he said, "What now?"

Dad told him all he knew and said to keep the alarms on, even when they were home. It wouldn't hurt to pull the blinds, either. Mark looked a little frightened.

"Remember, we are nearby, and you can always call us any time," he reassured Mark.

He also said that he would have Barry look into the person, but did not think they would be able to find him without a name. I suggested that Barry was very good, and has surprised us in the past, which Dad readily agreed to.

We told Mark that the bright outdoor lights would stay on all night, even after Bee came home. He thanked Dad and left with the game, saying he was going to have a great night.

CHAPTER 47

Fear Was Closing In

When Mark got home, he noticed the doors were locked and the alarms were set. His mom was in the living room with the blinds down.

"Is everything okay?" he asked his mother.

"Yes, but Nerissa thought we should be more careful for a while."

Mark answered, "I heard about the weird, pointed man."

"If he didn't give me the willies, I would think it was funny," she added.

Mark thought he would put the game aside and spend some time with her. He noticed the pictures on the wall and commented on how nice they looked. He said they made the house look like it was really home.

"How are you feeling, Mom? I mean, about living here. Is everything alright?" Mark questioned.

"Oh, I would say all was more than fine, until this strange man came around. I was reminded of your beating when Vinnie was around. It does frighten me to think there could be others as mean as he was," she replied honestly.

"Don't worry, Mom, we will be just fine. If you are scared at any time, just tell me so. Do you want to watch a movie and have some popcorn?" Mark asked.

She nodded, and he went to make the popcorn and settle in for a nice quiet night with his mom. They always had a good time watching movies and talking. The game from Josh would wait for another day.

It was a couple of hours later when they heard a car pass by. Mark checked it out and noticed Bee's car, with Kelly as a passenger. Everyone was home safe and sound. It felt good, and he wondered if a kid his age should even care about these things. He was used to being in charge and taking the place of the man in the house. He had learned to accept responsibility that other teens would not have or needed to have.

They finished their movie and were ready to retire. He checked all the doors.

CHAPTER 48

The Unlocked Door

"Mom, did you leave the back door open?" he called out.

"No, I did not, I remember locking it after Nerissa left," she replied.

"So, it was locked after Nerissa left, but before that it was unlocked, and now it's unlocked again?" Mark asked, then whispered into his mother's ear, "Let's just say we are going to bed, and then whisper the rest, okay?"

She looked frightened as she nodded. Mark texted Shawn to say he was checking the house for an intruder. He should not come over, as the alarms were set, but he would let him know when all was clear. He grabbed his baseball bat and gave his mom the fireplace poker that Josh's family had left for them. The kitchen looked clear, unless someone could fit into one of the cupboards. Angela stayed behind Mark, and they went back into the living room. The couch was against the wall, and there was no place to hide there. Now, to check the bedrooms. Mark motioned for his mom to stay in the hall as he walked into the room.

No one would know he was looking for an intruder. Mark loudly said, "Now, where did I put my baseball glove? I will need it tomorrow." He checked the spare room dresser and opened the clothes hamper.

He shouted as if his mom was in another part of the house, "Mom, do you know where my baseball glove is?"

He checked the closet, and it was pretty empty, only containing one large box. As he rifled through the box, he bent low to have a look under the high old bed. He saw a pair of pointed shoes.

He quickly said, "Oh, Mom, I know where it is, I left it at Josh's last week. I will tell him to bring it over after he finishes playing his games tonight."

She had backed into the kitchen and yelled, "Yes, that is fine, Mark, but does it have to be tonight?"

"Yes, I couldn't sleep well not having my entire equipment ready to go tomorrow. It's an important game."

She had already texted Shawn that someone was in the house and told him the back door was unlocked for him. Shawn was waiting outside the house for the text and opened the door quietly. He arrived with Barry, who he'd summoned to help. It startled Mark and Angela, as they didn't expect them so soon.

Angela said, "I will go to bed, Mark, just let me know when you are turning in, okay?"

Mark replied, "Sure, sounds good, Mom."

Mark whispered that he was under the bed in the first spare bedroom on the left.

Barry drew his gun and proceeded to go first, with Shawn close behind. Mark and Angela were to stay in the kitchen.

Shawn was glad he had painstakingly screwed down the subfloor so it would not squeak. They did not want to be detected, as they needed to surprise the intruder.

Barry lay on his stomach with his gun out in front of him. He was going to have this person in sight and command him to come out with his hands up while they were watching him.

He nodded to Shawn as if to say, "Are you ready?"

Shawn nodded back that he was and was waiting for a command.

Barry yelled, "Come out with your hands up!"

"Don't shoot, don't shoot! I'm coming out! Don't shoot!" the man yelled.

Barry commanded, "Toss your weapon out right now."

"Okay, don't shoot, I will," the intruder shouted.

Barry commanded, "Now, or I'll shoot."

"Here they are." He slid a handgun, a knife, and a Taser out from under the bed.

"Now, get out on the other side of the bed. Now!" Barry sounded forceful.

"I will, don't shoot, don't shoot," he repeated.

Barry watched carefully to make sure he wasn't doing anything stupid, and the man maneuvered his way from under the bed.

"Stay face down and put your hands over your head," Barry shouted, jumping to his feet in one smooth movement.

"Guard the weapons," he commanded Shawn, as he ran to stand over the man. Barry handcuffed his prisoner and stood him on his feet. He read him his rights and told him he was under arrest.

The police car was waiting outside for the word to enter, as Barry had told them to arrive without sirens for the element of surprise. The officers came in and took the pointed man to the car. The other officer gathered the weapons, being careful not to lose fingerprints on them.

Mark and Angela were still in the kitchen, quite shaken up. Dad and Barry sat down with them just as Mom and I arrived at the door.

"What happened?" I shouted, too hyper to care.

"They had an intruder," answered Dad.

"Was it the pointed man?" Mom quickly demanded.

Angela broke down and started to cry. It was too much for her. She had just realized what could have happened. It was overwhelming. Thank goodness, Mom was there and could console her by holding her tightly while she cried out her fears.

Barry told Mark he had done a great job in noticing the door was unlocked and making sure the house was clear of danger. He also asked questions regarding the timeline. Mom said she'd left around one, because she had looked at her watch and wondered if Grammy and Grammpy had eaten their lunch yet.

Then, Barry asked what Angela did for the rest of the afternoon. She answered that she had had a bite to eat and emptied some more boxes in her room, which was at the far end of the hall. Barry wanted to know if the doors were locked at the time. She thought carefully, then insisted that she locked them after Nerissa encouraged her to.

"So, you say after Nerissa left, the doors were all locked and the alarm was set?" Barry stated.

"Yes," she said, getting a little agitated.

"I am sorry, but this is important to the security of the house," Barry added. "I am guessing, then, that the intruder entered the house before Nerissa arrived."

"Do you think so?" Angela looked frantic.

"Can you tell me what you were doing between the time the stranger came to the door and when Nerissa arrived?" Barry drilled.

"Yes, of course, I was in the garage, sorting out what boxes I needed for my bedroom, as it was next on the agenda," she replied confidently.

"That must be when the man snuck in and hid under the bed," Barry surmised.

"You mean, he was there with a gun and knife the whole time I was alone?" Angela was totally overwhelmed with fear.

"I believe so, but what he was waiting for, I do not know. I also want to know why the door was unlocked," Barry questioned. "I need to go to the station to get some answers. Will you be all right?"

Shawn said, "We will make sure they are well taken care of, don't worry. Thank you for everything!"

As Barry left, he assured us that we were safe, as the man was in custody, and he would give us an update as soon as possible.

CHAPTER 49

Who is the Captured Intruder?

Everyone was safe, and the man had been arrested. Dad was going to stay here with Mark and Angela. That gave them a sense of security. He would sleep on the couch. They did not want to disturb the spare room in case it needed to be searched for more evidence. Mom and I walked home together and appreciated the bright lights Dad had left on. They shined all the way down the laneway, past the carriage house. I told Mom my concerns about this man hurting both of them and how uncertain life was becoming. Mom, again, reached deep down into herself and drew from her faith. She expressed that nothing was a surprise to God, and, although sometimes uncomfortable or even painful, God would bring them through every circumstance. The evil in the world would not win unless we let it.

"How could we let it, Mom?" I asked. "We can't control those that cause evil."

"That is true, but we can control how it affects us and how we live," she replied.

"What do you mean?" I was puzzled.

"Well, we don't have to live our lives in fear or be crippled by it. We can also treat others with respect, kindness, and love, not hate. That, and trusting in God, could change the world."

Mom was always the one with faith in people, no matter what. She would depend on God to change a bad situation and make it a good one. I figured God sure had his work cut out for him, as we were going from one bad situation to another. It did enter my mind, though, that every situation so far had been turned into something good. This one would be interesting. Surely, this man was not going to turn out to be a good man!

Of course, we had to fill everyone at home in on the weird and dangerous stranger. Everyone felt quite safe, knowing that he was in prison. We all said good night and headed for bed. I looked out of the window and down the lane once more, and my mind focused on the horrible night of Bee's accident. I had to shake it off and realized that, as terrible as that situation was, it did turn out okay. I was jolted back to reality as I watched a car pass the driveway on the road. I decided that the light sensor was the best thing Dad and Pa had installed. They had discussed a surveillance system, and I wondered if that was next. For now, we needed a good night's sleep, and I was off to bed.

The next day, Dad showed up for breakfast with Mark, which was not unusual, but also with Angela.

A place was set for them as Grammpy fried some more eggs and Grammy made some more toast. There were lots of hash browns, grilled with onions and bacon.

"What a treat, thank you for inviting me!" Angela announced.

Mom and Dad said she was welcome anytime, and that Mark was a regular at our table.

She said she had realized that. "My grocery money goes further than it used to," she laughed.

It was good to see her mood better.

"I can see Mark enjoying the food and the conversation around this table," she added.

I looked around the table. Even though it was one of the most gigantic tables I had ever seen, it was actually getting full. There were ten at the table this morning. It could seat another four, maybe six if necessary. I couldn't imagine a house where breakfast wasn't a big deal. It was always a special time in our home. Bee was messing it up just a little, with her crazy shifts at work and her all-over-the-map schedule for college classes.

Dad announced that he was having a surveillance system installed and said we should not be alarmed if the crew came to do some work. It would cover both our home and the carriage house. Mark and Angela thanked us, thinking they would feel much safer.

Kelly thought the entire happening was strange, and said they did not have this in Lancaster, though they kept their doors unlocked most of the time. I told him we never locked our doors until the beginning of this summer.

"What has changed?" He looked puzzled.

"We had some intruders. One was Mark's uncle, a very disturbed and dangerous man. The two men died falling over the gorge one night, but not before badly beating Mark. They wanted to kill him," Dad explained.

"Is this man connected?" asked Kelly.

"Barry has not given us the results of his interrogation yet," Dad answered, hoping there were no more questions.

"He said to come over after breakfast and he would fill me in on what he found," Dad added.

"What are you kids doing today?" Pa wanted to know.

"I told Kelly I would take him on the Niagara on the Lake, 'Whirlpool Jet Boats.' I need to see if he can take the adventure like a man," she laughed, giving Kelly one of her big smiles.

"I hope we see you tonight, Kelly," I said as everyone laughed.

He seemed to take the ribbing well and rather enjoyed it, taking no offence. Mom was going to email her parents' real estate agent and lawyer to see how the severance of property and the sale was going. They would be heading out in a day or so to go back. I could tell Mom was enjoying having them here instead of wondering how they were doing. She felt disconnected from them, as they did not text or call often and did not know how to use the Internet. I could not imagine living like that now.

"Well, I am going to talk to Barry, if you will excuse me," Dad spoke as he got up.

Mom let him know that she would be home all morning, and Dad left. Mark was going to help his mother with some chores and would check in later. Bee and Kelly were almost out of the door when Mom stopped them.

"You will need this baggy for your wallet and anything else you want to keep dry. Did you take your bathing suits?" she asked.

Kelly looked puzzled, and we all had fun watching his confusion. Nevin, a friend of Bee's, would give them a ride to remember. He had proposed to his wife while on one of these crazy rides, right in front of all the customers. Bee and Kelly were off on their adventure. I hoped they would buy the video.

I yelled after them, "Don't forget to hang on tight!"

CHAPTER 50

Organizing the Move

The elderly couple helped us clean up, while Mom and I discussed the rapids and how dangerous they were. Grammpy wondered if it was something he should do. We told him he should see how Kelly and Bee did today, then make up his mind.

Mom was busy with the lawyer, who said the land had been severed. He was faxing papers to sign, and she could fax them back after her parents read and signed them. They couldn't believe their eyes as the papers came through.

"Are you sure this is legal?" questioned Grammpy.

After he felt reassured, he expressed his joy in retaining a bit of his past, in the form of land in the place of his birth. After reminiscing a little, she phoned the real estate broker in charge of the sale. Mom was astounded to find out how much the property was worth. The man confirmed the property to be worth around three million because of its location. He surmised that her parents had no idea how much money they were dealing with.

She would have to help them understand. They lived from the land, the farm, and their gardens, and everything was homemade, even their clothing. She thought she would approach it after lunch, when they had time to digest the information she had given them.

Grammy had made some sandwiches for lunch, expecting others. She was used to providing a lot of food in short notice, as that was how the Amish people did things. The salami and cheese sandwiches, made with light rye bread and served with pickles and cabbage stuffed peppers, looked delicious. They were covered nicely and would not dry out. Mom felt she could talk to them now.

"Can we talk now?" Mom asked.

"Sure, is something wrong?" they asked.

"Oh, no, I just wanted to make sure you knew how much the farm was worth," she answered.

"Dear, we know that," Grammpy said. "It is no surprise. It is worth almost three and a half million dollars. Properties in Lancaster have sky rocketed in the past years."

He took some papers from the counter and lay them on the table in front of his chair, then continued, "I figured, with the cost of this addition being anywhere from $150,000 to $250,000, there would be at least three million left. Then we will need $1,500.00 for the lawyer. I figured a couple of thousand more for moving and incidentals would take care of it. Even if we bought appliances for another $10,000.00, there would be lots left over. I know things cost more here in Canada, but I was told of this great builder, 'Kenneth Homes,' who does a great job. He has done some renovations for a family who moved here from Lancaster. They were very pleased with his standard and quality. He has dependable trades like 'Radiant' doing the plumbing."

Mom was flabbergasted at the depth to which her father had done his research, and how he figured out his costs. She had not thought for one minute that he was stupid, rather, that his simple way of life made him unaware.

"I know you are worried about us, Nessa, but we know how to take care of ourselves when it comes to finances. We will need to buy extra healthcare, that is for sure, but it's manageable. We will not be a burden to you, we promise."

Hearing her childhood nickname was endearing. Mom continued to let them know, "You would never be a burden. On the contrary, you will be a blessing and delight to the family. I just somehow thought you lived such simple lives that you wouldn't understand the concept of this amount of money. I should never judge a person on how they live, should I?"

"You have been raised better than that," Grammy softly uttered, "But we do understand, Nessa."

Just then, Dad got back, and Pa and I showed up, as if the lunch bell had rung.

"Well, I knew there would be more for lunch," smiled Grammy.

We all sat down, and Dad said grace. Afterwards, Grammpy reminded Dad why he let his daughter marry him.

"I remember, Grammpy, you asked me to pray and I passed the test."

"Yes, you did, and I still like how you pray. So positive and strong, like you know God," Grammpy reported.

I wondered how you could sound like you knew God. Would I ever know God well enough for that? I finished my tall glass of cold milk while pondering.

Dad announced that we had some work to do outside after lunch. We were going to prune some low-hanging branches along the lane and in the yard. Pa and I said we would help. Dad wanted Mom's parents to think of things they wanted in their new home. The architect was going to start working on the plans as soon as Dad faxed him the present lot lines and existing house drawings.

They agreed to make a list that afternoon.

"You didn't tell us about the intruder, Dad. What did Barry say?" I wanted to know.

"I thought of it, but I didn't want to interrupt our lunch with the unpleasant details."

"With what unpleasant detail? What unpleasant details, Dad?!" I demanded.

CHAPTER 51

We Find Out Who He Is

"Where do I start?" Dad asked, then proceeded.

Barry interrogated the man, named Andy, after reading the report the first officer made. He seemed to tell the same story. The door was unlocked because he'd snuck back outside to go to the bathroom. Of course, he used the outdoors and forgot to lock the door afterwards. It checked out, as his fingerprints were on both sides of the doorknob. Angela was in the back, working in her bedroom, so he took advantage of the fact that her door was closed. When he returned, he took his position under the bed. He had been looking for his sister. She was last heard from in this area. Apparently, she was going to meet a lady at the old Royal George Theater years ago. It was a fundraiser for the needy, and his sister was to meet the woman in the parking lot afterwards. The woman was going to give her some money and a place to sleep for the night. Andy could not tell us the year, but that it was summer. His mother received the call from his sister after she met this lady. She said everything was going to be all right now, and her life was going to turn around. This lady promised. She said the lady gave her some money to prove she would be fine and to help her relax, but insisted that she call her mother. She sturted to cry and suddenly all that was heard were screams and then the phone was dead.

"Do you think that was Omz, Dad?" I asked.

"Why did he come now?" asked Mom.

Apparently, his mother was dying, and she pleaded with him to promise that he would take the address and find his sister. We all looked at each other. Who was his sister? We have never seen her.

Her name was Bella, but we had no idea what happened to her. The lady had to be Omz, it fit her description. She must have had a passenger that night.

"What happened to her?" asked Pa, who had been taking everything in with silence.

"Barry and I checked the report on the accident again, and no one else was found. I wondered if she got thrown out of the car, since she had no seat belt on."

"Something is wrong. Why did he have the weapons?" I smelled a lie.

"He said he expected his sister to be held hostage, so he bought some weapons from a second-hand store. He didn't have much money and apparently it checks out. The gun is a poor replica and won't even fire properly. He could have killed himself. The police verified where he bought it and for the amounts he said he paid for it. His mother is now gone, and he wants to find the only relative he has left. It brings up the death of Omz, and I didn't want you to have unpleasant memories over lunch."

"I thought everything Omz did and suggested to the girl, seemed like a good memory of her, don't you, Pa?"

"Yes, I do, son. It is how I remember Omz. Just like that." Then he asked, "What is the girl's last name?"

"It is Shantz. Bella Shantz and Andy Shantz," Dad informed. "Barry will do a search for her, and hopefully we will come up with something."

"Will he be staying in jail?" was my big question.

Barry had informed Dad that Andy would stay locked up if the charges were not dropped, or until proven not guilty. Andy had no one to pay his bail, and he had no money. Barry suggested giving Angela all the facts. Give her and Mark time to think on them, then see how they felt about it. He was going over now and asked me to go with him.

"It was so unexpected to think that Omz had someone else in her car. Why were they not found too?" I kept asking Dad.

"You will have to accept that I have no more answers than before," he said, looking straight into my eyes. "Sometimes we just don't have the answers, do we? Did you hear me, Josh?"

I replied, "Yes," but pouted.

CHAPTER 52

What is Happening to Josh?

What was Mark and his mother going to say to this information? My heart was trying to beat its way out of my chest. It looked like they were making him look innocent instead of guilty for what he'd done. What was Dad thinking? This man caused a lot of fear and could have hurt someone. You don't just take someone's privacy and invade their home like that! I had so much anger inside of me that I exploded right there on the driveway. I moaned from deep within and started punching a tree to express my anger. Dad had to hold me back, or I would have shredded my hands. He dragged me to the ground and forced me to stay there.

I started coming to my senses and felt pain in my bleeding knuckles.

"What is going through your mind, son? Talk to me. I want to help you," Dad encouraged.

"I don't know," was all I managed to get out of my mouth.

Dad sat on the ground beside me and held me tightly. I finally told him to let go. He didn't realize that he was strangling me. I felt awkward at this point, but Dad insisted that we talk. He was right, of course, but I didn't know what to say. He asked questions, and I answered. It finally came out that I hadn't dealt with the violation of someone ransacking our home while we were living in the carriage house and taping our conversations. It had been my safe place. I'd figured I would always be protected from danger there. Suddenly, I'd been left vulnerable. I didn't deal with my feelings and continued to go through the motions of being a tough guy, strong enough to withstand anything. There was a lot to do back then, and no time to deal with stuff that complicated an already-stressful time. Dad said he understood and should have tuned into my feelings much sooner.

"You have been so busy and focused on the tunnels that you haven't had time to sort out your feelings, Josh. You've had a lot on your plate for a young man, and I have taken that for granted."

I was back to my normal self, except for some very sore knuckles, and protested that I was enjoying all of the intrigue and danger. Any kid would be thrilled to live this life!

Dad agreed, but added, "When it hits the core of your security, your ultimate safe place, it shakes you up, and you have to deal with it. We will have to talk more about what is going on inside your head, okay, Josh?"

I agreed. I was never opposed to talking with Dad, or Pa, for that matter, "I just had no idea this was coming, I was blindsided."

Dad was compassionate and understood about stress. "We all deal with situations in different ways. It's important to deal with them, because they will surface again." He asked, "Do you want to go back home, or continue to Mark's place?"

I wanted to go on and figured if anyone in this world would understand me, Mark would.

We rang the doorbell and waited. We heard the locks being released, and Angela asked us to come in. We did, and it wasn't long before she noticed my hamburger knuckles.

"Mark, bring me the first aid kit," she shouted.

When he came in, he looked startled, but understood that only one thing could have caused this.

"Did you use a tree for a punching bag?" he compassionately asked. "I know, because I have done the same thing," he added.

"When? I don't remember."

"Now is not the time, but I will tell you. Did you win?" he asked.

After a quick deliberation, I was pleased to give a positive, "Yes, I did win."

While Angela cleaned and tended to my wounds, Dad asked if he could tell her about the intruder. He seemed hesitant to talk in front of me, but I kicked in some information on Andy to let him know I was good with it, and he continued. He gave her the story of his sister, Bella, and the one phone call, as well as what Bella had relayed regarding a ride from the theater that night to a place to stay. He told her about the promise Andy made to his Mother and why he bought his weapons. Dad felt Andy was quite innocent. Dad assured Angela that the man would be in prison unless the charges were dropped. He also told her to deal with the shock of the situation before making any decisions. I thanked her for bandaging my hands, which were now throbbing.

"We should talk soon," said Mark before we left. "We will let you know after we talk."

"I really don't feel like explaining what happened," I expressed.

"Well, there will be questions from people that love you, but they are also patient and will wait for answers if needed. See how it feels."

There was no one in the kitchen when they arrived back home. It was later than everyone expected, so they probably went on with what they had to do. I was going to go to my room for a while.

Dad organized himself and made plans for the new addition. He needed to have everything in place as soon as the plans were drawn up and permits bought.

Just then, Mom came in and asked what happened. Dad wondered how she knew, and found out she was looking out of her window and saw my outburst.

"How is he? Is he alright?" she was worried but knew he was in good hands.

Dad told her all of it, and she was sorry for not giving Josh time to deal with things. Dad assured her that I'd had no idea I had those feelings and just wasn't ready until it came time to release them. She wondered if she should go and see me, but Dad figured I needed a little time to think right now.

CHAPTER 53

A Sudden Good-Bye

"Oh, Shawn, Jake called and said that he could pick my parents up tomorrow. He was going to the Kitchener Market to pick up something and would swing by here at noon. I can't send Grammy home to pack alone."

"I think Bee would be happy to help her, don't you think?" Dad asked.

"She would be delighted. I think we have lost that girl to Kelly."

"Well, if I am going to lose her to someone, he is a very good one to win her," Dad added.

"I haven't even had a chance to catch up yet," Mom grumbled.

"I know. Why don't you make a date for the two of you to go for a coffee this evening? She needs to know that she is leaving tomorrow so she can extend her leave from work," Dad suggested wisely, then added, "You had better tell your parents that they are leaving tomorrow, they will want to pack today if I know them."

Nerissa went to give her parents the news, but she ached to look in on Josh. She was sure he would tell her when he was ready. The house would be quiet again soon. She would miss Bee and her parents. She had barely gotten to know Kelly, the man of Bee's dream. Nerissa thought Bee had fallen in love tunnels there was no turning back for her. She had another year of college to finish. Nerissa knew that was a long time for a long-distance relationship. She had also been looking forward to the whole family attending church together this weekend. It would have been so wonderful, although Grammy and Grammpy might have been shocked by the modern approach to the gospel. She was getting way ahead of herself and had to focus on the first task at hand, and that was chatting with her parents.

Much later that day, the family had a wonderful dinner together. The menu consisted of barbecued chicken and sausages, potato salad, and corn on the cob. Grammy had made two shoo-fly pies. We enjoyed dessert on our lovely, wide porch. It was the perfect evening, warm, with a lovely breeze blowing. This was the kind of evening that made everyone feel secure. The family sitting around, enjoying their dessert and evening coffee, on a porch designed for this purpose so many years ago. There were funny stories told, as well as sad ones. I could even talk about my wrapped hands, and how it happened. It was good to just be myself again. Grammpy asked Pa if he should fix that old Gazebo when he found time. I was surprised when Pa agreed that it needed a face-lift.

Pa suggested we add another step from the yard side, onto the gazebo as well, so the elderly people like him could also enjoy it. He quickly added that the stairs at the back should stay for nostalgia, although they would not be used. We all thought that was a great idea and looked forward to using the gazebo once more.

CHAPTER 54

The Ride of a Lifetime

Grammpy asked Kelly how the rapid ride was. By the look on Kelly's face, everyone knew it was pretty exciting.

Kelly started by saying, "If you had heart or back problems, you should sit near the front. Bee and I sat at the back, and we went flying. Nevin made that boat suddenly turn into the rapids, and it filled with water. We had to hold our breath as the water pounded us. When we came through that, there was water up to our knees. That was normal for the ride. Our clothes were soaked, and it is a good thing my wallet, watch, and passport were in the bag. I have the video if you want to see it." They all left to watch the video in the family room.

Bee suggested to Mom that they go for a walk instead of going into town for coffee. Mom agreed and loved taking a walk instead of sitting in a coffee shop. Bee told Mom she loved Kelly, and, yes, it was going to be a tough year, especially with Grammy and Grammpy being here. She could not visit as easily. Kelly only had one room and could not afford anything more due to his studies and part-time work hours. She said she was determined to make it work, although it would kill her.

"Has he ever thought of coming up this way?" asked Mom.

"Not so far," replied Bee.

"Sometimes time is the best problem solver, Bee. You will see."

They talked about Bee's dreams for the future. Bee mentioned how perfect she thought the gazebo would be for a wedding. She thought you could have chairs in a semi-circle around the gazebo on top of the hill for your guests, while the bride and groom could stand in the structure with the pastor. It seemed like she had given it a lot of thought.

That was a little scary for Mom. She mentioned that someone would have to go to South America to search for a few more descendants of the prisoners. They were going to send the young ones and Pa this time, and she asked if Bee wanted to go. Bee asked if she could be excused, as she was going to start some online courses to speed up her graduation. Mom liked her thinking and could accept that. That meant Josh and Pa would have to go. Shawn would be in charge of the addition. They decided it was time to get back to the house. The laneway looked so pretty as they walked down it. The porch had candles lit, and they were left with a lovely picture of this evening.

Bee and Mom decided to have breakfast on the porch in the morning. They would set up for breakfast outside and serve it buffet style. The weather was perfect, and they loved living outdoors whenever possible. They would have sausage and pancakes, muffins, fruit, and boiled eggs. There was something for everyone. Mom decided to invite Angela and Mark over, too. They would enjoy the fellowship.

Before I knew that some of the family was leaving, I arranged to meet Mac in the morning. Mom said to invite her for breakfast, too. It would be a party, of sorts.

One by one, the family appeared on the porch. The girls had set small tables with white linens and a bud vase with wild flowers. Bee took pictures, as it looked so inviting. Angela and Mark were a little taken aback by their first glimpse of the porch, until they saw everyone dressed as casual as always, just enjoying a different format. Mac couldn't believe her eyes, and Bee and Mac discussed all the layers that had taken place to make this look successful. They talked at great length regarding Bee going to Lancaster again and the courses she was starting online.

Mom took time to see if her parents needed anything else before they left. They were to stay in touch. Dad had Kelly in a corner, and

Mom wondered what they were taking about. They would take the morning to just be family and friends, without the drama of daily life.

The driver was on time at twelve sharp. Jake was driving today.

"Where is your regular driver?" asked Grammpy.

"His daughter ended up having her baby early, so he was needed on the farm to help out with the livestock," he replied.

"We could have waited," said Dad.

"I know, but we have people traveling every day this week, and I have had to hire more drivers, so this is better."

"We appreciate your concern for us," Grammpy added.

The luggage was loaded, and everybody was hugged good-bye. Bee had a snack for everyone, as she knew what to do by now. Pa was in the front with the driver. They were off, but this time, they had plans to return. It had been a lovely surprise to have them all here for Mom and Dad's arrival home. Dad, Pa, and I had gotten a chance to meet Kelly, too.

Mom was left as the only lady of the house again, but Angela helped her clean things up.

"What do you think about this Andy character?" Angela asked.

"I know he scared all of us, and you especially, but I do think he is harmless and should not be charged." Then she asked, "What do you think? That is more important."

She paused a while, then agreed that she should not charge him. She felt quite safe, even if he would be released. It was a very unfortunate circumstance. She respected a brother that went to those lengths to try to find and save his sister.

Nerissa agreed and suggested she talk to Barry and see how he would direct her.

There was a knock on the kitchen door.

"Well, speak of the devil," Mom announced.

"Why is that?" Barry asked.

"I just got finished telling Angela that she should speak to you regarding Andy," Mom stated.

That was why Barry had come over. He also wanted to talk about another matter, moving companies, and wanted to know where Mac was.

Mom informed him that Mac's whereabouts was the easy question. She was with the boys, off doing whatever they did.

That was what Barry wanted to know. What did they do?

"I assure you that their actions are honorable, they are well aware of how to treat a girl," Mom expressed.

"No, that is not what I am getting at. Where do they go on days like this?" He seemed agitated.

"I would punish my boy if he touched Mac in an inappropriate way!" added Angela.

Suddenly, the teens broke into the tense room, in the middle of a loud conversation.

"Hi Dad," said Mac, as if it was normal to see him there.

The three went into the family room to play some games, so Josh could unwrap his hands for a while.

"That is what they do, come and go," suggested Mom.

"I am sorry, but I was not implying they were misbehaving. I just wanted to be sure they did not go into places that could hurt them."

"Mark knows better than that!" Angela assured.

"Thank you for letting me be a concerned parent," Barry relaxed as he spoke.

"Nerissa you said your parents are moving from Lancaster. A word of caution for your parents: if you look online under, '10 moving companies have been charged' you will see an article about companies cheating their customers in many ways. It gives their names. Please check it out."

"Thank you, we will do that," Nerissa said, grateful.

"Now, the next thing on my list. Andy. Have you thought any more about him? Will you press charges?" He sounded like a police officer now.

Angela had decided to drop the charges. She was compassionate, and as long as there was no danger, she would let him go. She also asked Barry how he would find Andy's sister. Barry said they were working on that, and they would hopefully get some leads soon. He poked his head in on the family and said goodbye, as did Angela. We were so busy that we barely gave them a look. Mom reminded us of our manners.

Mom saw the two guests out and told Barry she understood what he was saying and knew how he felt. It was his job to be a parent and do the job well.

"Mom, since you are home, Pa texted that we should help him retrieve some of the gold bars. We are going to put them in the safe up here in the office. We need to clear out everything valuable, in case we have problems when we excavate. We will join Pa downstairs, if that is okay?"

"Is that what you came in to do?" she asked. "You could have fooled me. Yes, I will be here to guard the house. It should be much quieter then the last few days."

"I would check before I would ever bring the gold up," I told her.

"Be careful, please," she warned.

CHAPTER 55

Moving the Gold

"We will be all together mom, don't worry," we all said.

Josh went to the side ravine doors and brought in his old red wagon. He pulled it into the inner office and through the bookcase doors. Mom heard us and peeked her head in to see what we were doing. She gave a look of approval and let us carry on, making sure the bookcases were closed after her.

We continued to open the secret door and carried the wagon down the stairs into the next tunnel before putting it down. It made some noise as we pulled it, but it would be valuable in collecting the gold, as it was narrow and would fit through most tunnels. Once in the lower level of the tunnels, we could revisit all the piles of gold we'd left vulnerable.

"Where is Pa? He said he would wait for us," I reminded the others.

"Now, don't turn into a parent on us!" Mac warned.

We found Pa at the underground lake, not far from his small hideaway. He was sitting there, just staring into space.

"Pa, are you all right?"

"Josh, I was only taking a minute to appreciate all that has happened since I had to hide down here," he said. "I am truly blessed to get a second chance at life."

"We are all blessed to have you with us, Pa, you are special to me." I walked over and hugged him.

When I turned around to my friends, Mac had tears running down her face and Mark was wiping his eyes. I asked what was going on, and Mark announced that he did not have any relatives like Pa, but wished he did. Mac lost her Poppy two years ago and was missing him. I told them how sorry I was for them and they could share Pa with me.

"Hey, isn't anyone going to ask me? That is a lot of love to put out," he said as he stood up. He called a group hug, and it was awkward, but good.

"Now, let's get to work, kids," Pa commanded. "We have a lot of work to do."

We went from one place to another and gathered the gold. Unloading the gathered gold at the bottom of the stairs. This was no easy task, although the wagon worked beautifully and made our job a lot easier. Since we had gathered all the bars except the ones in the last tunnel I had found, I figured it was next. The wagons' width would fit through that crevice, too. Mac pleaded to go too, and it was decided the three of us would enter now that the bottomless hole was covered. Pa would stay and wait for us, then pull the wagon back through the tunnel with the gold bars when we were done. He could relax on his coat and even cover up with his sleeping bag.

I crawled in first, ever mindful of my exploration bag. It was nice, crawling right onto the board and knowing it wouldn't slip away. I stood in the tall crevasse-shaped tunnel and waited. Mac was next and came through in seconds.

"Woo, this is nice," she said.

"Mark, where are you?" I shouted.

CHAPTER 56

Mark is Frozen

He was halfway through the tunnel and couldn't move. Memories of his last visit left scars of fear, which were now painful. I got on my knees and crawled into the tunnel, coming face-to-face with him.

"Okay, buddy, I get it, look at me. Mark, look at me. The last time you couldn't find me, right? This time I am right here. See? I am okay, safe. Can you move and follow me?"

He nodded.

I shuffled backwards, and he moved forward, until I turned my body into the larger cave. He followed.

"Mark, we are past the black hole. You are on the other side. You can stand up now," I encouraged.

He followed my lead and stood up.

"I don't know what happened to me, Josh. I froze," Mark said.

"It happens to all of us," I reassured him.

Pa yelled in to make sure all was as it should be. We all yelled back, and that was all he needed to hear.

They followed me, and I made sure to go left at the crossroads, telling them to take note. I also told them we had not checked the tunnel in the other direction, but it was on the agenda. The wagon pulled behind, bumping the walls here and there. We finally got to the pile of sacks, and I uncovered the mangled skeleton of the soldier. I wished that I had been more reverent with his body. He was such a good man and had treated the prisoners with dignity. My friends had been filled in and helped me to gather the clothes and skeletal remains. We put them in one of the burlap bags to take with us. He would be buried in our cemetery, as we had no last name for him.

CHAPTER 57

A Whole Life in One Sack

We turned the wagon first, as there wasn't much room to do so when it was full. Mark and I loaded the twelve gold bars while we talked about what this could buy. Mac had all the soldiers' parts in a sack, and we were ready to go.

"Do you guys want to see where this leads?" I asked in a soft voice, all while walking forward.

They followed but wanted to know why they needed to be quiet.

"Because we are close to the opening, and getting closer every second," I told them.

I showed them where to look out. First Mac did, and then Mark. Mark jumped back and just about took us with him as he fell.

CHAPTER 58

Two Strangers

"There is someone out there," he mouthed.

I took another look. Sure enough, a couple was standing not more than ten feet away, having a conversation about the noise. We were very still for about fifteen minutes. They finally decided to move on, as they could hear nothing more.

"Were we ever lucky!" whispered Mac.

Mark and I both agreed. We would have to carry the wagon. We could not take a chance that it would be heard rumbling through the tunnel. I decided to text Mom, since we were near an opening, and have her look over the gazebo to see who the couple was. She answered and asked us to wait for a reply. It was difficult to wait, even for ten minutes. We couldn't imagine what Pa felt like, waiting for us all this time. Mom texted me back as soon as possible. I had my phone on silent. Her reply was, "The couple is just taking a summer hike to investigate the gully and see what they can find. They are crossing to the other side now, near the gorge ridge."

"Thanx Mom," was my reply.

We would still carry the wagon. It was a lot harder. We got to the tunnel and I pushed the wagon inside. Pa pulled it back into the small room.

"We will tell you later why we were so late, Pa. Do you want to join us? We are going to check out another tunnel in the opposite direction," I asked.

CHAPTER 59

The New Tunnel

"Do you all have lights?" Pa asked. "If so, I am coming through to join you. You grab my light. A new tunnel—this will be so much fun."

We continued on and filled Pa in on all that happened. We asked him if he knew that the soldier's bones and uniform was on top of the gold in the wagon.

He hadn't had the time to check that out.

I reminded everyone as we turned right into the other tunnel that it had not been investigated, so we needed to go slow and be very careful. There could be another black hole in the tunnel floor.

I gave everyone a job. I would check the floor, since I was first. Mark would check the right side of the wall. Pa took care of the left, and Mac would check out the ceiling.

"That should cover it," I said to myself.

"That is a very clever approach!" Pa announced.

We moved cautiously, at a snail's pace. I knew it could be danger-ous, so I wouldn't let them hurry me.

Pa shouted, "Stop! I see something."

He shone his light where he thought he saw a hole. There it was, large enough to fit your head through. What was it? He couldn't see anything.

"Let's mark it with some fluorescent tape," I said, digging in my bulging bag.

"You have got to be kidding! You have fluorescent tape with you!"

Mac looked impressed and shocked.

I put a piece over it, and our light caught it easily. We kept on going, and it seemed as though we had to hold our bodies back as we were descending.

Pa shouted, "Stop." Another hole.

The same way we'd done the last, we marked it.

After a while, Pa stopped us again and we marked a third hole. We reached a set of narrow, rough-cut stairs. They were difficult to maneuver, as the treads were short and irregular. They kept on spiraling down, and Pa kept on yelling stop as we marked holes. We reached some kind of bottom.

It was a cave, but we had no idea how high. We could only see vast darkness. Pa asked us to turn our lights off for a second to see if light came in from anywhere. It was quite scary to think how dependent we were on our lights. The light was put on again. We found seven holes in the walls. Our lights were searching the floor and walls of this unknown place until someone shouted again.

CHAPTER 60

Proof of Horror

"Stop! Stop! Look over there," Mark repeated himself.

Our flashlights hit the area he was shining on to enhance what he was looking at. We walked closer. "Oh, this is terrible, I can't believe it!" cried Mac.

Mark asked, "Is my grandfather, Joseph, here?"

Pa put his hands on my shoulders, and I didn't know if it was for his sake or mine. I knew he was saying his uncle, Friedrich, was here.

We neared slowly, at what seemed like a Holy Place. It was a pile of skeletons covered in ragged clothing. One body was lying on top of another.

"This cavern must go all the way up to where the men were sent down on ropes. They must have fallen hundreds of feet to their death," I sadly remarked.

Pa got closer and examined the skeletons. "We will bring the camera and document our findings. We mustn't move a thing," he directed.

"That reminds me, Pa, I didn't take pictures of the soldier before moving him," I confessed.

"That is okay, son, this would be to keep the bones separate for each person if at all possible," he continued.

"Pa, we have five flashlights with my little one. Can we leave the strongest two down here and see if they show from the openings in the wall you found?" I asked.

The others thought it a brilliant idea and gave me the thumbs up.

Pa took longer to consider, weighing the possibilities if one light went out or broke and so on. Finally, he agreed that we would still have enough light, as we were going straight back. He wondered how low we were, and if this was the lowest point of the system.

We left the brightest, most powerful flashlights with the ancestors and left. It was a very good workout going up, and I worried about Pa. We took our time and stopped many times. It was exciting, getting to the first hole in the wall and looking down, seeing quite clearly. We did the same thing at all openings and could see the light becoming dimmer and dimmer.

"I had another idea. We should bring at least seven very bright lights and put them in the openings, all the way up. Wouldn't that look cool?" I asked.

Mark added that we should also put a light in the opening from where the men fell to their death. Then, we could see where that was from the bottom. It was a plan, and next time we would illuminate the tunnel in that way we planned.

We needed to get back, as it had to be getting late. We would try to collect all the gold coins on another day. We also needed to figure out how to get the gold upstairs without carrying it. I had some thoughts on that and would let Pa and Dad know about them later. As we dropped the last twelve bars of gold off at the bottom of the stairs, we were astounded to realize that it didn't even excite us anymore. They were added to the pile in good order and left without much fanfare. We were some of the few people in the world who had actually seen a bar of gold; never mind twenty-four bars! Being tired, the climb up the stairs was slow, and we had lots to talk about. We were feeling our legs, and couldn't imagine carrying the gold up with us.

When we got upstairs, Pa went to rest before supper, although he only had a half hour. He figured we would fill Dad and Mom in.

"Mac, your Mom just called for you to come home for supper. Thank goodness you are back," Mom sounded relieved.

Mac was not happy, as she wanted to hear all the chit-chat about our findings and see my parents' faces when they heard.

"Fill me in later," she ordered as she ran off.

CHAPTER 61

Relaying Our Shock

Mark and I sat down to tell of our excursion when Dad said, "Just wait. Mark's mother wants him home in 45 minutes."

Mark was planning on leaving before we had dinner, so he would be early for a change.

Mom asked how we did, and we said we got all the gold in the area before the stairs. The coins were not yet collected, but we needed something non-breakable to keep them separate and carry them.

Mom asked, "How would large cookie tins do? They could be sealed with packing tape."

That sounded good. I asked, "How many do you have?"

"Not too many, but I can pick them up at the second-hand store," she announced. "I will do that tomorrow. Do you need twelve?"

"That's the magic number," we told her.

Our find of the tunnel, the stairs, the seven openings in the wall, and the cavern was nothing compared to the skeletons, all lying on top of one another.

"That discovery was awful," reported Mark. "It is a long way for Pa to climb. We don't know how deep, but it is very far down."

"It looks like you boys and Mac and Pa have done well once again. We are getting the job done. After retrieving it all, we just have the tunnels to the power station to find."

"Well, I had better get going and surprise my Mom with an early appearance," Mark spoke while getting the door to leave, "I am so glad we found Joseph. See you," and he was gone.

Mom had dinner ready and asked me to get Pa. I ran up the stairs, washed my hands, and knocked on his door. No one answered, so I peeked in. He looked like he was fast asleep... Or, was he dead? That could not be. I tip-toed over and put my hand in front of his mouth. He was breathing. I snuck back out and closed the door.

"Pa is sleeping," I reported. "I checked him because he was so quiet, but he is alive. It is funny how I would even think of such a terrible thing."

Dad replied it was natural and good that I checked. He would have, too.

Our evening prayer today was to be grateful for all we had including food, the people in our family, and the ones that gave their lives for a better world. It certainly summed it up as far as we were all concerned. Mom had a break today. Tonight, it was leftovers, which we loved. They were even better today.

We would let Pa sleep as long as he wanted, even until morning if he needed it.

"How did you make out with the architect?" asked Mom.

"He is making a special effort for us and will have the drawings by the weekend."

"Oh, so soon," she thought.

"Then, I will apply for a permit, which I am sure will not be a problem. I will get the application in on for Monday, as they have an opening in the planning meeting."

"Maybe if we can get some more help like we did today, we can gather all the coins. We can even bring up some of the gold."

"Dad, I had an idea on how to do that. We could take the wheels off of the wagon when we are done with it, or we can get another one. We could have a long rope and pull it up like a sleigh. We can secure the gold with a strap around the wagon, and tape it or wrap it or both. A few of us could pull it at the same time to make it a lighter load."

"Great idea, Josh! I think that will work."

Mom and Dad went to sit on the porch with their coffee to enjoy the evening. I made it my job to text Mark and Mac to see if they could get together in the morning. We could hang out all day, and they could have lunch here. I told them Mom would prepare a picnic lunch. Mark texted back that it was fine with him. Mac didn't text back for quite a while, then said she hadn't been able to find her phone. She thanked me for the invite and said she would show up around nine. I told her there was no rush. I wondered what was going on over there and if Barry was getting suspicious. After all, he was her dad. He needed to know she was safe. Did he know more than he was letting on? I dismissed the thought for now and went to play some games at Mark's for a change. He was expecting me.

CHAPTER 62

Collecting the Coins

Mom went to Value Village to get some large cookie tins. She got four there and bought the rest at the Dollarama. We had twelve, and that was plenty. I texted her a big thank you when she told me what she had bought. We were ready to get a lot done the next day. Mark and I decided to turn in at a decent hour, as we wanted to be well rested for our job. It was so much fun, planning on hanging out with my best friends in our secret hideout.

Dad was still crunching the numbers when I got in. The architect had worked all day on his plan, and Dad could pick it up tomorrow. Dad figured that was a miracle in itself.

He would meet us after he was done with his appointment.

I checked to see if Pa was still sleeping, and he was sawing logs. I covered him up, knowing he would sleep all night. We would be careful not to work him that hard again. For now, he was resting, and I was looking forward to the same. The next morning, Pa was the first up.

"You must have been up early with all the sleep you got, Pa," I said upon arriving in the kitchen.

"I sure was," he reported.

"Are you eating supper or breakfast, Pa?" I asked.

"Well, you are in good form," he returned.

"I was going to make French toast and bacon; how does that sound?" he asked.

I told him that was great, and I started to break the eggs as he got out the bread. The bacon was already sizzling and would be done soon. That meant that Mom and Dad would be down soon.

I was excited about getting a job done today. We could start the build with no apprehensions.

Pa and I were ready to eat when Dad joined us in the kitchen.

"Where is Mom?" I asked.

"I am not sure, but I think she has the flu. Or maybe it is a bad case of jet lag, or maybe she is just worn down. In any case, she is going to stay in bed for the day, or as long as she feels she needs."

"Should I stay with her?" Pa asked.

"Well, it would probably be a good idea to have someone in the house, in case she needs something."

"Consider her taken care of," Pa gestured a salute.

"You are sure spunky this morning," laughed Dad.

"What is that they say, Josh? I feel good, and I knew that I would, or something like that!" He tried to sing the words. We all laughed.

It wasn't long before Mark and Mac came to the door. They were just in time for breakfast. Our day started with a good chatting session. Breakfast was delicious, and Pa offered to clean up. We carried our dishes over and were glad to get going. Always cautious, we left through the inner office.

We decided that we would gather all the coins first, putting them into the cookie tins Mom had provided. We knew where everything was now, and, with the wagon, it was going very quickly. In no time, we were finished gathering the coins.

"Boy, that was quick," said Mac. "You know your Mom was sick this morning and didn't make us a picnic lunch, so can we make some mac and cheese?"

"Sure, but when we come back, let's bring lots of packing tape to secure the gold and coins."

"Are you kidding me?" said Mark. "That is impossible."

Mac forced us to go for lunch first and argue about how to do it later.

CHAPTER 63

In the Supply Room

I got the Coleman stove out, and Mark got the water from the pool. Mac spotted the mac and cheese. "It is a good thing there are two boxes," she said. "I will make them both."

The water was on and boiling. She drained the pasta and mixed in the cheese. I was looking at the slide and it hit me. If we got the gold up this far, we could maybe pull it up the slide with a rope. It was easier than using all the stairs and tunnels through the office. That would work. Maybe Dad and Pa could connect that electric pulley on a motor to assist in the job.

"Thanks for insisting we have mac and cheese, Mac. I have a great idea. We will get the stuff this far, then use a pulley up the slide," I explained.

"Let's talk about that later," she said. "Let's eat."

We had three spoons, and all ate out of the pot. It was so good, and I knew Pa would have enjoyed it too.

"Maybe we can leave a little for Pa's lunch," I suggested.

"Good idea. I am stuffed," moaned Mark.

Mac said, "Me too."

Now, we had to get the axle off the wagon, so it would slide. We took some tools and the packing tape downstairs with us. We removed the axle easily and effortlessly using our large pliers. We loaded the twelve bars of gold onto the wagon. They were well taped down inside the wagon. Then, we tied a long rope onto the handle. Mark and I were going to pull, and Mac would walk behind and make sure it sat on a step when we stopped to rest.

We were ready. We pulled hard. The weight was unbelievable, as we were pulling it up the stairs. Mac supported the back and helped push. It was hard work. We heard footsteps coming down the stairs towards us. I hoped it was Dad. As he came into focus, we saw he was with Pa.

"Just in time, Dad. With the three of us, it will work just fine."

He grabbed a hold of the rope, and we pulled together. It worked well. We rested after five minutes, and Mac made sure the wagon sat up on its end on the stair. Pa assisted. Ready to go again, we made it all the way to the storage room. There we unloaded, and I told Dad about the idea I had.

"Hey, did you have mac and cheese?" Pa asked.

"Yes, do you want some, Pa? We saved some for you," I asked.

"No, I shouldn't, I just had lunch, but it looks good! Sure, why not? This is special."

He devoured the food, and we wondered if he really did have lunch.

"Josh, your idea is very good. Depending on how long this slide is, we could pull it up from the top."

"How is Mom feeling?" I asked.

"I think a little better. When I tell her she doesn't have to feel bad about not making you lunch, she will at least lose her guilt over it. That will help."

After catching our breath, we decided to give it another try and bring up the other twelve bricks of gold. We had them almost all taped and ready to go when we noticed a visitor. Mac was going to reach out but noticed a sneer. There was something different about this visitor.

CHAPTER 64

Unexpected Company

Pa spoke quietly and directly, "Raise your arms and make yourselves look big. This is a male!"

Mac was the closest, and he told her to back up while facing the cougar. She couldn't and was frozen. The cougar was staring at her like she was dinner. It started to move and get into attack position. We had no fire or gunpowder. Pa tried to toss a brick of gold, but it didn't go far. Dad did the same. We started to yell in as low a voice as possible and waved our hands frantically. This was not happening. He would have to kill all of us or none of us. The wild cat was not giving up. What was keeping him here?

Mac was starting to shake with fear, and Pa kept saying, "Move back slowly, Mac, move now."

We moved towards Mac, yelling and waving our arms in the air until we were in front of Mac. No wonder she was terrified. It felt like we were standing no more than ten feet from the beast, and he was huge. His eyes were glaring at us as if to say, "I can take which ever one of you I want."

Pa started to become a martyr and stepped out in front of the rest of us. Dad demanded he stay back, but Pa took another step.

I yelled, "Pa! Pa, please don't!"

Mac suddenly came out of her trance and began to move. She realized she had scissors in her pocket for cutting the tape.

I almost freaked out when a hand came over my shoulder holding the scissor. Mac had enough sense to pass it to me, knowing I was stronger and might know what to do with it.

I said in a calm voice, "Pa, I have that scissor."

Dad said, "Pa, move back, we can do this together."

Pa did as he was told, but as he moved, the cougar became more intense and started to crouch again. It looked like he was going to pounce.

Suddenly there was growling and snarling noises we had never heard before. It was Girl! There was just enough room to fit between the male and us. Although relieved, we were still in danger and wondered what would happen next. Girl seemed so much smaller than the male. She stood her ground, looking at the male face-to-face. He finally turned and, with one huge jump, leapt onto the rock wall. He moved from one ledge to another and disappeared into thin air. We all took a deep breath. We didn't realize we'd been involuntarily holding our breath for so long.

Pa approached Girl and stroked her. "You are such a good girl," he repeated over and over.

She took it all in and seemed to put her head over for him to rub her ear. Was this possible? They had a unique relationship all right, and it might have just saved our lives.

Pa asked, "Where is your little one?"

It was like Girl understood, and she looked into the black hole. There, in the darkness, we could see her eyes. As she neared, her form became clear, we noticed how much she had grown. She hadn't grown her adult coat yet and still had the kitten look. She was adorable, and we just wanted to hug her.

Pa asked if we could pet Sweetheart. It was as if she agreed, and she walked over to Sweetheart's side. Pa was gentle and controlled in his movement. The kitten enjoyed his petting and might also be a friend if given time to get to know him.

"Can I touch her, too?" asked Mac.

"She should have your scent from before," said Pa.

Mac had lived for this moment since their last meeting and crouched down beside Sweetheart. The kitten almost jumped on her and knocked her over. She licked Mac's face and seemed to want to play. Girl just lay beside us as if to say, "I need a rest while you guys play." Mark and I went over and got in on the action. Mark had a protein bar in his pocket and thought he would see if she liked it.

"Not the kind of protein you are used to, huh Girl?" he said as she aggressively ate the bar.

Dad joined in with, "What a picture!" He took out his camera and snapped a couple of shots.

"Dad, you better keep those under wrap, or they will go viral," I suggested.

As if playtime was over, Girl got up and summoned Sweetheart that they were going.

We thanked her for saving our lives and enjoyed watching them disappear into the blackness of the cavern next door.

It was certainly an elating break. We'd gone from the fear of being near death to feeling more love from a wild animal then we ever knew was possible. We needed to be more vigilant. We had become so accustomed to our tunnels that we were not prepared for the dangers that lurked inside. We wondered how often that male cougar came here, and if he would come back.

We would take this load upstairs and then get the coins.

Our energy was rejuvenated. We made short work of the second twelve bars of gold. They were neatly stacked, and Mac did the cleanup from our lunch while we went to get the coins.

Dad liked the way we marked all the tins with names and where we found them. If there were discrepancies, we would have that to fall back on. The tins were sealed individually. They all fit in one load, as we stood them up on their side and secured them well. We could only imagine a tin of coins falling and where they would land, maybe never to be found.

This load seemed heavier than the last two. We had not weighed a tin of coins, but figured it was because we were getting tired. Once up in the storage room, the tins were nicely stacked beside the gold. What a haul! If anyone happened upon this, they wouldn't believe their eyes.

Since Mom was ill, Dad figured he'd better go and check on her. We decided that we would all go up and see if we could get a measurement of the slide. How would we do that?

Mom was still in bed, and Dad told her all the news, good and bad. He also told her that Mac had made mac and cheese down there, and she did not have to feel guilty about not making lunch. She smiled but expressed that it was too dangerous for the kids to go down by themselves now that there was another cougar. Dad knew that was coming, but honesty was the best policy. Even the thought of being honest made his stomach flip, as they were keeping so many secrets from so many people.

CHAPTER 65

The Measurement

Pa, Mark, Mac, and I were discussing how to measure the distance of the slope. Pa suggested to tie a long, heavy-duty string to something heavy and slide it down. We didn't think it would make all the turns and go all the way down.

I had an idea. I would go down the slide myself, holding the end of the string, and we would know just how far it was, provided we knew how long the string was.

As Dad came in, he noticed our enthusiasm and we filled him in.

"Ingenious," he said. "Who thought of this one?"

My chest was bursting, or at least, it felt that way when I admitted to the idea.

"Good work, son," he reaffirmed.

Pa had a few rolls of old spools of brick-layers' line in the attic. The nylon string liners ranged from 100, 150, 200, 250', and 500' each. He had picked them up cheap, because all the bricklayers were going into laser technology.

"I think we will tie two together, just in case. We can put the spool on a bar and let it roll as needed," Pa relayed.

We were excited to see this work. Pa went to get the rolls. We used one 100' string first and one 150' string next. We knew the fall's gorge was 188' at its highest point. We also took into consideration the twists and turns. With the two tied together, we wound one over top of the other, being careful not to knot the string. A copper pipe served as our rod. Pa had realized that whoever was holding this copper might need gloves, so he also brought a heavy pair.

I tied the end to one removed shoe, using the lace hole for extra security. I would hold it over my head as I went down.

I stood in place, and Dad and Pa moved back. Pa would slip a 2x4 in the door to keep it open a little, and Dad would hold the line while wearing the gloves. Mac was in charge of pulling the nail to release the trap door.

"Here it goes," I said, almost nervous.

"On the count of three," Mac said, counting, "One, two, three!"

I was off and sliding. Round and round so fast, I soon hit the floor on the supply room. I was still hanging on to my running shoe! It worked. I tied a knot into the line, so we knew where the distance ended. I noticed we had not finished the first 100' line. I cut it at my knot and took it upstairs to measure how much was left.

They were all waiting for my arrival and had the doors open for me.

"The slide is less than forty-six feet down. That is with all the turns," Dad clarified.

"I have an old winch with a fifty-foot cable attached to it. If we can attach it to the floor, then pull all that stuff up in two loads. It can pull about a ton, if I recall correctly."

Dad and Mark went to get the winch as Pa directed, and I got some plywood, screws, and a cordless screwdriver. Mac went downstairs to pile up the gold in one load and secure it. She not only used packing tape, but also duct tape. The wagon never looked so good. She knew enough to work to the side as someone would have to take the winch cable and slide it down to attach to the wagon. I wondered if the wagon handle was strong enough.

Suddenly, she heard someone sliding down. I arrived with a thump. I was holding the cable above my head. She laughed at how startled I looked.

"Do you think this wagon handle will be strong enough to carry that weight, Josh?" she questioned.

I studied it for a moment and thought aloud, "No, I think you are right. One screw has already given way from the journey up the stairs. We will have to remedy this." I took a piece of plywood from the wood corner and measured if the wagon would fit. "We will need a heavy-duty hook of sorts to attach to the plywood. I will support the back of the wagon with a piece of 2x4 screwed onto the plywood. Instead of unloading the wagon again we will just tape the wagon onto the wood platform."

"I will get that hook from upstairs, be right back."

Dad and Mark came down to help lift the wagon filled with gold. First, they attached the loop. The cable was supposed to hold 700 lbs.

They tipped the wagon on end, resting on the 2x4 attached to the plywood. That was difficult in itself. Mac wound the tape round and round, then around some more, until the guys shouted for her to stop.

"We want to be sure," she suggested.

It was pushed over in place, and the cable was attached.

Dad and Mark ran up to meet Pa, who was waiting to hit the switch. The motor started and worked steadily. It wasn't quick enough for the onlookers, but that was how it worked. As soon as it was out of sight, Mac and I ran to meet our load at the top.

We heard the phone ring. I ran to get it. It was Barry, and he wanted to speak with Mac. I called Mac, and she talked to her dad.

"But Dad, I am in the middle of a game, and I am winning! Can I stay for a little while longer? Please?"

He must have conceded, as she came back happy.

"I have to leave in an hour," she said, disgusted.

"Remember, Mac, your parents don't know about this and are just including you in their lives, right?" Dad said.

"You're right, I'm sorry."

Just then, we saw our gold arrive. The winch had no problem pulling it to the top. We slid the wagon over onto the floor. Mac cut the tape around the gold, separating it from the wagon. We loaded it into the safe in two large blocks. Now, we would repeat the process, and retrieve the coins from below.

After we were informed of the actual weight of the gold bars, we were shocked, and realized why we were so tired. Pa stayed upstairs and the rest of us went down to the supply room. I used the slide holding onto the cable. It took quite some time to load up, the way we had before, with tape holding all the tins in the wagon. Mark and Dad went up first and gave Pa the okay to hit the switch. Mac and I followed as soon as the coins were out of sight. Mac was getting impatient, as she knew she would have to leave soon and wanted to see the work completed.

"Only another few minutes," Pa said as he looked at his watch.

"There it is, it is coming!" exclaimed Mac. She would see the last load come up.

I dared to speak what I was thinking and almost got punished on the spot. "I would love to hang onto that thing and have it pull me up the slide, so I could see where it went"

Dad made me promise right then and there that I would never do that. He wouldn't let me go until I promised.

Mac said good-bye and we loaded the tins into the safe. It certainly looked like a safe now, except for the fact that no one kept cookies in safes. We would bring all the important papers up tomorrow and call it a day. We let the trap door down and cleaned up a little, leaving the winch and wagon attached to the plywood hidden in the secret hall behind the wall. Pa was ready to relax, although we hadn't made him work hard today. These little projects always took an emotional toll, as we never knew if they would work. Dad was going to check on Mom again, and Mark and I would play a couple of games. Mark texted his mom to make sure she didn't need anything. She was fine.

"Mark, are you free tomorrow to help with the rest of the important papers?" I asked.

He would check with his mom and let me know later.

"I will text Mac and see if she can come over tomorrow, and we will finish the game," I suggested.

She texted, saying that she was able to, and she would be the winner! I texted, "NO CHANCE."

Mark and I snacked on a bag of chips and talked about how successful the day went.

Dad asked if we had the energy to go back down and get the papers. We said sure. Dad had a bunch of files to keep separated and a garbage bag full for the rolls.

In our cozy living area, we put the separated piles of paper in the folders, marking them. The larger scrolls of paper were also gently put into the bag.

CHAPTER 66

Almost Caught

We had gathered it all and left for upstairs. It was so good to have the job done. As we neared the top, we heard someone say, "Hello, hello."

Dad went out and around to the family room. He made his way to the kitchen, where the voice was coming from. It was Barry. He came over with some homemade chicken soup for Mom.

"We heard how sick Nerissa was, and I knocked, but no one answered. I was going to leave it on the counter."

"That was so nice of Vanessa," Dad said as he put it in the fridge. "Thank Vanessa for us, will you?"

"Sure thing," said Barry. "I was wondering, are the boys home?"

"Oh, they are," Dad said, looking around the corner at the TV area. "They must have gone for fresh air. The bag of chips is still lying there. I wish they would clean up after themselves."

Barry took a peek and said, "I hope Mac cleans up after herself."

"Yes, if she wouldn't have gone home earlier, that bag wouldn't be there," Dad confided to his dismay.

"Well, I had better go. Wish Nerissa a speedy recovery," he said and left.

Mark and I came in and asked, "Who was it?"

Pa had heavily insulated the inner room, so no one could hear what was going on. It had certainly worked. Dad told us, and we agreed to be more careful. The papers were organized. The safe was not looking as huge as it had this morning. We used a clean office garbage can to stand the rolls up.

Dad and Pa had discussed a memorial service for all that died in the tunnels. They wanted Bee to be there, too. It would be a wonderful tribute to the men who gave their lives.

Dad told us details regarding the plans, and we looked forward to the event. He had made a list of the things that had to be done. There would be another trip to find descendants. Who knew what that would involve as the search unfolded?

They would have to check for the gunpowder cave and make sure there was no danger.

Pa was working on cashing in the gold bars, and we needed a buyer for the coins. We needed to build an addition for Grammy and Grammpy as soon as possible. Above all, the money would have to be divided for all the descendants of the dead. They needed to be honored, all the while keeping this immense secret for our safety.

I told Dad it would all fall into place, and as far as I was concerned, I was enjoying the whole process. I liked that my family was around, as well as my best friends. If we did no more, it was more than we ever thought or dreamt of doing. I reminded him of the short time span that it had taken to accomplish so much!

That was it for now, and that was enough. We would do everything on our list as soon as possible. I couldn't wait to find the long tunnel to the power station and discover more descendants in far off lands. Most of all, I couldn't wait to use this place as my own private hideaway.

Acknowledgements

It is an awesome experience to see your dream come true. My second book in this series of three is born out of the love of adventure, intrigue, and travel. It has been a pleasure to create this book, continually returning to my first love, the story of the tunnels of Niagara.

I would like to thank Ted Beaudoin. An author himself, Ted prodded me to continue the editing and kept me pursuing publication of my first book, back when it was just a dream and even before I knew of my publisher, Elm Grove. This man continued to encourage my unique way of writing and expressing my imagination. He introduced me to Elm Grove Publishing and here we are. Myself having no experience in publishing, EGP nurtured and helped me to realize my dream, Book number one. I am so grateful to them for the cover design and publishing *Past Secret Present Danger* winning the Finalist Book Excellence Award in 2018. I thank Shawn, my son, for his outstanding work in photography for the front and back covers. My never tiring models on the covers, Mac and Josh, were a joy to work with.

I am ever grateful to Harry my husband and the hours of dedication he has given to working with me in reading and rereading my work. Did I say I had the best husband from the number one shelf of choices? His patience and strength has been never-ending in my projects. His gifting so different from mine, is a never-ending blessing to me.

Those faithful people in my life that give of their time to read my material and help me in so many different ways. You know who you are and you are not taken for granted. I love how you inspire and cheer me on. In this book I salute another set of grandchildren. They have excelled this year in various facets of life and have done well. You will recognize yourselves and I congratulate you on living life with pride and joy.

About the Author

Margarete Ledwez was born in Germany, emigrating to Canada with her parents and brother when she was just a year old. She quickly developed a longing to create which has eventually manifested itself in her writing.

Growing up in St. Catharines, Ontario, she became fascinated by the tunnels that had been used to hide slaves as part of the Underground Railroad and later by bootleggers during Prohibition.

While she and her husband were raising their own children they lived in Niagara Falls, just 5 kilometers from the celebrated *Screaming Tunnel.* Her curiosity was once again piqued when she discovered the myths and legends surrounding the many tunnels under the famous falls, and when writing this series of stories, she drew from her knowledge as well as her unending intrigue that there could be many more tunnels yet to be discovered.

Niagara Tunnels Secrets Revealed is Margarete Ledwez's second novel, and is a sequel to *Past Secret Present Danger.* The story has been evolving in the author's imagination for many years.

Margarete Ledwez lives in St. Catharines, Ontario with her husband, Harry.